UNBRIDLED SPIRITS

UNBRIDLED SPIRITS

A SMALL BATCH MYSTERY

MICHELLE BENNINGTON

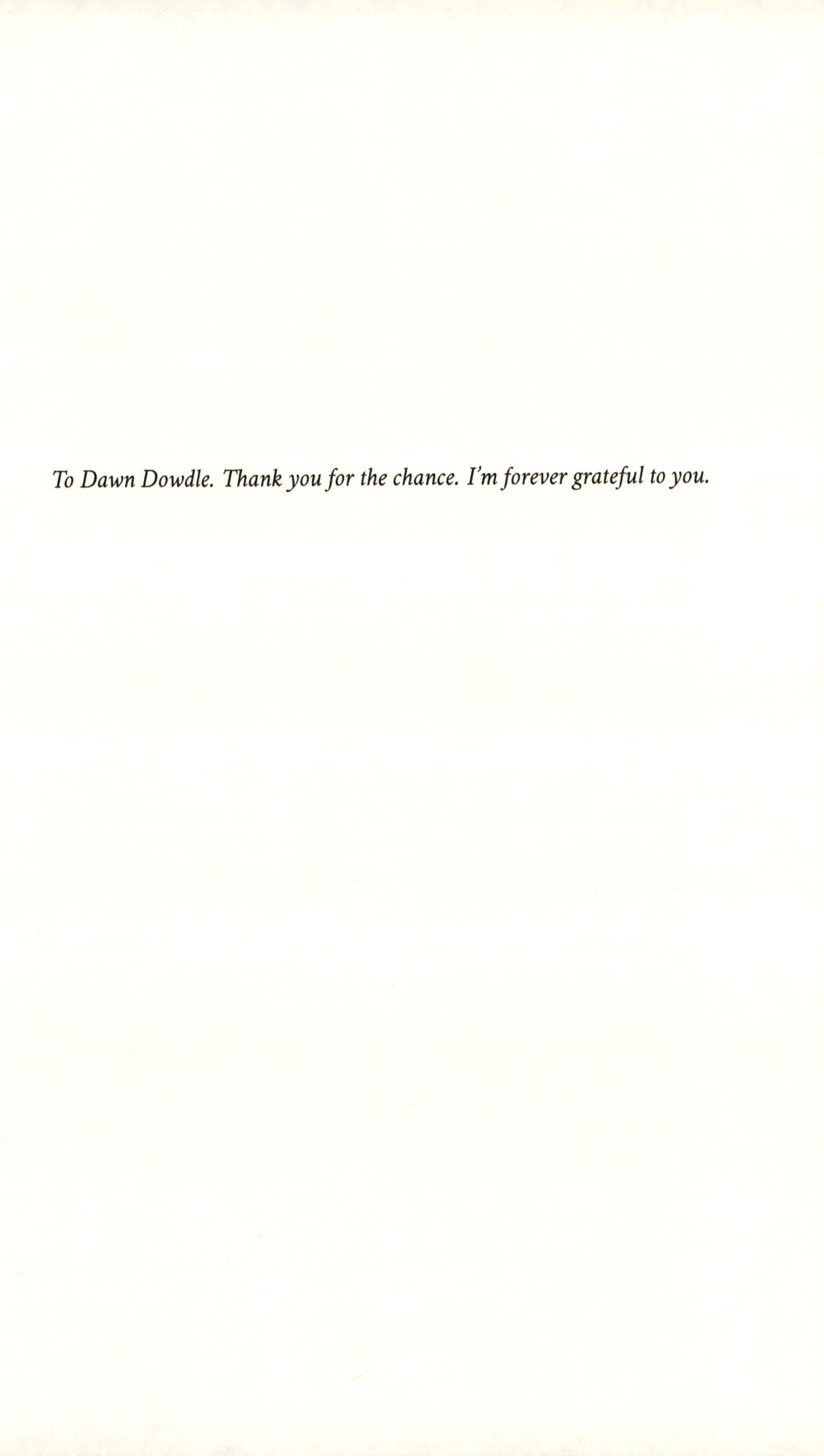

To Dawn Dowdle. Thank you for the chance. I'm forever grateful to you.

Chapter One

I returned from the grocery on a sunny Saturday morning to find Jimmy and Prim at the kitchen table. A few of the lavender roses from the bush Cam had given her stood in a vase, hanging their heads. She'd plucked them a couple days ago, and though they were beginning to wilt already, she loved those roses and was determined to hold on to them until they completely fell apart. Honestly, I was surprised any had managed to bloom this late in September. They looked at me as if they were a couple of kids I'd caught digging in the cookie jar.

I sat the bags on the countertop. "What's going on?" I said to Jimmy. "Why are you here so early? I thought we were going to your cousin's later."

"Yeah, I came across these files and thought I'd go ahead and bring them by."

He patted the stack of file folders by his right elbow. A file box sat on the floor by his chair.

"Is that about my mom's case?" I thought he'd forgotten. Or had been too busy to mess with it. After all, I'd asked him to look into it a few times since we'd started dating, but he always said he'd get around to it when he could. Yet, I hadn't heard any more about it.

"Yep." He smiled, rising to hug and kiss me. He filled out a gray T-shirt and worn jeans beautifully, and he had a clean, freshly showered smell.

Relief washed over me at his touch. I melted against him, glowing in our recent reconciliation. Though we'd had a bumpy beginning, each day drew me closer to him, and I could feel myself opening up to him in a way I hadn't done with a man since…well, since Cam. My ex-husband of about twenty months. I wasn't sure I could trust another man, but Jimmy chipped away, little by little, at the defensive wall I'd built around myself.

Prim pushed herself to stand. She wore a dark pink cotton dress under a lavender cardigan and house shoes. "I made some cinnamon pecan cake for breakfast..."

"Whoa there." I broke from Jimmy's embrace and put my arm around Prim's frail shoulders. I kissed her head and guided her back to her seat. "Don't trouble yourself. I'll get my own food after I put the groceries away. You sit."

"I'm tired of sitting," Prim groused. "I'm not used to this. I want to be out in my garden, cooking and canning."

"I know. You do plenty around here. You also need rest so you don't wear yourself down." Ever since she'd been diagnosed with cancer, my one and only mission was to keep what remained of my family with me as long as I could.

"Do you have more groceries to bring in?" Jimmy asked, peering out the window over the sink.

"Nope. I'm no two-trip girl." I smiled up at him.

He shook his head and laughed. "You're going to hurt your back one day, if you keep doing that."

"Think of it as strength training." I made a silly face, flexed my average biceps, and turned to put away the groceries. "So, what's going on with my mom's case? What've you discovered?"

Jimmy refilled his coffee and returned to the table. "I looked over some of the pictures in the files, and I noticed something."

A car door slammed outside. I glanced out the window. "Cam's here?"

"Yeah," Jimmy said. "I asked him to help over at Cassidy's today."

"Oh, uh, okay." Things had been tense with Cam. He and I split amicably, mostly, and had remained close friends. However, when I started dating his best friend, it had stirred up jealousy and put a strain on long-standing friendships. Many days I questioned my decisions.

Cam strode across the yard and entered the kitchen. "Good morning," he beamed from under his gray baseball cap. He wore a red Appalachia

Freedom T-shirt, worn jeans, and aged cowboy boots. "Hey, man." He slapped Jimmy on the shoulder, then leaned over to plant a kiss on Prim's head. "Hey, Prim. Looks like you need more coffee." He grabbed her cup and filled it up for her.

Prim said, "Mornin'. You want some breakfast, hon?" She stood and shuffled toward the cake.

"No, that's okay." He guided her back to the table. "My mom stuffed me full of biscuits and gravy this morning."

Then the battle of hospitality began, where Prim offered food to Cam in a variety of ways. Cam parried with a variety of declinations as he jumped in to unload the groceries.

"What're y'all up to this morning?" Cam asked.

Prim said, "Jimmy thinks he found some information about Annette's murder."

"Hopefully, something that can exonerate my dad," I added.

Cam looked pointedly at Jimmy, communicating a silent message I couldn't quite decipher. "Really? I'm glad to hear it."

Jimmy flushed a little and sipped his coffee. "Yep. I can't guarantee anything, but it might be enough to at least get another trial."

I knew it would irritate him if I said anything negative, but I couldn't stop my mouth. "I thought you'd given up on it. I wasn't sure you believed me when I said my dad was innocent."

A defensive edge entered his voice. "No. I believed you, but I had to consider the political side of things, too. I mean, my boss and superior officer was the lead investigator in the case. I have to go gently and quietly on this."

"Fair enough," I said. That was understandable. Sheriff Harlan "Bulldog" Goodman could be a force to reckon with, and if Jimmy wanted to keep his job, he couldn't go around openly embarrassing and challenging his boss.

Jimmy continued, tracing his finger along his cup handle. "Besides, if I'm right, and I need to be absolutely certain I am, this could give me incredible leverage."

I put the last of the groceries in the pantry and closed the cabinet.

"Leverage? For what?" I washed my hands.

Cam poured himself and me a cup of coffee.

Jimmy relaxed in his chair. "Well, there's an election this year. I'm thinking of running for sheriff."

I turned, surprised, drying my hands. "Are you serious?"

He nodded, eyeing me with a mix of hope and uncertainty. "I've been thinking about it for a while, but I put in the application today."

Filling my saucer with a slice of cake, I accepted a coffee mug from Cam with gratitude. We joined Prim and Jimmy at the table. I was shocked and a little hurt that he hadn't discussed this decision with me. "You've already put in the application?" Granted, we weren't married or engaged or even discussing those things, but how could he not at least mention such a life-changing decision to me? Maybe he didn't feel the same about me. Maybe I was more serious about our relationship than he was. I tamped down the disappointment with a chunk of cake and forced myself to seem gracious. "That's…I'm…happy for you." I hoped I hadn't let the hurt leak into my voice.

"Yeah. I'd been thinking about it for a long time." He wiped his hands on his jeans. "I'm kind of nervous, though. Bulldog probably won't take kindly to it. I'm afraid he might try to undermine me somehow."

I was no fan of Sheriff Harlan "Bulldog" Goodman, and he was no fan of mine or my family—especially my dad, who'd been a small-time crook long before he went to prison for my mom's murder—of which he was innocent. But if I considered him objectively, I couldn't imagine him being *that* petty. He seemed like the sort to appreciate a fair fight. "Why would he do something like that?"

Jimmy shrugged. "I think he'll see it as a threat to have a challenge from one of his…" He made air quotes as he said, "Underlings."

Underlings was a loaded word. It hinted that perhaps Jimmy had an embittered attitude or even a lack of respect toward his boss he hadn't shared with me. I wondered what was going on between them.

Prim interrupted, shifting in her seat. She patted the table. "Tell her about Annette."

Annette was my late mom. She'd died when I was young. Murder. My dad was blamed and was sitting in prison for the crime, though I remained convinced someone else was guilty and probably still wandering around free.

Jimmy opened a folder and put it in front of me. "Notice anything?"

It was a picture of a boot pattern on a gray carpet and wood paneling in the corner. A crime scene tag beside the muddy print. A border of lines marked the perimeter of the entire foot with star-type patterns in the middle of the upper foot and one at the bottom in the heel. I dove way back into the recesses of my mind where I stored childhood memories and searched for where that carpet and wood paneling would've been located in my old house. The downstairs den. "What am I looking for? All I see is a muddy shoe print."

"Look at the next picture."

I flipped to the next picture, revealing another crime scene tag beside another footprint. More gray carpet. In the background were clothes and shoes. A closet. The shoes were adult shoes, so they weren't mine. Mom and Dad's closet.

"Do you see it?" Jimmy asked.

Anxiety tickled just under the surface of my skin, annoyed that I couldn't see what Jimmy expected me to see. It was like looking for the back of an earring in a shag carpet. "I don't see it. What am I looking for?" Even I heard the tension rising in my voice.

Apparently, Jimmy sensed it, too, because he let me off the hook. "The boots."

"What about them?"

"The boots can't be in the closet and walking around, leaving muddy prints at the same time, can they?"

A light bulb flashed in my mind, awakening me to a whole new view of the pictures and my dad's case. I looked again at the boots. Pale tan Timberland work boots, the kind with the thick rubber soles he wore on the worksite. They were well-worn and dusty, but *not* muddy. "Maybe the mud was washed off."

"Well, I thought of that, too. But we now have a database and can sort through all the shoe sole patterns. Those are Timberland boots. The prints were left by Red Wings. They're similar, but not the same."

"You're sure they're different?"

"That's what the analysis says. But there's more."

I locked my eyes with his. "What?"

"I went back into the evidence locker and found some stuff with blood on it. Well, it turns out, there is blood present that doesn't match either of your parents. Most of the blood at the scene belonged to your mom. But we examined another item and found someone else's blood."

"Why didn't they find that before?"

"Better technology. Early on, we needed bigger blood samples, and it was difficult to separate commingled samples. Further, not only did we find different blood, we found two hairs mixed in with your mom's evidence. One is human. Not belonging to your parents. The other is feline."

"Feline?" Prim said. "Annette would've never had a cat. She was allergic. Her face would swell up all over if she got around a cat."

"That means someone else was in our house." The realization of that slammed over me like a massive ocean wave. I sat back in my chair, numb, trying to process this new information. "It wasn't daddy."

I had suspected for a long time that my dad, while no angel, was certainly no killer and had not murdered my mom, but I hadn't been able to prove it, and I didn't really know where to begin in finding out. Sheriff Harlan "Bulldog" Goodman was antagonistic toward me and my family, and since he was the lead investigator on the case, he wasn't interested in helping me prove himself wrong. Now I had some evidence that might prove me right.

Honestly, I wasn't interested in shaming the sheriff. Nor was I interested in some political anti-police stance. I was raised to respect authority and believed most police were interested in doing their jobs to the best of their ability. But I also recognized that the sheriff was human and all humans, regardless of their station in life, make mistakes; humans, even those in important positions, allowed pride to cloud their judgment; humans have always been fallible. So, for me, my father's case was never one of personal vendettas; it was about the truth. All I had ever wanted was the truth. And as hard as it would be to bear, if my dad did, in fact, kill my mom, then I would accept it and be content to let him sit in prison to pay the price for his crime. But if he didn't do it, he needed to be freed. And now to have this information…

Prim touched my hand. "You okay, hon?"

I gazed at her, unable to form words.

She said, "I know it's a lot to take in."

"Getting back to the subject at hand, how did they not find those hairs earlier?" Prim said.

He licked his lips and shifted in his seat. "That's more difficult to explain…"

Prim narrowed her eyes and nodded. "Ah. I get it. Sloppy work. Y'all were so happy to have *someone* you didn't care if you had the *right* one."

Jimmy sighed. "It doesn't happen often, but with small departments, with limited resources…" He leaned his elbows on the table. "Plus, in tiny towns like this where murders are rare compared to big cities, the officers sometimes aren't equipped or trained well enough to handle…"

Prim continued to glare at him.

Eager to defend Jimmy, I said, "Of course, Jimmy wasn't with the department back then, Prim. It's not his fault."

"I know that. Bulldog ought've known better with all his experience, but he didn't like your daddy, never did." She jabbed the tabletop with her finger. "It was personal."

Cam said, "It happens sometimes. Look at that JonBenét Ramsey case. One of the prevailing theories is that lack of training might've interfered with capturing the killer."

I finished the last of my breakfast and washed it down with coffee. "We have to move forward with this. We have to find out the truth."

"Amen," Prim said. "I want to know what happened to my daughter before I leave this earth." She looked at Jimmy. "If you think you're the one to figure it out, then you'd better get to work, young man. Time's a tickin'."

"I'll do everything I can." Jimmy checked his digital watch. "Well, we should probably get over to Cassidy's."

Cam and I stood, downed our respective coffees, and put the dirty dishes in the sink.

Prim said, "Is your cousin the new owner of the old J.T. Bolton House?"

"Yep." He smiled, gathering his dishes.

She pushed her glasses up, rhinestoned rims winking in the light. "I've heard for years

the house is haunted. Has she seen any ghosts yet?"

Jimmy snorted and chuckled. "Nah, there's no ghosts. There's no such thing as ghosts."

"Not from what I hear. I had a friend who cleaned houses when we were young. She had a job there once back in the sixties, and she heard strange noises in the upstairs bedroom, like footsteps. Except there was no one there. Scared the bejeezus out of her. She left and never went back."

"Old houses…" Jimmy shrugged. "They make all kinds of weird noises. The pipes creak. The floors settle. I doubt there's ghosts."

"Are you calling my friend a liar, young man?"

"No, ma'am, I—"

"Let it go." I patted Jimmy on the shoulder and nudged him toward the door. "C'mon."

Cam paused. "What about Prim?"

Prim pulled her cardigan tighter. "Don't worry about me. Batrene'll be here in a bit."

We kissed Prim goodbye, crammed into the cab of Jimmy's truck, and headed toward the debatably haunted J.T. Bolton House.

Chapter Two

The shaded street of Hickory Hollow Lane sprouted from the town square and sloped downward under a canopy of maple, oak, and hickory trees, bottoming out into a cul-de-sac crowned by a large late-Victorian era house smack in the center of a lush Bluegrass lawn dotted with catalpa, tulip, and pine trees along the perimeter and magnolia trees closer to the house.

The house had been built in the late 1880s by the supremely wealthy J.T. Bolton. As he'd made his fortune in bourbon, he was known as "bourbon aristocracy" or a bourbon baron. Though the house was highly fashionable for its time, it was easy to see how rumors of ghosts might attach to the building. The red brick structure boasted a lacy white trim tracing the three stories and white keystones around tall, arched windows and doors.

A dome-capped pentagonal turret stretched three stories high at one end of the house. Directly beneath the dome stood a space ringed with arched openings. A rooster wind vane nested atop the dome, interpreting the wind. A covered, wrap-around porch skirted the rest of the front and right side of the house. Pitched roofs spiked the top like the dark peaks of a mountain range.

A force of landscapers in jeans, long-sleeved T-shirts, and work boots scurried around with rakes, weed trimmers, hedge clippers, and wheelbarrows full of branches and clippings.

As we slid from the cab of his pickup truck, I shielded my eyes against the late-September sun. "This house is amazing." Jimmy had brought me out here when we'd first started dating. At that time, Cassidy and

Derek had owned the house for six months, and though they were making some headway, it was still in rough shape. They'd come a long way in the meantime.

Jimmy said, "Wait until you see the inside. I was out here the other day and it's a completely different place. There are still a few rough patches, but they can deal with those over time."

Cam whistled. "Man, look at this place."

"It used to belong to Jerome Taylor Bolton, the greatest bourbon baron to ever live in Kentucky," Jimmy said, sounding like a tour guide.

"A bourbon baron?" Cam asked.

I added, "Yeah, the rich men who owned distilleries back in the day." I had only recently learned about them myself when I started working at The Four Wild Horses Distillery. "They were the Elon Musk or Bill Gates of the Victorian and Edwardian eras. They made more money off of bourbon and whiskey than they could ever spend. And, like many rich people, they used their money and influence to impact and shape the political and social landscapes."

"Why aren't they hiring professionals to do this stuff? I'm afraid to mess something up in there." Cam said.

"You'll be fine," Jimmy said. "We're only removing wallpaper and painting. Minor stuff. They're getting professionals where they can, but as Cassidy tells it, the money is almost gone, so they need to cut corners where possible. Since they're opening soon, they're running up against a deadline."

Jimmy's cousin, Cassidy, sat on the gently angled roof over the porch, her legs swinging freely, drinking a glass of iced tea.

"Hey, y'all," she shouted as we crossed the yard. She wore a long-sleeve flannel shirt over jeans, work boots. Her too-large work gloves flopped on her hand as she waved.

Cassidy was a firecracker, and I'd taken an instant liking to her, rare for me, when I'd met her a couple months ago. It didn't surprise me at all to see her sitting on the roof of a giant Victorian home.

Jimmy shouted, "What the heck are you doing up there by yourself? Get down before you break your neck."

"I'm not by myself. Derek's inside." She swept her arm around, her long, blonde ponytail whipping with her movement, to point at the open window.

Something in Jimmy's tone annoyed me. He spoke to Cassidy as if she were a child. "She's an adult," I muttered. "I'm sure she knows what she's doing. Besides, the roof is practically flat."

"She needs to come down."

"Cass is fine." To be honest, I wanted to be on the roof too. It looked fun. It reminded me of when I was a young teen, when I couldn't sleep, I'd open my bedroom window at Prim's and sit in the window sill. My legs resting on a sharply inclined roof two stories above the ground, I listened to the crickets and tree frogs, and threw wishes at the moon hanging in the treetops.

"It's an old house," Jimmy said. "One rotted spot, she's on the ground with a broken back."

"Don't you think they fixed the roof?"

"Not necessarily. Roofs are expensive."

"The shingles all look pretty new to me."

"Okay, you two," Cam said. "If y'all are going to bicker all day, I'm going to work in a separate room."

Derek, Cassidy's husband of three weeks, poked his head out the window, a paintbrush in hand. He smiled and waved. "Hey, y'all. C'mon in."

"Gimme a minute, and I'll be right down."

Cassidy ran across the roof with ease and crawled through the open window.

Jimmy shook his head. "Crazy as a bed bug."

I chuckled. "I guess you'd have to be to buy a haunted house."

He looked at me like I had sprouted three heads. "Haunted? You don't really believe that stuff Prim was talking about?"

I shrugged. "Maybe. Why not?"

"Rook. There's no such thing as ghosts, and there's no such thing as haunted houses." "I don't know. There are stranger things in heaven and earth—"

"Quote all the Shakespeare you like. Doesn't change the facts. There are no ghosts here."

"Seriously," Cam said. "You two aren't going to be snipping like this all day, are you?"

"No," Jimmy said. "But I can't possibly take anyone seriously who says they believe in ghosts."

"Wow," I said. "Close-minded and insulting to both Prim and myself. You're on a winning streak."

"I believe what I can see and hear."

"You can't see DNA and atoms with your eyes, but do you believe in those?"

"Now you're just being difficult. Did you not get enough sleep last night?"

"I slept fine." That was a lie, but I sped right along to my point. "And I'm not being difficult. I'm simply making room for the possibility there are things on this planet that can't always be explained. Including ghosts."

Cassidy burst through the door and ran down the steps. "When's the wedding, y'all?" She charged at Jimmy, who swept her up as she leapt into his arms. He spun her once and squeezed her, as she laughed and called him a big brute. He returned her to the ground. "No wedding bells in the near future, for sure."

Ouch. That was honest. Admittedly, I'd been going back and forth. Though I'd been drawing nearer Jimmy in many ways, we still had some jagged rocks to climb. Yet, it hurt a little to hear the truth so openly and plainly stated. The sting burned in my chest, but I played it cool. Or tried to. At least I knew where I stood. I pasted on a smile.

"Well, if you ever do tie the knot, y'all *have* to get married here!"

"Marriage?" Cam chimed in, looking between us. "Y'all haven't been talking about marriage, have you?"

Jimmy screwed up his face and scoffed through a chuckle. "No."

I tried to make light of it to take the edge off my feelings. "I mean, we can't even agree on whether or not ghosts exist. How would we ever decide on where to honeymoon?" Even to me, my tone was sharper than I'd intended it to be.

If Cassidy noticed, she ignored it. She grabbed me up in a tight hug, slapping my back. "Oh, girl. I'm so glad to see you!" She rocked me back and forth.

"Ditto," I said, her Pantene-scented hair tickling my nose. "Did y'all have a great honeymoon? I can't wait to hear all about Scotland."

"It was only the most amazing trip ever. Hey Cam." She opened her arms and embraced him. "You doing all right?"

"Can't complain." He smiled. "Love the house."

"Thanks. Y'all c'mon in, and I'll show you around and show you Scotland pictures. I took about three thousand of them." She threw her arm around me and guided me toward the porch. "I've got some fresh sun tea made just yesterday. Probably be the last of the season until next summer."

"What were you doing up on the roof?" Jimmy looked up at the porch ceiling as we climbed the steps. "You got damage?"

I felt the implication of that question. I cut a side glance at him.

"No, no. Nothing like that. I had a ton of sticks and leaves in the gutters from those gale winds the other day, so I figured I'd clear out what I could. I'm tickled ten shades of pink our roof shingles held up."

"You need to get a professional. And get some gutter screens installed," Jimmy said over the clomp of our shoes on the wooden porch.

"Of course. Someday." She opened the double mahogany doors with stained glass windows featuring flowers, leaves, and swans. A polished bourbon barrel lid hung outside the door that read *J.T. Bolton House*. "Can't afford it right now, though. We sunk every bit of money we could find into the purchase of this place and the major renovations." We stepped into the dim foyer.

Jimmy would not let it go. "It's not safe to be—"

Cassidy nudged me with her elbow. "Here we go. Mr. Worrywart is going to tell me all the ways I could die." She rolled her eyes and laughed.

"Make fun all you want, but—"

She said to me, "Jimmy has always been a ninety-year-old grandpa."

"And you've always been…"

To put it in Southern language: Prim didn't raise no fool. Double negatives were a common Southern method of emphasizing a point, and it meant I wasn't about to get in the middle of this exchange. I laughed at them, throwing my hands up in surrender, and turned my attention to the beautiful dark cherry trim and wainscotting, a dainty floral pinstripe wallpaper, a dazzling crystal chandelier, fresh flowers on pedestals in the corners, extra-wide arched doorways leading to equally enticing rooms, and a red-carpeted staircase that most certainly led to luxurious bedrooms. Though the house dated to late Victorian, the decor was more Edwardian with modern updates designed to not interfere with the historicity of the place. If this house was haunted, these ghosts sure lived in style. And, if I listened close enough, I'd hear my wallet screaming from inside my purse.

Derek entered the room, wiping his wet hands on his faded, paint-smeared jeans. "Hey there." He was tall and thin in a wrinkled white T-shirt. He had close-cropped dark hair, a Roman nose, bright smile, and welcoming demeanor. He shook hands with Jimmy and Cam. "I'm really glad you guys could help us today." His accent had no detectable Southern accent, though he was apparently from Texas. I had learned at the rehearsal dinner before their wedding that he had been an "Army brat" who hailed from everywhere and nowhere.

After some small talk, Cassidy offered us a glass of iced sun tea and a brief tour of the house. Then we were all set to work and moved the painting party upstairs to prepare what would be the guest rooms.

As we climbed the stairs, I ran my hand along the wide banister as we stepped through the multi-colored light splashed on the floor from the stained-glass window. "None of the floors on the stairs or upper two stories have been done yet," Derek pointed out. "We're saving it until the end so they won't get all scuffed up."

When we reached the landing, Cassidy linked her arm with mine. "Rook, you're with me. We'll let the boys do those rooms over there." She led me toward the front of the house. "Bye, fellas."

We entered the giant room on the right. It was a pentagonal room housed in the turret. The large bay window looked out on the front yard over the catalpa and magnolia trees. "This used to be a family sitting room, but we're going to turn it into a honeymoon suite."

"It's beautiful." I was speaking of its potential because, in the moment, peeling, water-stained wallpaper and damaged wood trim marked the twelve-foot high walls. The floorboards were faded and scuffed and at least three inches of dust covered everything. The fireplace had been restored, with white-washed brick and new gas fixtures. Plastic had been taped over it, to protect it from paint.

"Yeah. It has a ton of potential. I love the chandelier." She pointed to a sparkling fixture hanging in the center of the room. "I love glittery things. Don't you?"

She plugged in a steamer. "I'll steam if you want to go around behind me and work on peeling off the wallpaper?"

"Sounds good."

She was more of a talker than me, so I listened while she chatted away. "I can't wait to decorate up here, but it'll have to be on a shoestring. Guess I'll be looking up lots of cute DIY videos on YouTube. Derek keeps hassling me about the money though, so if I don't make money on this place soon, I'm in big trouble. He's going to *kill* me."

Her laugh seemed to have some tension in it. I didn't want to pry, but since nosiness was scripted on my DNA, I signaled my desire to listen if she needed to talk, so I opened the door by saying, "Oh?" Sometimes, that one little word, said with just the right blend of curiosity and concern, was enough to draw someone out.

"Yeah. We borrowed a ton of money for this place. Plus, we have school loans. Derek hates to be in debt. He really didn't want a bed and breakfast, if I'm being honest." She ran the steamer handle up and down the wall, a puff of vapor wrinkling and bubbling the paper.

"Really? This place is gorgeous." I scrape off the dampened wallpaper with a putty knife.

"I know. I convinced him we could make it a profitable business. It's really put a strain on us, you know? I mean, I get it. He's tired. He works all day at the accounting firm, comes home to a half-complete home, and then spends all weekend working, too. And every penny he makes goes back into this house. Or school loans." She rolled her eyes. "I do what I can to ease his burden. But it's a lot."

I chuckled to try to relieve some of the tension. "But y'all just got married.

You're too new to have this many problems."

"Well, we lived together for a few years first. So, we aren't *that* new." She inhaled sharply. "But I will die before I give up on this dream. I want it so bad I can taste it." She turned her sharp green eyes to me, sparking with determination and fire. "I think I can make this house a wild success."

"I believe you will. Once you get this thing up and running, you'll be booked with something every weekend. People will be beating down your doors."

"I hope you're right."

Chapter Three

A male voice shouted up from downstairs. "Cassiiiideeee!" A pause. "Cass! Where're you at, girl?"

She stepped out of the parlor into the hall and shouted. "Up here in the turret!"

The rapid clomp of shoes on the stairs echoed as she returned to the room and squatted beside me.

"My older half-brother, Kenton." She whispered, squeezing the sponge in the soap water. "We have the same daddy. He hangs around here all the time. He's really trying to help, but sometimes he drives me crazy." She began washing the now paperless wall.

A man in a white golf shirt, blue jeans, and white Nike ball cap entered the room. He reminded me of Prim's chicken dumplings, all lumpy and doughy. Sweat beaded his tan, broad face, and he was a little out of breath from running up the stairs. With his thin lips, broad nose, and squinty eyes, I couldn't see an ounce of similarity between him and Cassidy. He pulled a blue plaid handkerchief from his back pocket, lifted his ball cap, wiped his face, and returned it.

He glanced at me and nodded. "How're you?" Which was a very southern way of saying *I'm only being polite by acknowledging your presence, but I could care less about you or why you're here since I have other business to attend to.* "Hey, Cass, I gotta talk to you for a minute."

"I'm in the middle of something. Can it wait?"

"I really need to go over this now. I've found someone who can handle the drywall in that one room on the third level, and I think he can probably fix those stairs in the cellar, too."

"We've discussed this." Ice infused her voice, and her green eyes flinted. "We have to wait on the third level. We'll worry about that once we've started making some money renting out the second level and hosting events."

I shivered a little and began to shift from foot to foot as a sense of awkwardness fingered my ribs. Grabbing my sponge, I washed the walls, pretending I wasn't listening.

Kenton pressed the issue. "Just come and look at what I'm talking about." He pulled a paper out of his pocket. "Look here, I got an estimate—"

"You did *what*? How dare you do that? I've already told you—"

He raised his voice. "I'm only trying to help. If you get the third level up and running now, you can make more money *now* instead of waiting. This guy–"

She raised her voice. "You had *no* right."

"I'll loan you the money."

"What don't you understand? We cannot afford to take out any more loans."

"You can take your time paying me back."

"Please, go. Stop talking to contractors. Stop interfering. You're not helping. You're making it harder. This is not your home or your business to run."

"About thirty grand of it is. And I aim to protect my share of the investment."

A heated silence filled the room, causing me to glance over my shoulder at the pair. Cassidy flushed and set her jaw. She sneaked a look of embarrassment in my direction. "Would you hush up," she hissed. "I will pay you back. I told you I would, and you need to shut your mouth right now. If Derek hears you, I'm dust."

"That money makes me practically a partner here."

"No. You're not a partner. Not even a little." Cassidy swept her hand through the air. "Which is exactly why I don't want to borrow one more dime from you. You've already built up all kinds of ideas about your role here. Now if you don't mind, I've got work to do." She shoved the sponge back in the water to rinse it and squeezed it dry with a huff. "Just go away and stop trying to help. This is *my* house, my business. *Mine.* And Derek's. Not yours. Cancel the appointment and get your money back. Now." She slammed the sponge against the wall and scrubbed with ferocity.

He growled and left the room, grumbling. "I don't know why you have to be so stubborn and difficult all the time."

Kenton's shoes sounded on the stairs, and then the front door slammed.

"Sorry you had to witness that," she said.

"It's okay." I was at a loss for what to say that wouldn't further embarrass her or aggravate the situation. "It's hard with family sometimes."

"Ain't that the truth. The lesson here is never do business with family. And, never, *ever* borrow money from them. Ever since I borrowed the money, he acts like he owns the place." She glanced over her shoulder and lowered her voice. "And Derek doesn't know anything about the loan, so don't say anything."

"Of course. I won't."

She rinsed the sponge again and scrubbed a new spot on the wall. "I'll admit I never expected running a B&B would be this much work. Or this much money." She stopped and wiped her forehead with the back of her wrist. "I knew we'd struggle, but everything is so expensive, and the loan wasn't enough to cover everything. So, I had to borrow money from Kenton and from my parents. Derek would flip out if he knew we owe about fifty grand more than the bank loan, but..." her voice broke, and her eyes grew watery. "If I can just get this place set up right..." Her voice trailed off, and she resumed scrubbing. "Anyway, Kenton is too much sometimes, and I wish he'd move out."

"He's living with you?" I rinsed my sponge.

"Yeah. For a little while. He and his wife have been having troubles, so he moved in here while they're trying to work things out. Worse, I think the money I borrowed might be contributing to their issues." She sighed, stopped scrubbing, and stared at the wall. "Why is everything so hard?" She rested her forehead against the wall.

I put my arm around her shoulders. "Aw, Cassidy. I'm sorry. I know it's hard right now, but I'm sure once you get the business up and running and you get the wrinkles ironed out, y'all will be fine. You just need time."

She lifted her head. "Thanks," she said softly. She rinsed her sponge and returned to scrubbing. "The craziest part is when I asked to borrow the money, he offered to buy us out. I never told Derek because I knew he'd jump at the chance. Sometimes I wish I'd accepted."

I didn't realize Cassidy was this unsure of herself. I studied her profile, surprised at how different she presented herself. From the moment we'd met, I'd believed her to be the most confident, together woman in my circle of acquaintances and I held her up as a source of inspiration. "You're struggling now, but keep pushing. You'll eventually come out the other side. What was it Winston Churchill said? 'If you're going through hell, keep going.'"

She looked at me, pensive, then she smiled. "Because there's only one way through, right?" She sniffed a laugh. "Alrighty, then. I reckon I'll do that. I'm sure things will get better once Kenton gets his marriage back on track and moves out."

Chapter Four

As Cassidy and I returned to work, I rolled her plight over in my mind. I knew all too well the burden of financial strain. It felt like dragging around an anchor day after day. The thread of her monetary crisis wove into my many concerns about work. The Four Wild Horses Distillery had suffered a major blow a couple months ago when some creeps stole a batch of rare bourbon and killed off a couple people—one of whom was my best friend. It caused a sensation in our tiny town, and it blew up our media. Though we weren't as small as the female-owned Mermaid Cove a few miles away, we weren't nearly as big with the same renown as Wild Turkey or Maker's Mark. At best, we were a middling size with distribution only in the Southeastern United States. When the bourbon heist and murders happened at Four Wild Horses, we lost a little face in the bourbon community, and our dreams of expanding our brand nationwide, even internationally, were threatened.

In light of the financial hit the company endured, rumors of layoffs loomed. The marketing department, in conjunction with management, concluded a new bourbon release would help us get back on track, and perhaps prevent job losses. But we still needed a winning idea for our newest label, Unbridled Spirits.

Then like a lightning bolt, it hit me. A beautiful Victorian era home with Edwardian touches, rife with the spirits of the Jazz Age, speakeasies, prohibition and whiskey-running. Spirits. Our new bourbon was called Unbridled Spirits, a play on the branding "Unbridled Spirit" the Commonwealth of Kentucky used to describe Kentucky culture as free and unrestrained as our champion thoroughbred horses.

What better place than the J.T. Bolton house to host a grand Jazz Age style party! And with Halloween around the corner, we could capitalize on the rumors of hauntings at the mansion and turn the event into a costume party. In an instant, we could time travel the J.T. Bolton house back to its Prohibition-era glory days. We could get a charity on board. Have a costume contest. Have ghost hunters thrill the crowd with ghost stories. A deluge of ideas poured into my brain.

I stopped painting and stared at the wall, watching the plan unfold against the gray paint.

Cassidy said, "Rook? Are you okay? You have a weird look on your face."

"Cassidy," I said, the excitement coursing through my veins. "I have an idea that could launch both of our careers." The more I talked, the more excited she became, too.

"That bourbon release could really boost the popularity of my bed and breakfast and start a word-of-mouth wildfire to bring visitors from all around! Thank you, Rook. I think you just saved me and my business!" She threw her arms around my neck.

I'd sold Cassidy on the idea. Now, I needed to sell it to my boss and the marketing department team lead. Even though it was a Saturday afternoon, I knew I had to strike while the iron was hot and before someone else came up with another idea. I also knew my boss, Pierce Simpson, had a Call Anytime Policy in matters of money. Though Four Wild Horses Distillery possessed a family atmosphere, there were moments when competitiveness prevailed. I started at the top. My team lead, Jeff, would be annoyed if I hadn't called him first, but I couldn't trust he would give credit where it was due. I needed credit for this.

"I'll put in a call right now," I said. "I left my phone in the truck though."

I jogged to the truck with Cassidy on my heels. She hovered nearby, double-crossing her fingers and saying a silent prayer with her eyes closed as I spilled the idea to Pierce. When he loved it and said I should move forward with it, I called Jeff to tell him. Thankfully, he didn't answer the phone, so I left a message. I could deal with his annoyance on Monday.

Cassidy and I held hands and jumped up and down to celebrate this shining career moment for the two of us. We were going to help each other climb the ladder to our respective successes.

A lanky man in dirt-stained jeans, navy ball cap, and gray T-shirt with the landscapers' green logo on the back approached us. His neck and arms were sunburned, and his face was sweaty from the day's labor. The ends of his longish blond hair clung to his neck with sweat.

"Hey, Cass. We're getting ready to leave."

"Hey. Trigg, this is my friend, Rook Campbell. Rook, this is Trigg West. He's an old friend of mine. We went to high school together and were in the school band together. Got our first jobs together at the Pizza King. We go way back, don't we?"

"Yeah," he smiled and nodded. His hazel eyes were clear and shining. "Sure do." He pulled a sheet of paper from his back pocket. "I've got this invoice for you. I need to collect some kind of payment before I can continue." His voice was raspy and weighted with a thick country accent.

"We paid you half already."

"Nawp. I ain't received any payment."

Cassidy glanced at me, dumbstruck. "I gave the money to Kenton last week and told him to pay you."

"I never received any money from him."

"I gave him two thousand dollars to give to you. And you're saying he never gave you that money?"

"Nawp." He shifted his ball cap, spit a loogie off to the side, and wiped his face in the crook of his arm.

"Well, maybe you forgot. I'll check with him."

"Nah. I'd remember two grand. Check with him all you want. I still need the money."

She took the paper and looked it over. "Wait. Uh." She hemmed. "Trigg, this isn't the price we discussed."

"Well, I had to add on some labor, and then that one dead maple in the back had to be dug up and split."

"You charge this much for cutting up a tree and removing it? That seems exorbitant."

"That's the going rate, Cass."

"That's crazy. Why is it so much?"

He shrugged. "Labor. Time."

She looked at me, aghast. "I don't believe this. This is at least twenty-five hundred more than you originally quoted. I could understand a few hundred dollars, give or take, but thousands?" She shook her head, staring at the paper.

"It's what it is. We need to get paid at least half of it today."

She looked around. "Why? You're not finished. And it took forever for you to get around to me in the first place. If I pay you now, what will ensure you'll return to finish the job." She turned her head and looked down. She clearly immediately regretted that statement.

"Are you accusing me of cheating you?"

"No, but something isn't right."

"I need my money." He claimed a power stance and crossed his arms over his chest. "Then we'll have to work you back into the schedule—"

Desperation entered her voice. "Trigg, I need this job done before the Grand Opening. Look at the front of my house. You haven't finished planting the shrubs. And what about the garden in the back? Have you replaced the pebbles?"

"I'll get it on the next trip."

"Which is when? It took me a month to get you here this time."

"All I know is I need a check before I leave today."

Cassidy set her jaw, glaring at the guy. Then she did the little half-chuckle common among southerners struggling to maintain politeness in the midst of fury while digging in their heels. "Well, I'm not paying one red cent until the whole job is complete. So, I guess you'll have to figure out how to finish sooner rather than later."

"I need the money today to pay my crew's salaries and cover the supplies we had to buy. We don't work for free, Cass. I'm sure you can understand that."

She crossed her arms over her chest. "I need the job finished first."

He snorted and laughed. "I can't believe you'd do this to me." Trigg pointed his dirty fingers at her and growled. "We're going home right now. But this ain't over, Cass. Not by a long shot."

She gasped. "Are you threatening me?"

"Don't get it twisted. It's no threat. It's a promise." He turned to his crew and whistled. Everyone stopped and looked at him. He cupped his hands around his mouth and shouted. "Wrap it up. Going home." He stormed off, shouting to his crew not to rake one more patch or fill one more hole.

Cassidy ran after him. "Trigg! Trigg! You have to finish this. You can't leave the job half done. I have a grand opening and a party!"

He ignored her, jumped in his truck, and peeled out of the drive. His crew ran to throw their tools in their trucks and followed close behind. Within three minutes, the yard was empty and quiet.

Cassidy deflated and ran her hands over her hair. She slumped up the porch stairs and flopped into the porch swing.

I sat beside her. "Oh, Cassidy. I'm sorry."

She rubbed her forehead. "I *know* I gave Kenton money to give to Trigg. I would've done it myself, but I was in a hurry and had to leave the house. Kenton said he'd wait around for Trigg to show up."

"A check should be easy to trace."

"Except I gave him cash."

I winced. "Oh."

"I know it was stupid, but it was money I had saved and stashed away. I didn't want to have to explain to Derek another bill coming out of the checking account. Besides, I was sure I could trust my own half-brother to do what he said he would." She sighed and dropped her head in her hands. "I'm so stupid."

"No. You're not. Maybe Kenton forgot. Maybe he still has the money."

She screwed up her lips and stared at me in disbelief. She shook her head. "I doubt it." She sighed again as if the world pressed down hard on her chest. "I'll talk to Kenton later. I'd hate for you to witness any more of my drama. Especially the family variety. It can get pretty ugly."

"I understand. I wish I could help in some way. Maybe Jimmy..."

She grabbed my hand. "No! Please don't tell Jimmy anything. I don't want him to worry. His worry will drive me crazy. I don't need him on my case, too."

I didn't like the idea of keeping things from Jimmy, but I wouldn't betray her trust and confidentiality. "Okay. I promise. I won't say anything."

"Besides, Rook, you've helped me more than you can possibly know. With this bourbon release you're planning, you're going to make us *the* premiere place for events and getaways. And most of my problems will be solved."

Chapter Five

The next few weeks passed in a blur as the Four Wild Horses Distillery marketing team prepared for the Exclusive Jazz Age Unbridled Spirits Experience, complete with a bourbon flight tasting, catered hors d'oeuvres, and ghost hunt house tour.

On the day of the event, I arrived early in the afternoon to direct the FWHD set-up crew as they rolled twenty-five bourbon barrels into the center of the ballroom floor and established a bourbon bar along the left wall. The jazz ensemble sat in the corner, warming up their instruments, filling the space with jagged and broken notes.

The room was as beautiful as the rest of the house, with dark polished wood floors, ivory-striped papered walls, ornate crown molding, and jeweled chandeliers dripping crystals.

I helped station high-backed stools around the barrels while answering random questions from the crew. We moved Victorian style red chairs and sofas into empty spots along the walls and together, we decorated the barrel tables with flameless candles and autumnal mums and gerberas in Mason jars. This was certainly a team effort.

I was already regretting my outfit choice. The heels pinched my toes and the teal satin dress, trapped heat against my skin, making sweat form in uncomfortable places. But when I was shopping for the event, I had fallen in love with the long mermaid-cut dress. I just had to have it.

Cassidy strode in wearing a strappy knock-'em dead red, glittery slip dress cut up nearly to where the sun doesn't normally shine, her white thigh flashing with each step. Her blonde hair fell in gentle waves around her face. She oozed 1930s screen siren vibes. Red rhinestone six-inch stilettos click-clacked across the floor, practically setting sparks as she walked. I felt wimpy for internally complaining about my little 3-inch heels when she was gliding around on stilts. My feet hurt more just looking at her shoes.

Behind her trailed a small team of hired wait staff dressed in black shirts, pants, shoes, and aprons. She stopped to issue directives. "It's real simple, y'all. Glasses stay full. No one should have to ask for a refill. The food circulates constantly. But your objective is to make drinks and food appear like magic, as if from thin air. Don't let them see you sweat. Don't let them sense you're in a hurry or anxious or irritable. Calm, grace, pure professionalism. Our goal is to make these people feel like kings and queens. C'mon. I'll show you where to place the food." She led them to a door in the left corner. "Right in here..." They all disappeared into the room.

"What's that room?" I asked one of the candle carriers.

The round-faced girl said, "The billiard room."

That recalled all those old books I had read as part of my literature degree. In the days before WWII, after dinner, the men would remove themselves to play billiards, smoke cigars, drink brandy, talk politics, and gossip while the women withdrew to the drawing room to have a cordial, play cards, or lounge, gossip, and talk politics. I could almost see the women and men in their Edwardian dining finery sitting at a long cloth-covered table, their faces aglow in candlelight, laughing and talking over glimmering crystalware and delicate china, like Downton Abbey.

I finished my tasks about an hour before guests were due to arrive, so I wandered through the house, taking in the high-polished dark wood, stained-glass and blown-glass windows, and the decor intended to recreate the Edwardian era. I climbed the stairs, running my hand up the wide banister. I turned the corner and started to climb the stairs to the next story when I heard voices. I paused on the staircase.

"I don't want to go over this again, Cassidy," Kenton said.

"I know you've been avoiding me. I want to know what you did with the money. I gave you two thousand dollars to give to the landscaper. Trigg says you didn't give him the money."

"Don't you think he'd lie to you to squeeze you for more money?"

"No, I don't think he'd lie to me. I've known him for a long time."

"I'm your brother."

"Half-brother."

"Why do you always qualify it like that? I'm still your brother. We're blood-kin. He's not."

"Fine. Then, as my brother, you should've paid the landscaper like I asked you to."

"I did."

"He says he didn't get the money, Kenton."

"He's lying. Plain and simple. And I don't have time to deal with this right now. I need to finish getting dressed for this party thing you're hosting." A door closed. Cassidy beat on it. "Kenton. Kenton! Come out here right now. I want proof."

Then Derek said, "Cass, we'll deal with this later. I'm sure there's a misunderstanding. C'mon. The guests will be arriving soon."

She growled.

I turned and jogged down the stairs so they wouldn't catch me eavesdropping on them. I rounded the corner and ran smack into a wall of a man. He stood at least a foot and a half over me. He had light auburn hair, a neatly-trimmed beard, a lean, athletic body with broad shoulders. He held my arms and smiled down at me.

"Excuse me," he said. "I didn't realize this was a full contact party." He wore a gray suit and a white shirt, casually unbuttoned at the neck. He must've just stepped out of a James Bond movie. The only thing missing was his vodka martini, shaken, not stirred.

Another man, bald and beefy in a black suit and blue shirt, stood behind him. He had a round, buggy brown eyes, and a bulbous nose.

"I'm so sorry." I flushed.

Derek and Cassidy came up behind me.

"Hey, Gordon. Louis." Derek said, offering his hand to the men.

"Hey, man." Gordon, the cute one, said, shaking Derek's hand. "What's up? The house is looking great."

Louis, the bald one, stepped around Gordon to shake Derek's hand. "Hey. Looks like we're early." Then he glanced at me. He looked at me as though a ghost had risen up and punched him in his puffy lips.

What was he staring at? Creepy-McCreepy. I averted my gaze to focus on the exchange between Gordon and Derek.

Cassidy interjected, "That's alright. People should be arriving any minute." She shook their hands, then looked at me. "I see you've met Rook Campbell. She's the event planner from Four Wild Horses Distillery. She's the mastermind behind this little shindig. Rook, this is Gordon Meece. He's a realtor and works with Kenton. This is his brother, Louis."

"A pleasure to meet you, Miss Rook," Gordon's dark green eyes lit with interest as we shook hands.

"Hi. Nice to meet you. I promise, and for the record, I don't normally tackle the guests."

Gordon ran his eyes over me. "I didn't mind the tackle treatment."

Minding my manners, I begrudgingly offered a weak smile to Louis and shook his massive hand with a simple. "Hello."

He was still staring at me. He said, "Where did you come from?"

I blinked. "Um, pardon?"

Gordon said to Louis. "What are you talking about, Lou?"

That seemed to snap Louis from whatever trance he was in. He laughed by blowing air through his nose. "Sorry, miss. I–I-I thought you were someone else. You look identical to someone…" He let his voice trail off. "It's freaky how much y'all look alike."

Yeah, that wasn't the only freaky thing.

Gordon said to Cassidy, "My father sends his regrets. He had a prior engagement. However…" He pulled a check from his inner chest pocket. "He wanted to make a donation to the charity. Who do I give this to?"

"I can take it." I held out my hand. "I'll ensure it gets to the proper person."

He handed me a check for ten thousand dollars. Just like that. No flinching or wincing or apparent pain. What must it be like to have that kind of money? I tried to keep my face blank as if I handled big money every day. "Thank you for your generous donation."

"I hope it will help many families in our area."

"I'm sure it will."

He removed a business card from his inside pocket and handed it to me. "And if you're ever in the market for a home or…interested in a cup of coffee…"

I accepted the card. It was black with shiny silver writing. In the corner was a silver logo with a phoenix rising over a large, jagged M in Meece & Ford Realty.

"Oh, thank you. But I have a home, and I'm drinking coffee with my boyfriend these days."

He ran his eyes over me in such a way that make me feel naked. "Too bad. If you ever stop drinking coffee with him, or you just need someone to tackle, you have my card."

My cheeks grew warm. "I'll keep that in mind." He was cute, refined, and rich, but I also wanted the temptation out of my sight.

Gordon turned his attention to Cassidy. "You know, I love what you did with the place. But…" He scanned the room. "Looks like it'll be costly and a lot of upkeep. So, if you ever want to unload it, my offer still stands."

"No, thank you. I'm going to hang on to it. It's a gem of Kentucky history."

"History is dead and gone. Land this size could hold two, even three, nice homes. And make you a lot of money."

"Not everything is about the money," Cassidy said, ice entering her voice.

The corners of Gordon's eyes crinkled. "We'll see if you feel that way in a year when you aren't able to rent enough rooms to make your mortgage."

Derek chuckled uncomfortably and clapped Gordon on the back. "Come on in here. I'll get you a drink." The men walked away. Gordon moved with a confident, leonine quality.

Cassidy glared at Gordon's back. "He's been trying to get this property from day one. He can't stand it that we outbid him."

Other guests in Jazz Age costuming arrived in support of Hero's Hope charity, a local organization providing scholarships and financial assistance to the families of fallen soldiers and emergency personnel. Soon, about a hundred people in 1920s attire packed the dimly lit ballroom, eating hors d'oeuvres, and sampling FWHD bourbon flights and cocktails made with our best bourbons. Soft jazz mingled with chatter and laughter.

I stood in the doorway, watching for mishaps or anything needing my assistance, glowing in pride and silently patting myself on the back for pulling off an elegant, fun, themed event. My boss, Pierce Simpson, made eye contact with me across the room and gave me a thumbs-up.

"We should probably go in and mingle, make sure everyone's having a good time," I said.

Something outside caught Cassidy's attention. "Are we expecting more guests?"

I checked the list. "No."

"Then who is this?"

A lady in a blue flapper frock and feathered boa wandered into the foyer from the hall. "Excuse me, hon, but the powder room is out of toilet paper."

Cassidy said, "Rook, will you handle that? I'll see who our newest visitor is."

By the time I finished filling the toilet paper, Pierce had caught me in the hall to congratulate me and introduce me to his wife, Margaret, and a few other people.

Derek sidled up to me and pulled me aside. "Where's Cassidy? We need to give the welcoming announcement."

"She stepped outside for a minute. I'll go get her."

I ran out to the porch where Cassidy was arguing with Trigg. Shrubs had been removed and lay on the ground like dead bodies. The sun had set, and moths battered the porch lights.

She said, "I understand you're mad, but you can't roll up in here on the most important night of my life and start ripping up shrubs."

"You owe me money. If you won't pay, then I'm taking back my work."

"I've talked to Kenton. He says he paid you."

"I'm not lying. He didn't pay me."

"Please, Trigg, I'm in a tight spot here. I will get the money to you, but I'm begging you. Please don't do this to me tonight. We're friends, right?"

"Hey, I've been cheated by friends before."

"I'm not cheating you!" She stamped a foot.

I said, "I'm really sorry to interrupt…"

Trigg looked at me with dead eyes and Cassidy snapped her face around to glare at me with a face full of pain, confusion, and anger.

"Derek's looking for you. It's time to make the welcoming announcement."

She threw up a hand and snapped at me. "I'll be there in a minute. Y'all go ahead."

I wasn't going to argue. I didn't want to frustrate her more, and I didn't want to hold up the event. As I shut the door, I heard her say, "Look, I have a little money stashed inside…" I lingered by the door to eavesdrop. "It's not much. Only a few hundred. But I'll give you that now, and then if you can come back tomorrow, we'll confront Kenton together. Just wait right here." When she turned to come back in the house, I ran back to the ballroom to find Derek, spotting him at the bar talking to Gordon and Kenton.

The conversation seemed serious, intense.

I slowed down. I didn't want to interrupt their conversation.

Derek nodded and threw back a shot of bourbon. Gordon clapped Kenton on the back, and they walked away, exiting the room through the door at the other end of the room, near the billiard room.

I whispered in his ear, "She's talking to Trigg right now. She said she'll be in soon and to go on without her."

"Why's Trigg here?"

"I don't know." I did know. But after what Cassidy had told me about their money troubles, I didn't want to open up a can of worms that would make things worse between her and Derek. I nudged him toward the front of the room. "Just go on."

Derek quieted the band and welcomed everyone to the event and introduced me, Pierce, and the FWHD bourbon sommelier who would guide the flight sampling.

I watched the crowd. Louis stood across the room, staring at me. I turned to focus on what my boss, Pierce, was saying about the faith he had in his team and how the distillery has grown, but still remains a family. When he'd finished his little speech, he, ever full of energy and the love of being at the center of attention, clapped his hands together and announced, "Enough of that. Let's drink some bourbon!"

The crowd hooted and cheered.

The serving staff poured into the room to place sampling flights on the tables. Our bourbon sommelier spoke about our new bourbon, Unbridled Spirits, gave a brief history of our distillery, and dove into the making of the Unbridled Spirits and its flavor profile. He held up the bourbon, which glowed a deep amber in the light. He described how a fifteen-year-old bourbon, typically bitter and tannic, was blended with a younger bourbon to create a balanced, but rich and complex drink. He then highlighted the oak, vanilla, and blackberry notes the tasters could expect to experience and encouraged them to sample it. Afterward, the sommelier guided everyone down the rest of the flight that Four Wild Horses had to offer.

After the tasting, the ghost hunters took over. They all wore black T-shirts with Bluegrass Boos Hounds written in bright green.

The leader was a large, doughy man with a Victorian-style top hat and tattoos sleeving both arms. He wore long denim shorts and Doc Martin combat boots. His deep, thunderous voice, perfect for guiding tours, carried through the room. "Hey, y'all. I'm Jinx. That's my nickname. I've been ghost hunting with Matt here since about age sixteen." He indicated a man with a head of unruly salt and pepper curls, a goatee, and glasses. He held some electronic contraption. Then Jinx pointed to a girl in skinny jeans, a wad of bracelets on her wrists, and her black hair tied into a limp ponytail. "This young lady is Piper. She's been working with us for about five years. And she's a very talented psychic." Jinx continued, "We're going to take half the guests at a time through a tour of the house with Miss Cassidy, who will help provide a history of the house."

Piper said, "I'm certain there are ghosts here. I can feel their presence. Look!" She showed her arm to Matt. "The hairs are standing up on my arms."

"That's one sign," Matt added. "And I'm getting some interesting readings on my EMF gauge."

An excited rumble waved through the audience.

I had to admit this was the part I'd been waiting for all evening. My practical side, which didn't believe in ghosts, warred with a vivid imagination that thought it was possible something existed beyond the human plane. More than anything, I enjoyed the stories about the history of the place, the people who had once lived in this grand, beautiful home, and what their lives might've been like. And if a few ghost stories were sprinkled into the mix, so much the better.

Derek came in behind me. He seemed edgy, maybe a little panicked. "Have you seen Cassidy?"

"No." I looked around the room. "She should've been back by now."

"Huh." His eyes darted, and he smoothed his hand over his chin. "She was supposed to go with the ghost hunters to talk about some of the renovations we did to the house as the tour stopped at each room. She had also researched a bunch of stories about the owners through the years at the library. I have some notes here…" He showed me some papers in his hand. "But I don't know the details as well as she does." He scanned his notes, then checked his watch. "The tour is going to start in a few minutes."

In my desire to help, I said, "Well, why don't you go on with the ghost hunters, and I'll go find Cassidy and send her your way."

"Okay, sounds good. Thanks." He looked around nervously and headed toward the ghost hunters.

Jinx clapped his hands together. "All right, folks, we'll take tables one through twelve now. Then we'll do another tour with everyone else. We'll only be gone for about thirty minutes. At the end, we'll gather everyone to see if we were able to pick up any spectral evidence. Please be sure to bring your phones to take pictures and recordings." The people at the first twelve tables rushed to join the hunters, giggling and fidgeting like school kids.

With the crowd adequately distracted, I stepped out of the room and ran upstairs ahead of the tour group. No, Cassidy. I ran down the servants' stairs and searched the main floor while the tour group headed up the main stairs. Still, no Cassidy. Maybe she had gone back outside. I stepped out on the porch and shouted for her. I leaned over the porch railing, craning my neck to search the darkness. Trigg and his truck were gone. Cassidy was gone.

A shadowy figure darted between the giant catalpa trees beyond the porch lights.

"Hey! Who's out there?"

I charged down the steps, but my heels and aching feet impeded my ability to move quickly. I kicked them off and grabbed them, running in bare feet across the damp grass, shoes in hand. "Hey! You!"

The shadow picked up pace, darting between the trees. He was simply too fast for me, which wasn't saying much since I'd never been much of a runner. A side stitch formed in my right ribs as a car door slammed about a hundred feet from me—the car shielded by the large evergreens. Holding my ribs, trying to rub the pain away, I doubled over to catch my breath. The car sped away.

Though there were a few street lights, they were too dim and sparsely placed to offer much lighting assistance. Worse, there were so many trees in the front yard and lining the streets that the light was nearly completely blocked. I squinted, ducking and weaving to see through the trees, but couldn't track the vehicle. I returned to the house to search for Cassidy. The house was huge, so we might've missed each other.

Instinctively, I searched my hips for my phone to call Jimmy to tell him about the suspicious person sneaking around in the yard. My dress didn't have pockets. As I cursed fashion designers for failing to put pockets in a large number of women's clothing items, I remembered my phone was in my purse. I had tucked it in a cabinet in the blue room where Cassidy said it would be safe. I entered the house and pushed through the tourists collecting in the foyer. I didn't want to interrupt the tour. I could slip in unnoticed to get my purse when they entered the room.

Jinx stood in front of the closed double doors. "Back in the late 1800s, a beautiful opera soprano from Europe had visited Kentucky during her tour of the United States. She wasn't very famous, but was building a name for herself. After her show at the music hall a few miles away, she came here as a special guest, met our local dignitaries, and sang a beautiful aria for the private audience. Afterward, she stepped outside for some fresh air, the summer heat making the house too warm. But she never returned. Everyone thought she had retired to her hotel room down the street.

"Later, the next morning, they found her body floating in the creek at the back of the property. She had been strangled with the silk stole she was wearing. No one ever discovered who killed her or why, but to this day, if you listen closely, you can still hear her sing the beautiful aria she sang in this very room that fateful night." Jinx put his hand on the doorknob and said, "Let's go inside, stand very quietly, and see if we can hear anything." He put his finger to his lips, opened the door, and stood aside to allow people to enter the room.

Instead of a haunted aria, a very human scream tore through the air.

Chapter Six

I pushed past the people lingering in the doorway, rubbernecking. The room was as pristine as the first time I saw it, except for the lifeless body of Cassidy, her legs and arms akimbo. Her blonde, wavy hair splayed on the floor like a spiky crown, as if someone had taken the time to fix it for display, and a blue plaid handkerchief lay over her face. My breath stalled as I stared at the cloth, willing it to rise and fall. I dropped to my knees beside her. Reaching to check her neck for a pulse, I snatched my shaking hand back. A weed eater string snaked around her throat, cutting into the flesh of her neck. *Trigg?* I was too late to do CPR.

Oh, nonononononono. I glanced around. I shrunk internally from the worried faces staring at me, waiting for me to speak. The murderer could still be inside the house with us. Though I was about a thousand percent sure she was dead, I couldn't suppress the spark of hope compelling me to feel for a pulse on her wrist.

Nothing. *No, Cassidy. NO!* My heart sank, heavy as a barrel of bourbon. My hand automatically reached for hers, to hold hers tight and let her know that she wasn't alone, hesitating when I realized I might mess up evidence. That right there was what the police would call a clue, and I'd seen that pattern before…

A female voice said, "Her spirit has moved on."

I jumped. Piper from the Boos Hounds loomed over us. *Thanks, Miss Obvious.* One didn't need to be psychic to know that.

I didn't want to scare everyone with the proclamation of murder, nor was it my place to make such a determination, though the weed eater string made it apparent. While I wasn't a police officer, I knew enough to know they'd want the cleanest possible crime scene.

"Y'all need to get out of here." I looked at the people standing around us, gaping. "All of you. You need to get away from this room right now. We need to preserve evidence for the police when they get here."

Some people ran from the room, others took videos or photos, while others began making phone calls, presumably, I hoped, to 9-1-1. I pushed myself to my feet and ran on tiptoes to the cabinet by the window to retrieve my purse.

My fingers found the small silver clutch purse I'd brought with me and fumbled with the latch. With shaking hands, I extracted my phone and dialed Jimmy. As it rang once, twice, three times, something tickled the back of my neck, and a cool breeze washed over me. I turned to face an open window. My jaw dropped open. That window was closed earlier. Had someone come in through the window to attack Cassidy? Or maybe the attacker came in a different way and left through the window to avoid detection? Maybe that was the person sneaking around in the yard earlier.

"What's up, babe?" Jimmy finally answered, the noise of Planet Fitness music blasting in the background.

I spoke in a low voice. "You need to get out to the J.T. Bolton House immediately. Cassidy is dead."

"Wait. What?"

I repeated myself.

"Oh, God. Are you sure?" His voice was shaking with his movements. The music faded, and the background noise shifted to parking lot noise, indicating that he was clearly running to his car.

My voice quaked with rising emotion. "I'm sure. She's got something like a weed eater string around her neck. Eyes glassy. No pulse. Also, she'd had a fight with the landscaper tonight. That Trigg guy who was out here. You remember him?"

"Yeah. I think. I guess."

"Also, the window is open in the blue room, and I noticed someone creeping around the property earlier. I was about to call you about the creeper when we discovered her."

"We who?"

"The tour group."

He groaned. "How many people are in the vicinity of the body?"

"About fifty people."

He hissed a curse. "Try to clear the area so we can preserve as much evidence as possible."

"I did."

"Good. Don't put yourself in harm's way. I'm coming." His car door closed, and the engine started. "Ask people if they will stay. We can't force them, but it would be helpful to get as many fresh statements as possible. I'll be out there ASAP."

"Okay."

"Oh, and hey…"

"Yeah?"

"Don't get in the center of this. I need everything by the book, because when I catch this guy…"

"Hey—" I was gearing up to resent his statement, even though he was right. After all, this wasn't the first case I'd been entangled in. He hung up before I could say anything else.

I had to take control of this situation. "I need your attention, please. The police are on their way. Please exit the room now so the evidence can be preserved and isn't tainted. It's the most important thing we can do to help them investigate and find out what happened to her."

A lady in a sparkly peach flapper dress spoke, the feather in her headband bobbing as she asked, "Was she murdered?"

A low rumble of voices rose up.

Good Heavens, woman, hush.

"I don't know. We're going to stay out of this room and let emergency professionals do their job when they get here."

I guided people away from the area and blocked the phone cameras with my hand. "Can y'all put the cameras away? Show a little respect?" But panicked people and rubberneckers were horrible listeners.

Jinx and the other Boos Hounds seemed to still have their wits about them so I implored them. "Please, can y'all help here? I'd like to get everyone back to the ballroom."

Jinx, Matt, and Piper jumped in to guide the crowd to the foyer. I closed the blue room doors behind me and planted myself in front of it. I looked around for Derek, but I didn't see him. Where was he?

I tried to speak to the crowd, but no one was listening. I shot a pleading glance at Jinx and he whistled loudly, which brought everyone's voices to a hush.

He said, "Listen up."

I held up my hands, my clutch purse dangling from my wrist like a hooked fish. "Thank you. I've spoken with the police. They would like everyone to stay here until they arrive. Please, we need everyone's cooperation to make this go as quickly and smoothly as possible. They'll be here any minute." A small rumble of voices filled the air.

A gray-haired man looking for a fight said, "You can't make us stay."

"You're right. I can't, but I'm hoping you'll decide to do the right thing and help the police."

"We don't know anything," he shot back.

"It won't hurt to talk to the police anyway. Sometimes the tiniest detail can help them."

They grumbled and mumbled to each other. I needed a way to placate a crowd that threatened to turn ugly in a blink, so I did the only thing I knew to do: offer them free bourbon. They were supposed to buy the bourbon after their initial flight sampling, but desperate times called for desperate solutions. "If y'all will please return to your tables in the ballroom, we'll get you some food and drink. The drinks are on us." My gut twisted into a pretzel. "Please." To my surprise, almost everyone turned like a herd of sheep and entered the ballroom through the door Piper held open. The gray-haired man and his wife, along with a few others, left.

"Matt..." I waved him over. "You and Piper watch this door until I get back. Not a soul enters this door. Got it?"

Matt nodded. "Yes, ma'am."

I rushed into the ballroom and spoke to the bar staff to tell them to give everyone free drinks. They hustled drinks to the fidgety crowd as I searched the room for Derek. Where was he? I ran to the foyer.

Pierce ran toward me from the hallway. "What's going on?" he asked.

"Cassidy, our hostess, is dead." I swiped my eyes. I lowered my voice. "She's been murdered."

Pierce deflated and stepped back as though I'd shoved him. "Oh, my…" He clapped his hand over his mouth. "Are you serious?" He looked around, panicked. "I-I-I don't even know what to say or-or-or…" He squeezed my arm. "I'm so sorry. She was a friend of yours, wasn't she?"

"Yes, thank you. She was my boyfriend's cousin."

He shook his head, his brow wrinkled with concern. "Gosh. That's awful."

"I want to keep people here for the police to get their statements, so I offered them free bourbon."

He ran his hand over his thick, white hair. "You did *what?*"

"I'm sorry I didn't clear it with you first. I did what I had to do. A bunch of them were trying to leave, but Jimmy said he'd prefer they didn't. It will make it easier on the police if they can collect as many statements as possible tonight. And I had a bunch of people rubbernecking, taking pictures and videos, so I had to get them away from the murder scene."

He groaned and rubbed his face.

"I'm sorry, but murder trumps pricey bourbon. Don't ya think?" I didn't have the time to think through the particulars about who I would upset or who would pay for all the bourbon. In one of my Scarlett O'Hara moments, I'd have to think about that later. Right now, I had one mission: try to keep the people here and keep them happy until the police arrived. And I was going to do it come hell or high water.

He waved his hands, his eyes closed. "You're right. You did the right thing." He rubbed his forehead. "We'll figure out how to recover on Monday."

"I need to find her husband. You met him earlier tonight. Have you seen him?"

"No."

A flood of police and forensics techs poured into the house as I stepped into the foyer. Harlan "Bulldog" Goodman entered first, looking like a brick wall in his brown sheriff's uniform and wide-brimmed hat. His russet mustache twitched as he barked orders for the deputies to set up the perimeter. Sheriff Goodman earned the moniker "Bulldog" as a result of his tough-on-crime campaign several years ago. He had been successful in terms of cracking down hard on criminals, but our poor commonwealth had been so deeply overrun with the demons of illicit drugs and dangerous pharmaceuticals that it proved a larger job than one man and his team of deputies could manage. He planted his hands on his hips and leveled his gaze at me. His chestnut brown eyes hardened into pebbles, and he shook his head.

"If this don't beat all." He pushed his hat back and scratched his forehead. "Rook Campbell. How is it that *you* always happen to be where the trouble is?"

I shrugged. "Lucky, I guess."

Goodman and I were on a tentative truce. I'd been angry with him for a long time because he'd been the lead investigator in my mom's murder case when he arrested my dad. And his apparent resentment of my father had prejudiced his impression of me. But over the past several months, the sheriff and I had come to understand that neither of us meant the other any harm. While we wouldn't be inviting each other to our family barbeques, we were no longer openly hostile to each other.

"With luck like yours, it's probably best to have no luck at all."

"I can't argue with that logic, sheriff. I'd sure sleep better at night if I saw fewer dead people."

Goodman said, "Well, Miss Rook, we have at least one point we can agree on."

Jimmy rushed in. He was in his gym clothes, a pair of jogging shorts and a T-shirt with his badge on a chain around his neck. I wanted to hug him, but I didn't want to put him in a weird position with his boss. So, I gave a sympathetic squeeze to his arm. He barely acknowledged me as he passed by to the blue room. He took a knee beside Cassidy, gently touched a tendril of her hair. He pressed his fist to his mouth and turned his head away so we couldn't see his face. But I could tell by the shake of his shoulders he was crying. After a few moments, he wiped his eyes with his T-shirt sleeve. Emotion clenched my stomach, and my throat tightened. I wanted to comfort him, but I couldn't enter the crime scene, and I knew any words or hugs I offered would be futile. I hugged myself.

Goodman said Jinx. "How're you doing, son?"

"All right, sir." Jinx shifted from side to side, visibly uncomfortable.

"Your brother staying out of trouble?"

"Yessir. He got out of rehab about six months ago. Still clean. Got a job at the recovery center as a counselor."

Goodman offered a stiff, congratulatory nod in the way manly men do. "That's terrific news. I like to hear when young men turn their lives around." Goodman looked at me again. "Who found the body?"

"We all did. The tour group, led by Jinx and his friends. The tour group filed in, a woman screamed, and everything went sideways from there."

Jimmy returned to my side. Goodman said, "Do you know the victim?"

"It's my cousin," Jimmy said. "Cassidy Wallace." He sniffed.

"Really? I'm sorry to hear that, son."

Jimmy continued. "She appears to have been strangled with a weed eater string."

I added, "I witnessed her arguing with a landscaper prior to that. They had been having a pretty heated back and forth for a few weeks overpayment for a job he did."

"Alright." He pulled a pen and notepad out of his front shirt pocket. "What was the name of the landscaper?"

"Trigg West. He had come to talk to her tonight." I recounted both conversations I'd overheard between Trigg and Cassidy a few weeks ago and tonight. I added, "By the time we found her, Trigg was gone."

The sheriff nodded. "Okay. Do you know where he lived or if he had an office? Any kind of location information?"

I shook my head. "No. Sorry."

He called over a deputy and asked her to search out Trigg then he turned to Jimmy. "Do you know of any enemies your cousin might've had? Or anyone she was having issues with?"

Jimmy said, "I can't think of anyone. If she was having problems, she didn't tell me."

Guilt pressed down on me. Cassidy had shared a lot of her issues with me and had made me promise to keep her confidentiality and not say anything to Jimmy. She didn't want him to worry, and she didn't want him to pester her with his worries. Now I wish I'd said something. I had to say something now, though. Even if it was going to upset Jimmy. "Well…" I hemmed.

Jimmy focused on me with intensity like a bird dog on prey.

I licked my lips and pushed forward. "She complained about how she and Derek were in pretty desperate financial straits." I unpacked the situation with Kenton and how she'd borrowed a bunch of money from him and from her parents behind Derek's back.

Jimmy's face grew darker as he glared at me. "Where is Derek?"

"I don't know. I was on my way to look for him after I settled the crowd. I'm not sure he and Kenton even know Cassidy is dead."

Jimmy said, "I'll check downstairs. They should hear it from family." He whispered to me. "We'll talk later." He strode toward the stairs.

I sank. He was not happy with me.

"How many people were in the room?" Goodman asked.

I thought back to what seemed like a year ago. "I'd say about fifteen people inside the room. Everyone else was standing out here, waiting to get in. But the people in the front stopped and held up the group. I pushed my way into the room to get a look at what was going on."

"Of course you did."

I crossed my arms over my chest. "For your information, I was headed into that room because my purse was in there, and I needed my phone to call Jimmy. I'd seen someone stalking around the grounds earlier, and I thought he should know."

"Who was it?"

"I don't know. Whoever it was drove off. But maybe it was Cassidy's killer. Because the window in the blue room is open, and it was closed earlier tonight."

"You're sure?"

"Yes."

"What car did they drive?" He was primed to write down the information.

"I don't know. I couldn't see. It was dark, and trees were blocking my view."

He sighed. "All right. If you think of anything else, let me know." The sheriff turned to a deputy. "Deputy, get a few other deputies, and y'all start pulling people out to interview. Start with the ones who were actually in the room with the body." The officer rushed off as Goodman stepped into the blue room to inspect Cassidy's corpse.

Since Jimmy was checking downstairs for Derek, I moved to check upstairs. I couldn't abide not being useful, standing around gaping like everyone else. I slipped through the stream of techs and officers and up the stairs to Derek and Cassidy's bedroom. He wasn't there. I checked the next room, a corner room at the end of the hall. It appeared to be an office or study. Boxes were piled everywhere. They hadn't finished moving in yet. The desk stood in front of the window, which was flanked by built-in bookshelves. The shelves were sparsely filled with books, pictures, and knickknacks. Bubble wrap and brown packing paper filled in one corner of the room.

The stacks of papers and files on the desk called out to me like a siren song for the chronically nosy. I checked behind me, closed the door, and rushed toward the desk. Maybe there was more to Cassidy's story. Maybe she was in more trouble than she let on, and someone decided to get her out of the way. I shuffled through a few of the files on top of the stack. Nothing spectacular. Some old college papers. Some old credit card and bank statements. Money poured like water through Cassidy and Derek's hands. They sure loved to spend what Derek brought in. There were some client files. Files concerning decoration ideas. A file for keeping up with expenditures and receipts. It was strange that all of this was still hard copy. I thought I was the only weirdo who kept both paper and digital files because I didn't trust my computer to always work. I'd had far too many computer issues.

Beneath these files was a legal pad of yellow paper with Cassidy's name written over and over and over. I looked closely at the signatures. As a former middle school and high school student who sometimes wanted to get out of school or gym class and took it upon herself to forge her grandmother's signature on an excuse note, I recognized the familiar sight of signature forgery: the shakiness of the letters, the varying slants and garlands of a hand trying way too hard to be careful and perfect. That was weird. I took a picture with my phone. Clearly, someone was trying to forge Cassidy's name.

I shifted through a few more papers and files to find something Cassidy would've signed. I wanted to compare her writing to this. I found a furniture delivery form signed by Cassidy. The difference was obvious. Her writing was round, puffy, measured. Her Es and As were more open and welcoming; there were fewer garlands as she mixed print and cursive. This other writing was narrower, sharper, the Es and As closed off and uninviting, more garlands connecting the letters. I took a picture and found another example for comparison. And found a list Cassidy had written. I took a picture, discomfort settling in. Unhappy and dark suspicions began to form in my mind about Derek. The practitioner of the forgery had to be Derek. But why? I shook my head and continued rifling through the papers. I didn't really want to know why. I didn't want to think he might've had something to do with—

Then I saw it. A life insurance form. Completed. For one million dollars. That right there was known as a clue. It was also known as a motive. I looked closely at it. Cassidy's signature wasn't quite right. It more closely resembled the signatures on the legal pad than the forms and lists Cassidy had written. My stomach twisted. *Oh, this is not good.* I snapped a picture of that, too, and made my way to the door. I didn't want to get caught snooping. I opened the door.

Jimmy.

My heart jumped into my throat, and I clapped my hand over my heart as I fell back against the wall. "Crap! Dang it, Jimmy. You scared me."

He glowered at me, then his eyes darted around the room. "What are you doing in here? I hope you aren't doing what I *think* you're doing because that would be interfering with an investigation."

Well, this presented a quandary. I could lie about my presence here and keep from getting in deeper hot water with him. But to do so might slow down Cassidy's murder investigation, and I wanted the killer caught and punished to the fullest extent of the law. Or I could tell the truth, take the heat I'd receive, get my feelings hurt, but hopefully get closer to justice. I sighed, blowing my cheeks out like a pufferfish. Sometimes, taking the heat was the only way. Remembering Churchill and the quote about getting through hell, I steeled myself for the inevitable.

"I have something to show you. You need to get a warrant. Now."

Chapter Seven

Jimmy rolled his eyes. In one move, he grabbed my arm, pulled me out of the room, and shut the door. His fingers digging into my arm, he marched me away from the office, down the hall, into the pentagonal room, and through the double French doors where he shut us out of the house on the widow's walk. The ultimate privacy.

"I don't even know where to begin with you," he said. He rubbed his face and paced, hands on hips, in tight little circles. "I swear if you do anything to mess up this case, of all cases, Rook, I'll—I'll—" He lifted his hands as if he might reach for my throat.

I glared at his hands. "You'll what?" I narrowed my eyes. "You'd better think through your next words very carefully, Deputy Duvall."

That seemed to snap him awake. He dropped his hands. "Sorry. I'm sorry. You know I'd never…" He huffed and leaned on the railing. "I'm upset about Cassidy. About a lot of things."

"I know. I'm sorry." I put a hand on his back, hard as a stone.

His voice broke. "Why didn't you tell me what she was going through? Why didn't you tell me she was having such money troubles?"

"She asked me not to, Jimmy. She knew you'd worry, and she didn't want to trouble you."

He shook his head. "You should've told me."

"And break my promise? Break her trust? Really? That's not the sort of friend I am."

He pressed his thumb and forefinger into the bridge of his nose. "You're right. I guess. I just can't help but wonder if she'd still be alive if I'd known about her struggles and been able to help her somehow."

"You can't do that to yourself, Jimmy. You'll drive yourself crazy. The only one to blame is the killer. That's it."

He sniffed and stood up. "Maybe. I feel like I failed her, though."

Maybe I should've broken my confidence with Cassidy. Maybe Jimmy was right. Though he didn't come right out and say it, the implication was there: if he'd known, he might've helped, and she might still be alive. He blamed me for not making it known. I hadn't missed that.

After a brief silence, he said, "So why do you think I need a warrant?"

"Because of this." I showed him my phone and explained what he was looking at. "So you need to get your hands on those papers before Derek gets any bright ideas about destroying them."

He looked at the pictures, nodding. "Yeah. HM. Or, a crafty girl I know could sneak them out."

I scoffed. "Whatever. You know better. Such evidence would never be admissible."

"I know, but an officer can dream for it to be so easy, right?"

Then he grew pensive. "Hm."

"What?"

"Don't you think it's kind of stupid to leave something so obvious lying around, though?"

"Well, criminals do stupid things all the time."

He nodded, chewing on the inside of his lip. "Yeah. Maybe." He opened the door to the pentagonal room and stepped inside. "Well, I have to get back to work. Thanks for the information. I'll work on getting the warrant. Hopefully, I can get hold of the papers in time." I followed. He turned to me, rubbing the arm he had earlier gripped. "Hey, I'm sorry I lost my temper."

"Given the situation, apology accepted. This time."

"Understood." He wrapped me in his arms and held me. But I couldn't melt into him like before. It was as if a wall had dropped between us, dividing us. We separated, and he kissed my forehead. "Let's go. I have to get back to work."

As we landed in the foyer, Kenton rushed from behind the staircase, with a beer in one hand and a cell phone pressed to his ear in the other. When he saw all the officers and forensics techs milling around the foyer, his face twisted in confusion. He spoke into his phone. "I-uh-I gotta go. There's a bunch of cops here." He looked flushed and hectic.

I studied Kenton to figure out why he was sweaty and flushed. Could he have had something to do with Cassidy's death? Why else would he be so sweaty and panicky? They did have big money issues between them and their relationship in general seemed strained. After all, she always referred to him as her half-brother, certain to emphasize the distinction. Further, she talked about family drama and how it sometimes grew ugly. Sounded like grounds for murder to me.

Many things in my life had made me a suspicious person. I stopped myself in my tracks. *Good Lord, Rook! What is wrong with you?* He's her half-brother. Perhaps I'd been reading too many true crime books. Not everyone was a murderer. Kenton was clearly out of shape. It wouldn't take much exertion to put him out of breath. Then I remembered something else. The very first day I'd met him, he was sweaty then, too.

I was about to mark him off my list when I recalled that first day in more detail. He'd pulled a blue plaid handkerchief out of his pocket to wipe his face. A blue plaid handkerchief. Much like the one over Cassidy's face. It wasn't likely many men on the premises owned such an item. Shock yawned in my brain as I marked him down on my suspect list again. It was hard to believe, but not impossible, for Kenton to kill his own half-sister—especially if their relationship was as contentious as it seemed. After all, family members killed each other all the time. Kenton hung up his phone and engaged the nearest officer to find out what was going on.

I sat on the staircase. It kept me out of the way, but allowed me to watch the sad spectacle in front of me. This was a time to employ Occam's Razor: the simplest explanation was usually the correct one. Derek was likely the killer. The insurance policy I'd uncovered upstairs pointed clearly to him. And, though he wasn't a stupid man, maybe he had, like many criminals, grown too confident and cocky; so, he didn't feel the need to get rid of the evidence. Besides, in almost every *Forensics Files* or *Dateline*, the killer was usually the person closest to the victim. Trigg, Derek, Kenton. The clues and suspects were adding up.

Then I saw Derek sitting in the dining room, sobbing, red-faced, with tears and mucus covering his face. His whole body shook as he keened for his dead wife. He implored the deputy hovering nearby to tell him why and who, but the deputy could only say they were looking into it. Kenton stood by his brother-in-law, and hand on his shoulder, and tried to answer the deputies' questions.

Would a wife-killer be so distraught over the woman he had just killed? I didn't know Derek very well, but the little interaction I'd had with him pushed him further down my list of suspects.

My boss, Pierce, came into the foyer with his wife. He stopped by the staircase where I sat until someone needed me.

"You all right?" He asked.

I shrugged. "I will be. I'm sorry if I caused any problems by giving away drinks. I didn't know what else to do. I panicked."

"It's okay. It's small potatoes compared to everything else going on here. Though we will have to find a way to redeem this situation. But we'll talk more on Monday. Hopefully, this won't get too much attention."

I tried not to look at him as if he'd just sprouted another head. What was he thinking? Had he just crawled out from under a rock? This was a murder in a historic home in the tiny town of Rothdale. This news was going all over everything. And as if thinking about the news willed it into existence, I saw through the open front door, the WTVB news van crawl down the drive. "Speak of the devil," I said.

Pierce sank. "This won't be good will it?"

I shook my head. "Probably not."

"Hell's bells," he groaned. "I'm getting out of here before the reporter finds out who I am. I do not want to be involved in any interviews."

People climbed out of the van and began unloading equipment.

Pierce whispered to me. "Please do not say anything to the press. Don't even let them know you work for us, and tell the crew they are *not* to speak to the press at all. We'll deal with all this Monday. We'll release an official statement then. We need to circle the wagons. This could hurt us if anyone talks."

Surely, he was only panicking. After all, Cassidy didn't die on our property. He probably thought any association with the death would hurt the distillery and the brand. In an attempt to assure him and give him a small measure of comfort, I jumped up, ready for action. "I'll handle it. I'll talk to the crew now." I sent a group text for everyone to gather at the wet bar in the ballroom immediately. "Rest assured, I'm not going to say anything to anyone and will do everything I can to protect the distillery, but you know there's no way to keep this quiet. Our name is all over this event on social media, fliers, and invitations. Besides, we even did a promotional spot and interview on the TV station, so there's no way to keep our name out of it."

"You're right. I'll call our lawyer. I'll see if I can run some kind of damage control."

"Sounds like a plan. Keep your cool. This will all be okay. Y'all go home before you get trapped. I'll see you Monday."

Pierce and his wife rushed out the door. The reporter made a beeline for the house while the crew began setting up. A deputy posted on the front porch stepped forward to stop the reporter and speak with her. I ran on blistered feet to the ballroom to prepare the distillery crew to keep their silence.

Chapter Eight

All this running around in a cocktail dress was heating me up. I flapped the top of my dress to cool my face and chest as I made my way to the front porch to bask in the cool October air. In spite of the circumstances, it was a beautiful night. Crickets chirped in the darkness; a light breeze rustled the leaves. I checked the time on my phone. I couldn't stay much longer. The event, including breakdown and cleanup, was planned to end in about thirty minutes so we could be out of the house by ten. I needed to get home to Prim. I texted Patrice Dawnson, my best friend Millie's mom, to let her know I might be a smidge late. I hated to keep her longer than necessary. Normally, I would've had my neighbor, Batrene Bishop, sit with Prim, but Batrene couldn't do it. She was attending a wedding with her sister.

I sat on the window sill, removed my shoes, rubbed my squeaking pinky toes, and poked at the grouchy blister on my heel. I watched people come and go. Deputies stood around talking to each other, to techs, to frightened guests. The news crew set up their camera and lights. Techs rushed to and from their vans. Cassidy's smiling face kept popping up in my mind, haunting, chilling. A dull throb settled behind my eyes. Only a few weeks ago, I was in this very house, talking to her, laughing with her, helping her paint, listening to her hopes and dreams, and rallying behind her to cheer her on. It was as if I had *needed* her to succeed as if her success would somehow fix something for me, show me what was possible.

Tears filled my eyes. And in a snap, the light was snuffed, the life ended. Life was such a strange and wonderful thing, both beautiful and painful.

It was so easy to forget it was finite, and at any moment, the people we've loved are just—gone.

Sufficiently cooled off and not wanting to be alone with my grim thoughts a moment longer, I stuffed my feet in my shoes and with a cleansing exhale pulled myself together. It was time to alert the crew to start breakdown and cleanup so we could go home.

As I turned to enter the house, Gordon Meece stepped outside and lit a cigarette. That took him down about ten points on the attractive meter—not that I was really interested in him anyway. But I wasn't dead. I could appreciate a handsome man when I saw him.

The news reporter—a shiny, young blonde—put her microphone in his face. "We understand there's been a murder here tonight. Can you elaborate on what transpired?"

He ran a cool gaze over the woman, blowing smoke slowly from his nostrils. "Who told you it was a murder?"

She wasn't going to be asked anything. "Can you say who was involved? Has the family been notified?"

"Sounds like someone got it twisted, sweetheart." He took another drag from the cigarette. A smirk crossed his face. "No comment." Spotting me, he walked toward me. "Miss Rook."

I stopped. "Yes, Mr. Meece."

He put his hand to his heart and pretended to be pained. "Oh, so formal." He motioned his head toward the corner of the porch, indicating I should follow him. He leaned against the brick. "It's a shame, isn't it?" He shook his head and blew smoke away from us. Little good it did since the breeze blew it back in my face. When he noticed, he apologized and said, "Sorry. I'll stand downwind." He lifted the cigarette. "My greatest vice. I can't seem to kick these things no matter how hard I try." He took another puff and blew it over his shoulder, the wind effectively carrying it away from me. "Yeah, a shame. I'd only met her a couple times, but I liked her."

"Yeah, me too. She was a special person."

"So, what do you think happened?"

I stood with my back to the yard to shield our conversation from the prying eyes and ears of the reporters. "Clearly, it's murder," I whispered, trying to hold my breath against the cigarette smoke. "She'd been strangled."

He frowned and shook his head. "Awful."

"It is. I can't imagine who would do such a thing."

"Can't you?" He tipped his head.

I blinked. "Well, that's blunt."

"Sorry, hon. I don't mean to speak ill of the dead, but Cassidy Wallace had a few enemies. Even her husband didn't like her most days." He stroked his beard, releasing smoke from his nose.

I eyed him suspiciously. That didn't sound right. She and Derek seemed solid. "What makes you say that?"

He drew from his cigarette, the ash glowing orange. "From what I understand, she and Derek were discussing divorce."

Bells went off in my brain. That definitely didn't seem truthful. They had married only a couple of months ago. I had attended their wedding. Everything seemed perfect—so perfect I was actually briefly, mildly jealous, but that was another matter. I felt compelled to defend her. "I don't think so."

He shrugged. "That's what I heard. Seems Derek has a bit of a gambling and alcohol problem."

I crossed my arms over my chest. "Then wouldn't *she* be more interested in getting rid of *him*?" Besides, from what Cassidy had told me, she was the one spending all the money on the business, causing Derek to be upset with her.

"Exactly. She was on his case all the time, then threatened to leave him, keep the business, take a chunk of his money for alimony…" He shrugged. "Apparently, they fought over money all the time. Money issues can kill a marriage faster than anything."

True enough. I didn't want to believe him. After all, I didn't know Gordon Meece from Adam. Derek seemed like a nice guy, a loving husband. But I'd been alive in the world long enough to know that sometimes people lie and put up fronts and pretend to be something they weren't. And I'd read and seen enough true crime stories about black widowers who married women, took out insurance claims on them, then killed them for the money. If Derek had placed a million dollar insurance policy on Cassidy with hopes of collecting money from her death—especially if he was desperate for money—then she'd decided to leave him, he would be pushed to act sooner rather than later. Then, knowing about her recent disputes with Trigg and Kenton, he might've used the weed eater string to distract police and planted the plaid handkerchief to cast attention on Kenton. But Derek? I thought about the man in the dining room crying his eyes out. No. I shoved the thought away. It didn't match up.

I shook my head. "Eeeh. I'm not sure about your information. They seemed pretty happy to me."

"Well, I can tell you from my own experience with divorce that married couples can often put on a peaceful act for others."

I thought back to my own divorce from Cam almost two years ago. I didn't remember us putting on a peaceful act. But then we didn't exactly drag things out, either. Of course, we didn't have any money or assets to fight over, which inevitably seemed to make divorces more bitter.

He added, "Ever see the movie *War of the Roses*? My divorce was similar. But then my ex-wife was a she-devil." He chuckled. "Should've listened to my parents. They never liked Trish. They tried to warn me." He shook his head. "She took nearly everything. I'm only now beginning to recover from our divorce ten years ago."

"That's unfortunate. Especially when kids are involved."

"Got lucky there. We didn't have kids."

"That's good." But I wasn't completely convinced about Cassidy and Derek's purported divorce. "How did you know about their pending divorce?"

He pulled a final drag on his cigarette. "I didn't know them as well as I know her brother, Kenton. He and I have worked together for over a decade." He shrugged. "So, you know, we talk about our families." He put the cigarette out against the brick and tossed the butt into the grass.

I nodded. "I see." I needed to speak to Jimmy now. My brain was about to explode with everything I was learning. "Well, I'd love to chat more, but I've got some stuff to take care of. There's a lot going on tonight."

"Of course." He walked with me and opened the door. "Beauty first."

The flattery was obvious, but Prim raised me to be polite, so I thanked him and stepped through the foyer to find Jimmy, almost running into Derek.

He looked like a zombie, his face blank, his eyes distant. I squeezed his arm. "I'm really sorry about Cassidy. Are you okay?"

He nodded, dazed.

"Is there anything I can do for you?"

He blinked at me. His glazed eyes stared through me. He nodded. "I-I don't know what to do."

He seemed to be genuinely in shock, but maybe he was pretending. I searched his face and eyes to see if there was any pretense, but I couldn't spot any. Was he such a fine actor?

A deputy stepped up and took Derek by the elbow. "Mr. Wallace, we have a few more questions. Can we speak to you over here?"

Derek nodded.

"Derek," I said. "If you need anything at all, you let me know, okay? I'll help however I can."

He nodded and followed the deputy like a toddler.

Heavy with grief and exhaustion, I returned to the ballroom and found Jimmy in a corner interviewing a pudgy woman in a black-fringed flapper dress.

I informed the distillery crew lead I would be leaving soon and instructed him to round up everyone to begin breakdown and cleanup so they could go home, too. I watched the time on my phone, anxious to get home to Prim, and paced while I waited for Jimmy's interview to end. When the lady walked away, I swooped in and spilled my guts, telling him everything about my conversation with Gordon.

A light of suspicion brightened his face. "Is that so?" He thought for a moment. "Interesting."

"Do you think it's that simple though? Do you think Derek would be so stupid as to take out an insurance claim so soon before killing her?" I put my finger to my bottom lip. "Of course, if he had a gambling issue and was desperate for money, he might've been forced to act if she was talking about leaving him."

"Rook—"

"And then there's the matter of her brother. Half-brother. He'd loaned her money. They were fighting over that. I'm also willing to bet he didn't pay Trigg the money he was owed. But why?"

"Rook—"

"I'm almost certain Kenton's handkerchief was over her face."

He raised his voice. "Rook!"

I blinked at him, my face growing warm.

"You do remember me telling you to stay out of this?"

"Of course. And I will. But I had this information, and I'd rather give it to you than to Goodman. You want to be sheriff, right? Wouldn't it help you to be the one to solve this case first?" I shrugged. "I mean, I assume. I don't really know how any of this works."

He shook his head and put his hands on his hips. "Just stop. Okay? Stop. Quit interfering. Quit sticking your nose where it doesn't belong. I don't want you getting involved in this, doing something to cause our case to get tossed on a technicality."

It wasn't what he said so much as *how* he said it. His tone rubbed me all kinds of wrong ways and raised my hackles. "Don't talk to me like that. Especially when I'm only trying to help."

He growled and emphasized each word by chopping one of his palms with the side of the other hand. "You. Are. Not. A. Cop. You're doing things that're going to get us both in deep trouble, destroy any of my chances of election, if I decide to run, and screw up this case." He poked me in the temple. "Get that through your head."

I smacked his hand away in instant rage. "How dare you. I'm not a dog to be ordered around, and I'm not a child to be scolded and lectured. And I don't care how annoyed you get with me; you aren't allowed to touch me while you're upset. You may be grieving and worried, but that doesn't give you the right to treat me this way." Angry tears bubbled into my eyes, which only made me angrier. "Now get out. I have work to do."

"Will do. Stay out of the way of *my* work, which is far more important. You play with bourbon. I catch bad guys."

I bit the side of my mouth to keep from crying and struggled against the overwhelming desire to pounce on him like a rabid wildcat. Logically, he was right, but his tone, demeanor, and lack of even a scintilla of gratitude left me seething. It might've taken him twice as long to figure out any of the stuff I'd handed him on a virtual platter. I shouted at his back. "Fine. I'll stay out of your way. Way out of your way." I popped open my clutch and dug out my keys. "You won't need to worry about me bothering you for a long while."

Clearly, I wasn't wanted or needed. The crew could handle things on their own. I had a bubble bath, a Kentucky Spice soda, and Moon Pie calling my name. I was D-O-N-E. I strode out of the room, pushed my way through the crowd and chaos in the foyer, and out of the house to my car. I jammed the key in the ignition, cursing under my breath.

The car wouldn't start.

Chapter Nine

I tried again. *Click, click, click, click.* I knew less about cars than anything else on the planet, but even I knew that was not a good sound. There had been no indication earlier in the day that anything was wrong with my car. Then, all of a sudden, nothing. Nada. Zip. No juice.

"Blast it all!" I shouted, pounding the steering wheel and throwing a good old-fashioned hissy fit. I got out of the car and slammed my door. Hands on hips, I paced in circles, trying to figure out what to do. Millie was out of town. Prim couldn't drive because her medications made her woozy, and Patrice would want to get home. Cam. Maybe. He was probably working, but I called him anyway.

He picked up. The background was filled with loud voices. "Hey. What's up?"

The sound of his voice soothed me. "I don't suppose you could pick me up at the J.T. Bolton House? My car won't start."

"What's wrong with it?"

"I don't know. It won't turn over. It keeps making a clicking sound."

"Ew. That's not good. Sounds like your alternator."

"I don't know what that means."

"It means a hefty mechanics bill."

"Great." I leaned against my car. "Exactly what I needed."

"Are you okay? You sound…upset."

"Oh, Jimmy's a jackass."

"Ah. Been fighting?"

"Yeah. When *aren't* we fighting?" I didn't want to talk about Jimmy.

"Well, he's always struggled with keeping girlfriends. He has a hot temper, and he's too involved with his work."

"Great. I picked a winner. Why didn't you tell me this?"

He scoffed. "Like you would've listened. If I'd told you all his faults, it would've only made you more determined to date him."

"That's not true."

He laughed. "You've met *you*, right?"

I rolled my eyes. "Okay, fine. Whatever."

"You're one of those unfortunate people who can only learn the hard way. Most of the time."

Was this beat up on Rook night? "Okay. Okay."

"Besides, Jimmy really is a good guy. And he needs a good woman in his life. I think the right woman could take the edge off of him. He's my best friend, and I figured he deserved the best. I figured you're the best thing to happen to him in a long time. Once I got over being mad at you two, that is."

"That's sweet of you. Thank you. But I don't think it's working out."

He sighed. "I'm sorry, Rook. And I'm sorry about your car." His voice was edged with genuine disappointment. "I wish I could help, but I can't. We're swamped. We're short-staffed tonight, and we have a huge crowd for the U of B versus Florida Gators game. It's fourth quarter, fourth down, thirty seconds, and U of B's ball. They have a real chance to win. And people are drinking and eating like it's their last night on earth."

The U of B Thoroughbreds and Florida Gators had a fierce rivalry stretching back to the invention of college football. "I get it. Be careful. There'll probably be a few couches set on fire on campus tonight, a few cars overturned, and lots of other drunken revelries."

He laughed. "No doubt." He paused. "Who are you going to get to take you home?"

"I don't know. Maybe I can wrangle a co-worker." One thing for certain: I'd eat broken glass before I asked Jimmy.

Hey, I've got to go. I'll call and check on you later, though, okay?"

"Okay."

"And, hey, text me when you get home so I know you made it okay."

"Okay." I hung up.

That was everyone I knew who might be willing or available to help. I couldn't call an Uber or Lyft because I hadn't hit payday yet, and the last student loan payment I'd made, along with helping to pay for Prim's medications (for which she'd fought me like a bobcat), had tapped me out. Since the big game was going on tonight, Uber and Lyft would cost a lot more. I looked up the road, briefly wondering if I could make the ten-mile walk to my house along country roads with no sidewalks or streetlights. Looking down at my feet, I determined, "Not in these shoes." My pinky toes were already rebelling against me.

I huffed out a breath and looked back at the grand house buzzing with activity. Police and techs jogged up and down the stairs; reporters milled about in the front yard, hoping to snap up a story. I ran through a mental list of my co-workers. I didn't want to ride with a man because I didn't want to further aggravate Jimmy, nor did I want to start up the rumor mill at work or give the man any ideas about my intentions. So that left the three women. Paige lived thirty minutes in the opposite direction, so I didn't want to ask her. Blair was a little weird and scary. Amy was chatty, ditzy, shallow, and, frankly, annoying, but she was my best bet.

"Looks like you're going to have to suck it up, buttercup." I started back toward the house.

Louis Meece stepped out of the shadows.

I jumped and chuckled nervously. "You scared me."

"Sorry about that. Didn't mean to." Something about his smile seemed off, as if it was a mask. He held up his phone. "I came out here to make a phone call. It's kind of noisy around the house."

"Yeah. Kind of a wild night, huh?"

"Yeah." He pointed at my car. "You having trouble?"

"My car won't start."

"Oh. Bummer." He sympathized. "I'm kind of a car geek. You want me to take a look at it?"

"Uhm…" Honestly, I didn't want him anywhere near me. He made my skin crawl. However, if he helped me get out of here, then I'd suck it up.

"Sure."

We walked back to my car together in silence while I said a mental prayer *pleaseohpleaseohpleaselethimfixit.*

Louis sat inside the car, door open, with one leg hanging out. He tried to start the car.

Click, click, click. He got out of the car, shut the door, and handed me the keys. "Well, I've got good news and bad news."

"Uh-oh."

"Good news. I know what it is."

Hope bloomed.

"Bad news. It's your alternator. You ain't going anywhere in that car tonight. You'll need to get it towed."

The hope shriveled up and dropped dead. The urge to throw myself on the ground and kick and cry like a toddler was almost too much to resist. I sighed and rubbed my face, hoping I didn't smear my dark eyeshadow and eyeliner everywhere. "How much does it cost to repair?"

"Depends on the mechanic. Could run you between four, five hundred, or even a thousand."

The acid shot up my esophagus like a bottle rocket, and my brain filled with static. The first tears breached the hold and slipped down my face. "I don't know what I'm going to do." There was actually a lot more I could've said about my student loans. Medical debt. Terminally ill grandmother. Fights with Jimmy. Cassidy's murder. Instead, I whirled around to rest against the car and put my face in my hands. My head throbbed against the pressure to collect myself and regain composure.

Louis put a hand on my back and I jumped away as if I'd been shocked. Oddly, in the

heat of my mental fizz, I'd forgotten about him, but his touch snapped me back.

"Oh. Sorry." His hand was still lifted. "You seemed upset."

I backed away. "Uh. Yeah. I am." I glanced around the yard. "I should probably get back to the house."

"Do you need a ride home? I could take you."

The thought of asking Amy for a ride seemed less daunting. She would probably annoy the bejeezus out of me, but it was better than getting in a car with this guy. Of course, I was assuming she could even take me. She was young and sociable; she might have plans.

"Oh, uh. Thanks for the offer, but my boyfriend is inside." I didn't need to tell him my boyfriend was a big jerkface I wasn't speaking to.

He lifted his chin. "Ah. Who's your boyfriend?"

"Deputy Jimmy Duvall." I started back toward the house.

Louis followed after me. "I didn't know you had a boyfriend."

I frowned. A strange thing to say.

"You know, you look just like a woman I once knew."

"Yeah. You said that earlier when we first met." I picked up my pace, trying to ignore my screeching pinky toes. So did he.

"It's amazing how much you look like her."

"Yeah?" I didn't care to hear any more about this guy or the woman he knew.

"I was crazy about her."

"Huh."

"But it didn't…work out."

Why was this guy telling me his life story? How was I supposed to respond to this? I didn't want to be a jerk, but he made me uneasy. I was afraid any sympathy I showed him would only encourage him. However, he was also the brother of a major donor for tonight's charity. All I could say was, "Sorry to hear that."

"How long have you and your boyfriend been dating?"

"A few months."

"Is it serious?"

"Extremely," I lied. It was a necessary lie.

I wove through the news crew on the front lawn, but I couldn't seem to shake Louis. We climbed the steps.

Gordon was on the front porch and called out to his brother. "Hey, Lou. We need to go."

Louis said, "Oh, hey, Rook, sorry. I have to go. I'll see you soon, though.

Okay?"

Relieved, I said, "All right." I waved to Gordon. "Bye. Thank you for your donation."

He waved. "My pleasure." He and Louis headed to their car.

I found Amy in the ballroom, sweeping. "Hey, Amy, I was wondering, could I catch a ride with you? My car stopped working."

"Sorry. I'm going out with friends as soon as I get out of here."

That was understandable. She was college-aged, cute, bubbly, and it was Friday night. "Where's Blair?"

"I think she's, like, gone already. She said something about needing to pick up her kids."

I didn't know Blair had kids. This night kept getting better and better. "Okay. Thanks." I stepped into the hall and saw Jimmy taking notes. For a moment, I considered swallowing my pride long enough to ask for a ride home, but I slammed the door on the notion. No. I was still mad at him. He was being a jerk. While I was willing to make many allowances for his ill-processing of his grief, I could not deal with him anymore tonight.

I called Cam again. As soon as he answered, I said, "Are you one hundred percent certain you can't come get me?" I explained the situation.

He sighed. "Hold on."

After a few moments, he came back, but tension edged his voice. "Okay. I'll do it. But I have to come right back to work after I drop you off."

"I understand. I'm sorry. Thank you."

"Okay. Be at the end of the drive. I'll be there in twenty minutes or so."

"Okay. I'm really sorry." I owed him one. Maybe I could make him his favorite hummingbird cake. No, not big enough. Season tickets to U of B games. I'd have to save up for a while to afford those. I'd keep thinking about what I could do. Cam had bent over backwards to help me lately. Guilt and exhaustion weighed on my shoulders. And I was thirsty. I had time for a glass of iced tea. I dragged myself toward the kitchen and flipped on the light.

Derek sat at the kitchen table, staring at the floor.

"Derek?"

He flinched, proving he'd heard me. But he didn't move.

I approached him and put my hand on his arm. "Derek? Are you okay?"

His head turned slowly, his gaze trailing even slower. His mouth and eyes were drawn downward, making his face appear like a melting candle. Distance opened in his eyes as if he didn't recognize me. "Huh?" But there was something else there under the surface of his behavior—a sense of hyper-grief. He reminded me of an actor from one of those cheesy old black-and-white films where the actors *over*-played their roles.

I hemmed, wondering if he was trying to manipulate me, which would irritate me beyond measure. Reminding myself that everyone grieves differently, I played along. "I'm getting some iced tea. You want some, too?"

He continued to stare through me. I poured a glass of tea for each of us and I sat at the table with him. "Is there anything I can do for you?" I drew deeply from my tea.

He shook his head absently. "I don't know what to do." Then he broke down in gasping sobs. "I don't know what to do." He slapped the table, then held his head between his hands. "I don't know what to do."

I wanted to comfort him, but, at the same time, something seemed off. Was he jerking me around?

He rocked back and forth, still holding his head and sobbing.

"Hold on. Let me see if I can find someone to help. Maybe you need a sedative tonight or something." I stood and turned to find Jimmy in the doorway. My skin tightened. He watched Derek and waved me over. Jimmy was the last man I wanted to talk to, but I went to him anyway. He motioned for me to step into the hall.

He whispered. "Everything okay?" He looked over my shoulder at Derek.

I shrugged. "I guess."

"Something's not right."

"I know. He's a wreck. Are any paramedics still here? Maybe they can give him a sedative so he can get some rest?"

"Nah. It's weird. Like he's acting how he thinks a grieving husband *should* act."

I glanced back at Derek who now sat catatonic in a chair at the table.

"Are you saying he might've killed Cassidy?"

He shook his head. "Don't know. And I can't discuss it with you anyway."

"Right."

"I'll deal with this. When are you leaving?"

I stiffened with resentment. How could he stand here and start a conversation with me as if nothing had happened? "Soon. Cam's coming to get me because my car won't start."

"Cam? Seriously? Why him?" His anger was rising. "I'm right here and you call him for help?"

Jimmy and Cam had been best friends. There was a bit of a dust up between them when Jimmy and I had started dating. They'd since reconciled, but it was tenuous. And Jimmy still had little bouts of jealousy over my continued friendship with Cam.

I explained everything to him, then added, "And you're working a crime scene."

"You called your ex-husband and went to all those other choices *before* you decided to come apologize to me and ask me for a ride." He squinted. "If I'm putting this together correctly, I'm your last resort."

There it was. The jealousy thing again. I slumped against the door jamb and rubbed my face. I didn't want to expend the energy to explain my reasoning. "Number one, I don't owe you an apology. Number two, it's getting late, and I don't want to hang around here all night waiting for you. I don't want to fight. I just want to go home. So I can check on Prim and let Patrice go home."

"Got it. I read you loud and clear."

I checked my phone. "I have to go. Cam will be here soon."

It felt strange to leave the J.T. Bolton House. Cassidy had been murdered in her dream home, and to just leave and go on with my life as if nothing had happened seemed callous. A compulsion to do something for her, to remember her, memorialize her, overcame me. "Hold on a minute."

I turned to her husband. "Derek?"

He looked up. His face was red but lacked the puffiness from recent tears.

"Yes?" His voice was adequately watery.

"I'd like to have a memorial service here on Sunday to celebrate Cassidy's life, if that's okay with you. You know, since this was her dream home, and she died here."

"Well, we can't have the funeral that soon. I don't know when we can bury her. How long does an autopsy take?" He looked at Jimmy.

Jimmy said, "Maybe a day or so."

"Will the house be released to me by then?"

"I think so," Jimmy said. "We're working quickly, and there doesn't seem to be a lot of evidence to process. I figure we should be done in several hours."

I put forth my idea again. "So…how about the memorial service? I'll take care of everything. You won't have to lift a finger. I just thought it'd be nice to celebrate her life."

He shook his head. "Oh, uh…" Then he nodded and rubbed his face. "Yeah, sure. That'd be great. Thanks."

"Do you have any pictures you would like included?"

"Oh, I-I-I don't know."

"Maybe I can come out tomorrow and look through your pictures?"

He shrugged and slumped in his chair. "I guess." He removed his phone from his pocket and stared at the screen.

I checked my phone. "I have to go."

Chapter Ten

Cam pulled up just as I reached the end of the driveway. He ducked his head to watch the scene unfolding at the house. His demeanor was a mix of fascination and irritation. It wasn't hard to guess which part was for me. He greeted me with an annoyed "Hey" as I jumped in his truck, panting from my sprint. I immediately kicked off my shoes and rubbed my feet.

Cam sped away. "Looks like a crazy night tonight."

"For sure. Cassidy's dead, my boss is all freaked out, Jimmy's being a jerk, these shoes are killing my feet, and my car died."

"Did *anything* go right?" He hung a tight curve, pressing me against the passenger door. I gripped the handle.

"The hors d'oeuvres and cocktails were pretty tasty."

He chuckled. "That's something."

"Thank you a thousand, million, trillion times. Seriously. I owe you big time. I swear I'll come up with something to pay you back."

"You don't have to pay me back." His tone softened.

"How about I get my act together and quit being so broke and needy?"

He chuckled. "That would help. It's a full-time job looking after you."

I playfully smacked his arm. "I really do feel guilty."

"Sorry. Don't feel bad. I know you can't help it, and I wouldn't be here if I didn't want to help. If you pay back anyone, pay back my crew for the tight spot I'm putting them in."

"Fair enough. Please apologize to them for me. Do you think one of Prim's cakes would smooth things over?"

"Might," he smiled. "I guess Jimmy was too busy to bring you home."

"Yeah, I think so." I didn't want to go into details.

"How's he handling Cassidy's death?"

"He's struggling. I think that's part of why he's being difficult tonight. He's trying so hard to keep it together; he's coming off mean."

"Hm. Mean how?"

"Grabbing my arm, fussing at me. Stuff like that."

He glanced between me and the road as we flew through the town's center. "He put his hands on you?" His voice darkened.

Crap. I'd said too much. *Way to go, Rook.* I scrambled to recover. "Not like that. No. It's fine."

He looked at me in disbelief.

"Seriously. It's fine."

"If he even tries anything like that with you, and I find out about it, I'll make him regret it."

"Please. Forget I said anything. You know how my mouth runs sometimes."

We stopped at a light and sat in tense silence for a few moments. Then he said, "So, did you find out what's wrong with your car?"

"Nah. Some guy named Louis checked it out for me and said it could be my alternator."

He turned right onto the darker country road leading to my home. The truck lights beamed against the canopy of trees flanking the narrow, hilly road.

"Well, I know a couple of mechanics who can give you a pretty good deal. And one of them has a tow truck."

"That sounds fantastic. Are they inexpensive?"

"I don't know how much they'd charge, but I'm sure they'd be willing to give you a bit of a discount because they know me."

"Sign me up!" I smiled.

"I'll text you the details later."

"Thank you! You're so awesome."

"No problem. I know you're tight on cash."

After a few moments of thought, he said, "Would you ever move?"

That was a weird question. "Uh, no. I haven't even entertained such an idea. I landed this job a few months ago. Then there's Prim. I'd never leave her, and she's too fragile to move. Batrene needs my help, too, now that Bryan is gone. My life is here. Though I sure would love a vacation."

"Yeah? Where to?"

"You know me, I love the beach. Maybe Florida."

"Oh." He nodded. He seemed dejected.

Was there a full moon tonight making all the men in my life act weird? I frowned at him, puzzled. Why was he asking me this? Was he thinking of moving there? My heart sped up. I sat up straight. "Wait. Why are you asking? Are *you* moving?"

"No," he laughed. "I'm not moving."

"So, why are you asking?"

He pulled up in my driveway. "It's nothing. Just wondering."

"There must be some reason you'd ask me such a weird, random question."

"Seriously, I was just curious." He parked the truck in front of my house. "Sorry, Rook, I've really got to get back to work. I hope you can get that vacation real soon."

I had already inconvenienced him enough, so I grabbed my shoes and purse and slid from his truck, my feet hitting the gravel. "Yeah. Okay. Uh, thanks again for the ride. Text that mechanic info to me."

"Sure will."

I eased my way on sharp edges around his truck and then dashed through the chilly, dew-laced grass to the house.

I dragged into the backdoor through the kitchen, dropped my shoes on the mat by the door, and beelined to the fridge. I grabbed a cold bottle of Kentucky spice ginger-citrus soda, and one of Prim's fried apple pies instead of a Moon Pie. After all, nobody made apple pies like Prim.

Patrice came out of the living room, speaking in a low voice. "Hey, hon. How was the event?"

Patrice was my friend Millie's mom. Patrice had recently been kidnapped, and I had played a role in finding her. She had always been a petite woman, but it seemed she had lost more weight since her terrifying incident about a month ago. Where she had once been lean, she was now bony. She looked over the rim of her wireframes from under a mop of tousled gray hair. Her eyes were blue mingled with green, rendering them nearly teal in color. Her skin, once clear and pale, was sallow, and the smile lines around her eyes and mouth, once faint, had deepened some, making her fifty-eight years more apparent. A small silver mermaid dangled from a chain around her neck—a token she and her partner had gifted themselves with when they opened their own distillery, Mermaid Cove, which had the distinction of being the only all-female-owned distillery in the Bluegrass.

I slouched against the counter, chewing on the fried apple pie, its cinnamon, clove, and brown sugar melting away the evening's stress. "Horrible." I spilled the awful details of the evening.

Patrice sank into a chair at the kitchen table. "My goodness. I can't believe it." Her eyes watered as she toyed with the mermaid on her necklace. "That poor girl. How is her husband handling it?"

I didn't want to start the rumor mill churning, so I gave a noncommittal answer. "As well as could be expected."

Patrice shook her head. "What can I do?"

Glancing at the clock, I said, "It's already eleven. It's so late." I finished off my apple pie.

"Don't worry about that. What do you need?"

"Well, I was going to put together a small, informal memorial for her closest family and friends on Sunday after church. Derek said we could set up at the J.T. Bolton House."

She clapped her hands together. "That's a wonderful idea. We can turn it into a potluck. What can I do?"

"Perfect." No Southern woman worth her salt ever turned down an opportunity to host a potluck or contribute to one. I grabbed a steno pad and pen from the overstuffed mail holder on the wall and sat at the table with her. We set about planning.

Flipping open the pad, I wrote down my name and Patrice's. Under my name, I wrote as I spoke. "I'm going to go back out to the J.T. Bolton House to go through pictures of Cassidy to use as a centerpiece. Then I'll run to the grocery to pick up some things to make a hashbrown casserole." Honestly, as strangely as Derek was behaving, he didn't really deserve Prim's famous hashbrown casserole that was the hit of every church potluck, but this was the South, and nothing short of mortal enemies would obstruct the dictates of condolence food offerings to the aggrieved family. Besides, the hashbrown casserole was to honor Cassidy and her memory, not Derek.

"Oh, the hashbrown casserole will be perfect."

"Since I'll be at the grocery anyway, I'll also pick up some stuff to make Sprite punch, some lemonade, and a couple of gallons of iced tea."

She laid her hand over the paper. "Now, I can't have you taking on all this yourself. You tell me what to do, and I'll do it."

"I'm getting to it. What can we do that would be a lasting memory, something that can't be thrown away?"

"Something like a memorial garden? Or a stone marker?"

"Kind of. But something Derek wouldn't balk at too much. He might get grouchy if we start digging a whole garden."

"How about a couple of white rose bushes?"

"Perfect! I'll clear it with him tomorrow. I'm sure he won't mind."

"And a bench with a nameplate on it to sit by the tree. My cousin can engrave the nameplate in a hot minute. I can get a bench at the Clay's Home & Garden and take it out to my cousin. He'll get it fixed up in no time."

"That would be amazing." I wrote everything on the paper. "Now, I'm also going to contact all her friends and family in the area and give an informal invite. Can you also pick up an easel from the church or have someone bring it to us?"

"Yep. And I'll tell the ladies at the church. We'll have more food and flowers than you can shake a stick at."

"Perfect."

After we had settled who was responsible for each task, Patrice gave a report on Prim. All was well. She ate a little bit, but complained of pain and nausea between cat naps. She had finally got Prim upstairs and settled in bed. I thanked Patrice and offered her a room for the night since it was so late. She declined and headed out.

I changed into a pair of fuzzy socks, cotton pajama pants, and a jumbo sweatshirt. It was the time of year where the days were warm and the nights chilly. But, because Prim's illness gave her night sweats, we tried to keep the house as cool as possible. So, I dressed warmly to refrain from running the heat too high. I settled in on the living room sofa, flipped on the 24/7 *Dateline* channel on Roku, and opened my laptop.

My nerves danced along a sharp edge, snapping and popping. I went to Cassidy's Facebook page. Her sister had already posted about her death, and messages were pouring in. I'd take them to get copies printed for the memorial board. I pulled several pictures and saved them to a thumb drive. I would wait until the next morning to post the information about her memorial because tonight, I couldn't bear the weight of the grief any longer. I needed a distraction.

I checked my email. Dad's lawyer, Glenn Winston, had emailed me. He said he'd located some old police reports my mom had filed. He said he'd like to discuss them further and to call him when I had a chance. I opened the attached reports, scanned them, and saved them to my computer. I added calling the lawyer and the prison to my to-do list for the next day.

My phone vibrated, ringing on silent. *Cam.* It was about one in the morning.

I answered. "Hey. What's up?"

Kitchen noises and loud music rattled in the background. He was still at work. "Did I wake you?"

"No. I'm up. Planning a memorial service, checking emails from my dad's lawyer."

"What?"

I explained everything to him.

"Got it. Well, I was about to text the mechanic information to you, but then I got to thinking. Maybe I should be the one to talk to him so he knows you actually know me."

"Okay. I appreciate it."

"Also, how are you going to get around tomorrow if you're planning a memorial thing?"

"I hadn't thought about it. Maybe try to borrow Prim's car. But it got pretty beat up under my last watch when I got Patrice out of her situation, so Prim might be reluctant to let me borrow it again."

"If you can wait until a little later in the morning, I can take you around."

A spark of hope leapt in my chest. "How late?"

"Maybe around ten or so? Can you wait that late?"

I ran through some quick mental math. If I got up at eight, got dressed, helped Prim get up, get breakfast and get settled, got Batrene to watch her, and then made a few quick phone calls, I could be ready by the time Cam arrived. "That sounds fine. I really appreciate it, and I don't mean to sound ungrateful, but why do you want to do that?"

"I'll be out anyway. We can go by the mechanics first so I can give Martin a heads up."

"Okay. Then we can go to the J.T. Bolton House. I need to go through some of Cassidy's old pictures and run through the memorial details with Derek. Maybe you can look at my car. You might be able to tell what the problem is. Are you sure ten isn't too early for you? I mean, you don't even close up the bar until two."

"I'll cut out a little early tonight, and now that I'm living with Mom and Dad and helping them with the farm, I don't remember what sleep even is."

We chuckled. I could relate. Caring for Prim and the house was a full-time job on top of my actual full-time job at the distillery. "Well, I guess I should get off here and try to get some sleep before I run you all over Rothdale tomorrow. G'night, Cam."

Chapter Eleven

The next morning was a flurry of phone calls and rushing. I launched myself out of bed at eight and flew to the shower. I threw on a pair of jeggings and a long pink sweater. I coiled my damp hair into a bun and went with barely-there makeup. Then I helped Prim out of bed, gave her a sponge bath, slipped a loose-fitting navy floral dress over her head, and topped it with a lavender sweater. I brushed out her hair and clipped it back with clear rhinestone barrettes.

After capping her feet with non-slip, fleece-lined slippers, she held the banister with both hands, my hand on her elbow and back to brace her, as she inched down the steps to the kitchen, slower than frozen molasses. I got her seated in a chair and began the breakfast routine. I poured ginger ale in a glass and handed it to her with her pills. Fortunately, the coffee was auto-perk, so I fixed my coffee while she worked on her pharmaceutical appetizer.

Then I fixed her a bowl of apple cinnamon oatmeal. It was the fake stuff from the packets, but she liked it so I wasn't going to fight her on it. As far as I was concerned, she'd officially reached a point where she could eat whatever made her happy. I also made a slice of toast for her, smeared with the blackberry jam she'd preserved last summer. Prim nibbled at her toast and oatmeal while I made a sandwich of peanut butter and blackberry jam. I ate standing at the counter while I reviewed my list from the night before and thought out my priorities.

It was already nine. I posted on Facebook, apologizing for the short notice, but inviting close friends and family to the J.T. Bolton House for a memorial gathering for Cassidy and inviting people to bring a dish if they felt so inclined. Phone calls were next on my list. My first call: Batrene. I needed her to sit with Prim while I was gone. She said she didn't mind at all and she'd be over right after breakfast. I thanked her profusely and promised I'd be back as soon as possible and hopefully wouldn't be gone more than a few hours.

Then I talked to Dad's lawyer, Glenn Winston, while I unloaded the dishwasher. He was from the Innocence Project and had given me his cell phone with the promise I could call him any time. He had received a letter from my father in prison, and after going through the initial interview, believed my dad had been railroaded by inadequate representation—which was probably true given we didn't have enough money to hire a fancy attorney and had to settle for a state-issued defense attorney. I'm not saying the lady hadn't tried her best, but, according to whispered conversations I'd overheard as a child between Prim and Papaw, the lady had been drowning in caseloads. In those situations, things get overlooked, and the poor people are going to get chewed up and spit out faster in the system.

Glenn answered, breathless as though he was walking at a fast pace.

"Morning," he greeted me brightly. "I'm walking my dog. But I'm glad you called me back. I won't keep you long. I just didn't want to put all this in an email."

"Okay. What's up?"

"Well, I have some interesting news. Good news, I think."

"Okay..." Hope sprang up, but I held it down. I couldn't let hope start running wild before I had the whole story.

"I've been looking through the case files from the sheriff's department, and it looks like they overlooked some evidence. So last time we talked, you told me your mom and dad had split up before they got married?"

"Yes," I said tentatively.

"That's not completely true. They had actually split during the marriage for about six months and were considering divorce."

"What!" I dropped the bowl in my hand, thankful it was plastic. Prim looked up at me, puzzled. I imagined I was giving her the same quizzical stare. Had she kept things from me? I paused and stared out the window over the kitchen sink, watching a squirrel breach the bird feeder for the precious sunflower seeds Prim put out for the cardinals. I picked up my memory box and shook it to see if something new would fall out.

I remembered Dad had been there when I went to bed one night and was gone the next morning. For the first couple days, I didn't think much of it. But by the third day, I had known something was wrong. I asked Mom, and she said Dad was on overnight trips for work. I pretended to believe it, but I knew better. Most of his clothes were gone. His shaving equipment was no longer in the bathroom. And why wasn't he calling to check on us? Then there were a bunch of calls from some guy. A voice I'd never heard before when I answered the phone. The man always asked for mom. Mom had grown shy and playful on the phone. She seemed to drop about ten years when she talked to this man in quiet tones. Plus, Mom had been leaving me with Prim and Papaw more, and I'd had more overnight stays with Millie and Patrice.

So that meant—and here came the freefall—when everyone had told me mom had dated that Will Decker guy during her split from dad, it wasn't *before* they were married. It was *after.* I suddenly felt like a Halloween pumpkin cut open, and all my guts scooped out. My mom. Who had always been the image of an angel in my mind, stainless of sin and the grimy parts of life fell to ashes. It was like forcing a puzzle piece in the wrong spot. I couldn't reconcile the woman I'd created with the one who had once existed. What had happened? Had she been with another man while she and Dad were separated? Is that why I spent all those nights with Prim, Millie, and Patrice?

"Rook? Are you there?"

Tears formed in my eyes, and gravel formed in my throat. "Uh, yeah. When was this?"

"From what I gather, it was around the ten-year mark of their marriage, a little over two years before she was murdered."

Well, they'd made it longer than Cam, and I had before troubles set in. That was something, I guess. A cacophony of thoughts loud as crows rushed at me.

"Um, okay." I stared at Prim. She and I were about to have a conversation.

My tone must've conveyed everything because he said, "I gather you've been misinformed."

"You could say that. I'd been sheltered from much of the trial."

"I'm sorry to be the one to tell you." He sounded sincere. Children laughed and played in the background.

I stared at my empty yard. I couldn't deal with the hurt and all these feelings bubbling up. I almost felt betrayed, misled…hurt. Right now, I had to focus. "So, uh, how is this relevant? I figure the separation would be a main subject at trial. I mean, wouldn't the prosecution paint my dad as a jealous husband? It doesn't seem to help his case."

"It seems there was a police report about someone following her during their time apart. I think the sheriff assumed it was your dad. Not long after these reports were filed, your parents reconciled. There was one more report filed after their reconciliation."

"How long after?"

"Several months."

"And did the report involve my dad?"

"That's the thing. It had nothing to do with him."

"Who was it then?"

"Don't know. Neither of the reports name anyone. There was a break-in; some things moved around on one of the reports. On the other occasion there was someone staring in the window at their house while your mom was alone. Unfortunately, she couldn't describe the person, so no action was taken."

"Why wasn't any of this considered in the case?"

"According to the statements, your dad did tell the sheriff about these things, but they simply didn't believe him because they supposedly had a witness placing your dad at the scene."

"What?"

"One Tommy Jenkins, the son of a well-respected businessman in town, said he'd witnessed your dad going in and out of the residence on the night in question."

"How?" I racked my brains, mentally sifting through all the information I'd read about the case over the years. I didn't remember anything about Tommy Jenkins.

"Apparently, Tommy was at a house across the street in the neighborhood you grew up in."

I recalled the roomy rural suburb, brick ranch homes spread far apart. The neighbor across from us was the Wheelers. They had large oak trees in their yard. "At the Wheelers' house?"

"Yes."

"*How* did he see anything? There were trees everywhere in that neighborhood. And if it was dark…"

"Exactly. But it gets better." He paused. "Tommy Jenkins and his twin brother Trace were no strangers at the Wheeler house. They were there all the time. They played football with the Wheeler kid. They were having a homecoming party that night. It was noisy and crowded. In their original statement, they said they'd witnessed your dad enter the house."

"Okay."

"However, they confessed later to a friend who brought the information to the sheriff's department, but the department didn't look into it. The officer who'd taken the statement had been killed in the line of duty. The files transferred to new officers who probably just missed it. I found the statement buried deep in the files. I then went to Trace and Tommy, questioned them both, and they admitted the truth. They were both too drunk and stoned that night to know what they saw. They did see someone, a shadow, enter your mom's house, but they *assumed* it was your dad."

"So it boils down to bad witnesses and some shoddy work?"

"Essentially. And gullible jurors and bad defense. It doesn't happen often, but sometimes things go wrong. Really, really wrong."

"Can you send me copies of what you have?"

Cam pulled up in the driveway and honked the horn.

"Sure. I'll email you copies. I'll keep you updated as we proceed."

"Thank you." I hung up and looked at Prim. She munched her toast and wouldn't look at me.

"So that was the lawyer." I began gathering my keys, list, and purse. "He had some information I'd never known. Stuff that had been hidden from me. You and I need to have a talk later." Cam honked again. "I don't have time to talk about it right now, but I have questions."

"Mm-hm." Prim avoided eye contact and sipped her coffee.

"I'll be back in a few hours."

My face burned as I stomped to Cam's truck. How could the people in my life keep such important information from me? I climbed in Cam's truck, turned my face from him, and swiped my eyes.

"Hey. What's up?"

I blew out a breath. "Same junk. Different day." I ran my hands up my face and over my head. Flopping back against the seat, I buckled myself in.

He leaned forward over the steering wheel to look at me. "Are you crying?"

"No."

"Then why's your nose red and your face puffy?"

"Can we go, please? I'll be fine."

"Okay. Sure." He put the truck in gear and backed out of the drive. But he just couldn't let it go. "Seriously, what's wrong? Is it Prim? Is she worse?"

Dang. I didn't really want to talk about this, but I also didn't want him worrying about Prim. He really loved her. "Prim's fine. Well, fine enough." I related what the lawyer had said to me. "Can you believe they lied to me about my mom?"

He propped his elbow on his open window and hooked his other wrist on the steering wheel to guide it. "Yep. I sure can."

The cool wind whipped my hair. I reached in my purse for a clip, gave my hair a twist and clipped it into place. "You're okay with that?"

"You were a kid. You weren't going to understand all those complicated adult relationships. And it could be, knowing Prim, she was probably embarrassed over her own daughter's behavior *and* she probably didn't want you to grow up with a bad opinion of your mom. Especially after she'd died."

I turned to stare out the window at the sun glinting off the leaves of the underbrush and trees. He was right, of course, now that I stopped to think about it instead of reacting. I needed to learn to be less reactionary. Prim was devastated after Mom's murder. She would've wanted to protect me, my image of my mom, and my mom's reputation. And I was young, not quite finished playing with Barbies. There was a great deal I wouldn't have understood or might've misinterpreted. I sighed. "You're right."

"It's good you can finally admit that."

I rolled my eyes to look at him. He winked at me. I pursed my lips, then stuck out my tongue at him.

We stopped first at Martin's Motor Medic, so Cam could talk to his buddy about my car. Once we squared away that business, we jumped in the truck and headed to the J.T. Bolton House.

We entertained ourselves with conversation about his parents, Prim, and Jimmy while he passed through the older neighborhoods on the fringe of downtown Rothdale, all named after trees and flowers. He turned left down Old Hickory Lane. Lined with large Victorian and Edwardian Era homes and trees, the road sloped downward into a gentle valley toward the J.T. Bolton House.

We parked beside my poor little lime green Fiesta. Sliding out of Cam's truck, I said, "I'm going to try again to start my car. If it doesn't work, we'll call for the tow truck." I unlocked my car and sat in the driver's seat to start the car. *Click, click, click.*

Cam stood with his hands on his hips. "That's not a good sound. It's not even worth trying to jump the battery. It's probably your alternator."

"That's what I was afraid of." I closed my car hood.

He pulled his phone out of his pocket. "I'll call Martin. Have him send out a tow truck."

Derek stepped out on the porch in bare feet, shorts, and T-shirt, holding a beer. "Y'all alright?" he shouted.

"Yeah." I wiped my hands on my jeans and approached the porch, with Cam lagging behind. "Cam brought me by to look at my car and to get some pictures of Cassidy for the memorial service."

"Come on in."

I eyed the beer bottle. I threw a hint that it was too early to be drinking.

"Are you out of coffee? We can go get you some."

He lifted the bottle of bourbon barrel ale to his lips, a gleam of rebellion in his eyes. He released a satisfied sigh. "Nah. I'm good."

The engine of a large truck sounded behind us. I waved at the driver of the Four Wild Horses Distillery. Cy and another guy jumped down from the truck and made their way to us on the porch.

"There's the guys. I need to escort them into the house."

"Okay," Cam said. "I'll wait out here for the tow truck."

The distillery truck backed up to the house, and a grizzled man jumped out of the driver's seat, and a couple of other men slid from the passenger side.

"Hey, Cy," I said. "I'll show you where the stuff is."

The men followed me down the hall to the ballroom. The bar and crates of unused Unbridled Spirits bourbon lined one wall. I almost felt sorry for the sad, unused bottles, symbols of hope for our little distillery now tainted with murder.

The men set to work with dollies and back braces to protect their heavy-lifting backs.

My phone rang, and I stepped into the hall. It was Pierce, my boss at the distillery. I thought about silencing the call and dealing with him later, but couldn't bring myself to do it. He was freaked out about the death and its implications for the Unbridled Spirits release. And with all the crazy things happening around Four Wild Horses Distillery lately, he was probably worried about the future of the company. "Hello?"

"Good Morning, Rook. Are you busy?"

"Hey, Pierce. Not really. I'm out here at the J.T. Bolton House. The guys are here loading up what they can now."

"Again, I just wanted to tell you how very sorry we are for your and your boyfriend's loss."

"Thank you."

"When you know the funeral details, please let me know. We'll send some flowers from the distillery."

"Thank you. That's very nice."

"And Margaret would like to bake a cake. She makes a fantastic bourbon pecan cake, and we'll just send the flowers along with it today."

"That'll be nice. If you'd like, wait until tomorrow. We're having a small memorial for friends and family. Her favorite flower was white roses."

"Perfect. We'll send a wreath of those." He paused. "I won't keep you much longer, but while I have you…" He paused again. He wanted to talk business and was trying to soften the blow of it. "I hate to bring up a crass business concern at such a time, but…"

But life goes on for the living, huh?

"Considering what's happened during the release of the new bourbon, I'd like us to put together another exclusive tasting event to try to salvage the bourbon's reputation and ours. After a respectable time, of course. Maybe during the Christmas season. Since, you know, people will be adding spirits to their holiday activities."

"Sure. I understand. I'll start thinking about it and try to come up with another location."

"Sounds great. We'll talk more on Monday."

I turned around and Gordon Meece stood at the end of the hall between me and the kitchen. His white button down and khaki slacks gave him the appearance of a politician trying too hard to relate to the "common" people. He gave me a once over and flashed his dimples.

"I think I can help out with that."

Okay. He was super cute. I said something intelligent like, "Uhhh…" Then my mouth kicked in before my brain. "What are you doing here?"

He chuckled and stepped toward me. "I'm here discussing some development plans with Kenton." He held up his phone. "I stepped away to make a call when I heard you." He stood close enough for his fresh cologne to tickle my nose. "I didn't mean to, but I overheard your predicament, and I think I can help. My father and I own a real estate development firm, and we sit on the board of directors for the Homes for the Holidays project."

"I haven't heard of it. Is it a new charity?"

"It is. We just finished filing our nonprofit and grant paperwork a couple months ago and getting all our key people in place. Our vision is to build at least one home and give it away to a needy family each Christmas. Of course, if we could generate more funds, we'd build more houses."

"That sounds pretty amazing, though. So what did you have in mind?"

"A fundraiser. An exclusive bourbon-tasting…" He opened his hand toward me as if giving me a gift. "Featuring your new Unbridled Spirits."

"Where were you thinking of hosting it?"

"Well, we could host it at my father's home. He has a large event space in a renovated barn on his property. It's quite nice."

"That sounds awesome. However, we already have a charity. Heroes Hope."

"No problem. We could work together. Maybe we can give away a home to a veteran in need?"

My eyes widened. "Heck yeah!" My mind began working on the plan, ideas springing like grasshoppers in summer grass. "Maybe we could tie it into Charles Dickens' *A Christmas Carol*? You know, because of the spirits of Christmas Past, Present, and Future?" I patted my back pockets. "Ugh. I don't have any business cards on me—"

"No worries. You still have my business card, I hope." A corner of his mouth tipped into a deep dimple. "Just give me a call when you're ready. I know you're in a mourning period right now."

"Well, would your father approve?"

"He's president of the company in name only. I actually run the company until he retires at the end of the year." He shrugged. "So, it's really my decision. And I've decided. I'd like *you* and your distillery to host our fundraiser."

Maybe I was misreading this guy, but he seemed to be flashing a Colin-Firth-Mr.-Darcy level of smolder at me. I needed to shut it down now. I didn't need him getting any ideas. "I'll be in touch, Mr. Meece. Thank you for the offer. The distillery looks forward to partnering with you. If the terms are right, of course." I flashed a smile. There. Clear. Professional.

"Of course."

Louis and Kenton appeared in the hall. "Hey man," Kenton said. "You ready to go take a look at the potential job site?"

Louis stared at me for several seconds before nodding and saying hello. "It's so good to see you again. I didn't know you would be here today."

My skin crawled. "Hi, Louis."

"How's your car? I noticed it was still here today. If you want, I can arrange to have someone—"

I cut him off. "That's okay. My ex-husband is making arrangements."

"Ex-husband?" His face grew red, and there was a hint of accusation in his voice. "I didn't know you were married before."

Yeah. There's a whole lot you don't know about me, buddy. I glanced at Gordon. I didn't want to damage what proved to be a potentially great working relationship between Gordon and me, so I needed to play nice. Forcing a chuckle, I said, "Well, we just met, so I wouldn't expect you to know."

Gordon clapped his brother on the shoulder. "C'mon, Lou, we need to go." He nudged him toward the door. Gordon looked back at me. "Hey, Rook, we'll get together and talk about it. I'll be in touch." He glanced back over his shoulder at me as he left the house.

Louis looked back at me, his dark eyes intense.

Cam leaned on the balustrade. "Who's the goober in khakis?"

I rolled my eyes at him. "A potential client. He offered an event space to do a re-release of Unbridled Spirits bourbon."

"I heard. He was flirting with you. Does Jimmy know about him?"

"There's nothing to know. And Jimmy doesn't need to worry." I shoved him playfully. "So stop trying to aggravate me. This is not the time or place."

The FWHD workers came through with the last of their loaded dollies. Cy paused and said, "I think this is everything, if you want to double check…"

"Oh, no. That's okay. If I see anything else, Cam and I will grab it."

"Alright then. See ya later."

"See ya. Thanks a bunch, and have a good weekend."

"Yep." They stepped out of the house.

I turned to Cam. "Where's Derek?"

"Oh, uh, he and Kenton went somewhere…" He pointed down the hall on the other side of the stairs. "That way."

"Okay. Well, I need to square away some of the details for tomorrow." I passed down the hall where I heard some low voices coming out of a sitting room on the left.

I was about to open the door when Derek said angrily, "Does this have to be done right now?"

Kenton replied with equal vigor. "Yes. The sooner, the better. Gordon Meece is breathing down my neck on this. You know how he and his old man can be."

"Look, Cassidy *just* died. The *police* are breathing down *my* neck, which matters a whole lot more. Because if Gordon gets his way, I might get some money, but if the police get their way, I lose everything, including my freedom."

"You can't be serious," Kenton scoffed. "You don't honestly think the police think you had anything to do with Cassidy's death."

"Yes. I do. I'm the husband. Also, that blasted Deputy Duvall keeps sniffing around here, asking me a bunch of questions. I'm telling you, he suspects me."

"Just turn the property over to me, and I'll handle everything," Kenton said.

"Yeah, and let you take a big chunk of the profit, too, I suppose. I don't think so."

"Look…" Kenton snapped. "Y'all owe me a big chunk of money anyway. Money I'd lent to Cassidy to keep this place afloat. So, as I see it, you owe me this."

"Is that so?" There was a brief silence. Then Derek said, "What if I've decided I don't want to sell now."

"What!" Kenton shouted.

"Shut up, man." Derek hissed.

"You'll regret it if you don't sell."

"Oh, really? Seems to me you're the one who will have regrets if I decide to keep it. I don't know. Maybe I'm in the mood to own a bed and breakfast now. In honor of my wife."

"You don't want to mess with me, Derek. I'll make you wish you'd never been born."

"And how would that be different than any other day?"

"I'm serious, man—"

"Kenton, you can go back and tell the Meece's I'll think about it."

"They want an answer now. They're eager to get started. The crew is waiting for the go-ahead and —"

"Well, they aren't getting one until I'm ready."

The doorknob rattled.

Dang it! I'd stayed too long. I needed to get away from the room before I was discovered eavesdropping. I turned to run, but I hadn't realized Cam had followed me, so I ran smack into him. We fumbled and fluttered to get around each other, but we weren't fast enough.

Kenton emerged and pushed past us, and Derek mosied out of the room, his eyes glittering with suspicion. "I guess you heard that?"

I tried to play it cool. "Heard what?"

"Me and Kenton fighting?"

"N-n-no. I-I-I didn't hear anything. I was, uh, just looking for you to discuss the memorial for Cassidy." I was too fidgety and nervous to be believable. Cam put his hand on the small of my back, which, oddly, helped to calm me.

He put his hands in his pockets. "Sure, shoot."

I eased into my ideas about Cassidy's memorial, watching him closely, trying to read him. I couldn't reconcile what I'd believed about his and Cassidy's relationship and their undying love with this seemingly man in front of me and the things I'd been learning about him. It wasn't clicking together. It didn't make sense.

Derek agreed to everything I suggested. "Thanks for doing this. It sounds really nice. Here, let me pay for something. You're doing so much; it's the least I can do." He pulled out his wallet and handed me a fifty.

"Okay, thanks." I accepted the cash. "Thanks for the pictures. I'll make copies and return the originals to you as soon as possible."

He waved his hand. "Don't worry about it. Just use the originals."

I frowned at him. Was this an awkward attempt at affability? Or was he this cold? I wanted to slap him and scream, *Did you love her at all?* "Okay. Can I look through your pictures for the memorial poster?"

"Yeah, sure. Up in our bedroom."

The doorbell rang.

Derek said, "I wonder who that is." He opened the door. Jimmy.

I stiffened. We hadn't spoken or contacted each other since last night. Tension filled the air. Jimmy's eyes darted between me and Cam, but he was in professional mode and greeted us with a simple hello and nod as if he didn't know us.

Jimmy said, "Derek, if you don't mind, I have a few more questions." He pointed to the dining room. "Can we step in here?"

"Sure." Derek turned to me. "Hey, Rook, just help yourself to the pictures. They're upstairs in our closet in a blue container."

"Okay, thanks."

Cam said, "I'll come with you, Rook."

We climbed the stairs and turned left toward Derek and Cassidy's bedroom. A light on the right caught my eye through a cracked open door. It was a laptop in a dark room. Curious, I pushed the door open. Sunlight poured in through the curtains, spilling on the rumpled bed.

"What are you doing?" Cam whispered.

"I think this is Kenton's room." I recalled his argument and strained relationship with Cassidy. "He and Cassidy had been fighting over money the night she died. She was really upset because it caused a dispute with Trigg, the landscaper."

"Okay?"

"I thought I might poke around a little to see if I can find out anything."

"If we get caught…"

"If you hush and stand in the hall to be my lookout, we won't get caught."

"I'm standing right here." He leaned against the door jamb, his back to me.

I flipped on the light. Kenton was messy. His suitcase stood in the corner, filled with a pile of clothes in disarray. Dirty clothes were strewn about the room. His laptop sat open on a nearby table, the screen black, but a blue light on the side blinked. It was a red Alienware laptop with a glowing alien face in the center of the lid. Below this was a sticker from the Red River Gorge Railway Experience. On the screen was some sort of plot layout for a land development, but at first, I couldn't tell where it was. Then I looked closer, studied the picture. There was an old barn, a stretch of land and, in the bottom corner, stood the J.T. Bolton House. Why would Kenton be looking at something like this? I snapped a picture.

I took a giant step over a pair of shoes to get a closer look. There was a used drinking glass and a few empty packs of candy and chips. Under the table was an unopened bottle of Unbridled Spirits bourbon that he'd clearly stolen from the event since these weren't for sale yet. Irritated, I was tempted to take it away from him. Instead, I took a picture. Just in case. I took the paper and slipped it into my bra. I opened the drawer, nothing.

Near the wastebasket was a crumpled ball of legal paper. The yellow kind that I'd seen in Derek's office earlier. I opened the paper. Weird. It was Derek's name written over and over. Just as Cassidy's name had been written over and over on Derek's paper. But if Derek was practicing to forge Cassidy's name, why would Derek's signature practice be in Kenton's room? Was Kenton actually the attempted forger, and he put the pad in Derek's office to point authorities toward Derek?

I folded the paper and tucked it in my back pocket. I noticed something sticking out from behind the bed frame. I knelt down and pulled it out. A manila folder. It was several copies of Derek and Cassidy's life insurance policy. One of them was doctored with wite-out. The others had obvious forgeries of their signatures. Another form looked like a land deed. Kenton was cooking up something shady, for sure. Maybe Cassidy had caught him, and he had to kill her to silence her? I didn't have time to read any of this, but I was keeping the folder. I'd give it to Jimmy before he left. He could just be mad at me.

Cam said, "Are you done yet? Hurry up."

"Hold on."

I stood and scanned the room and noticed the edge of a paper sticking out of his suitcase. It was an envelope with Cassidy's writing on the outside: *Trigg.* Inside the envelope was a wad of cash and a note from Cassidy thanking Trigg for his work with a promise to pay the balance in a few weeks. I didn't have time to sit and count it, but I took pictures of the note, envelope, and money. I struggled against the temptation to take the money and give it to Trigg. I returned the money to its hiding spot and took a picture of that, too. I grabbed the folder, turned out the light, and pulled the door to the position I'd found it in. "C'mon," I whispered to Cam as we headed to Derek's bedroom.

"What's in the folder? Why'd you take it?"

I stepped into Derek's bedroom and explained. "I think this has something to do with Cassidy's death. It looks like Kenton was trying to forge life insurance claims to make himself the beneficiary." I removed the paper from my back pocket and showed Cam. "Look. He'd been practicing Derek's signature." I put the paper in the folder with the other papers. "I'm going to give this to Jimmy when he's finished talking to Derek."

"I don't think that's a good idea. He's not going to be happy with you interfering." He sat on the other side of the bed, scanning through his phone.

True enough. I tossed the file on the bed and took a look around the room. "Well, it won't be the first time Jimmy's upset with me, but if this helps find Cassidy's killer, then I don't care."

There were moving boxes stacked in the corner. I lifted the lid on one. I lifted up the top item. A woman's shirt. "This is Cassidy's." I looked in the box. It was full of Cassidy's things. I jerked open the closet door. Cassidy's clothes were cleared out. I turned to Cam.

"He's already packing up her things." I gaped at Cam.

"Really?"

"That jerk! How could he do this? I could never…" I thought about Prim. It took her years to box up Papaw's things, and she still had a couple of his jackets hanging in the hall closet.

Cam shook his head. "That's cold, if you ask me."

This didn't look favorably for Derek. "You can bet your sweet patootie I'm telling Jimmy about this."

"Are you saying you think Derek had something to do with his wife's death?"

I pointed at the boxes full of Cassidy's things. "This doesn't exactly make him look innocent."

"There has to be an explanation. Derek doesn't seem like a killer."

"You'd be surprised how many killers never seemed to be." I ducked into the closet to find the box of pictures. I found the container, a little bigger than a shoe box, in the corner. I sat on the bed, and Cam sat across from me to scroll through his phone.

I lifted the container lid and sifted through the images of Cassidy's short life. I found a few of Cassidy in beauty pageants, equestrian competitions; some of her with her mom, sisters, dad, and aunts and uncles. There were pictures of her as a child at the zoo, hayrides, soccer games, beach visits, fishing, and so much more. There were pictures of her as a ballerina, a cheerleader, a soccer player, and graduation photos. Tears flooded my eyes to see this buoyant, happy girl through the years, her life big, full, and active. A girl with big hopes and bigger dreams, all snuffed out, and a husband who married this precious life and didn't seem to care that it was now gone. Anger rose, sharpening the edge of my grief. I wiped away a few tears and selected a few from each phase of her life, careful to include pictures with her family, and stuck them in the folder with the papers I'd taken from Kenton's room.

My phone rang. It was Dad. I waited for the automated voice to ask me if I accepted the call from the prison.

Once I accepted, Dad's voice came on. "Hey, baby girl. What's up?" There was a lot of noise in the background, people shouting, laughing, and talking loudly.

"How are you doing?" I stared at the gray floral pattern on the bedspread. It was a stupid question. After all, the man was in prison.

"All right. Haven't heard from you in a while."

"I know. Sorry. I've been working a lot and stuff. It'll take too long to go into details. So, I wanted to tell you I received some emails from your lawyer and spoke with him this morning. Has he called you yet?"

"Not yet. What did he have to say?"

I shared with him what the lawyer had told me.

"Those two kids lied, and I went to prison for it? Why didn't they come forward sooner? Why did they wait so long?"

"I don't know, dad. The world is full of people who do things that don't make sense or do things that are plain wicked. And it didn't help that the jury was gullible. They believed those Jenkins' boys over you. The upshot is Mr. Winston is going to get you out. He says it looks like the sheriff's office might've overlooked some evidence in your case, plus with the bad witnesses, you have a pretty good chance."

"That's a relief. Did he give you a timeline?"

"No. I didn't think to ask. I was in a rush this morning."

"That's okay. He calls about once a week. Maybe I'll hear from him soon."

We paused. "He also mentioned you and Mom split during your marriage for about six months, and y'all were considering divorce."

Cam looked at me, listening to my side of the conversation. I looked away.

"Ah…" He sighed. "Yeah."

"Why didn't you or Prim tell me this?"

"I don't know, hon. I guess since your mom and I eventually got back together, nobody thought it was a big deal anymore."

"Kind of a big deal to me."

"Why?"

My voice raised a couple notches. "Because it's part of my family, my history."

"It was our marriage. And you were a kid. You didn't need to know about all the adult stuff. I'm just glad you had somewhere to go, someone who would take you in and love you and be good to you. That's all I cared about."

My throat grew tight with the pressure of tears. I swallowed them down like a cup of marbles. "But why were y'all talking about divorce?"

He blew out a heavy breath. "Look. I've done a lot of things I'm not proud of. Your momma was an angel to put up with me. She said if I didn't straighten up, she'd leave me because she wasn't going to raise her daughter in a bunch of craziness."

Clearly, Mom's warning had fallen on deaf ears, but I asked anyway. "Did you even try?"

"I did. I really did. She let me move back in, and I tried to walk the straight and narrow. But I didn't always have steady work, and I wanted to be a good provider, so I did things that weren't—"

The call was being recorded, so I stopped him. "That's okay, Dad. You don't have to tell me. Remember, we're being recorded."

"Statute of limitations is passed anyway. I was a construction worker. Got into business with a rotten developer. He sold the lots to people, and I built the houses based on the specs they chose. But he wouldn't pay me until a project was done. Sometimes, I needed money or supplies to start another job. So I would borrow supplies from the job sites to build other houses and projects I was selling on the side. Sometimes, I'd sell the stuff to other builders to get by."

"Ohmigosh, Dad." I rolled my eyes. "That's so illegal. Didn't the other builders wonder where you got the stuff?"

"Darling, there's the licensed and bonded folks, then there's the folks who are just trying to eke out a living. The ekers aren't too concerned about many things as long as they make money and can feed their families."

My head was beginning to throb. I gripped my forehead with one hand and tried to rub the tension gathering there like a storm cloud. What on earth compelled my mom to get involved with a man like my dad? I loved him, but he certainly wasn't the gold standard of men. I'd always figured my mom had had better taste or that Prim and Papaw would've prevented the union.

"Look, I did some bad stuff. I've never denied it. But I am not and never have been a murderer." His voice cracked. "I haven't been honest about a lot of things, but I swear on my life, I loved your mother more than any person on this earth. I'd die for her." His voice grew watery. "I wish every day of my life I'd been home that night. That the attacker had killed me instead of her. I'd die right now if it'd bring her back. I *never* laid a hand on her."

I held my head in my hand. I was crying now, too. But the timer was ticking. I had to move on. I swiped my tears. "I'm sorry, Dad." Years of guilt pressed down on me. "I'm sorry I haven't done more to help you. I didn't know. There was so much I didn't understand or know how to do."

Cam handed me a tissue from the bedside table. I grabbed it, flashed him a look of gratitude, and blew my nose.

"Don't worry about it, hon. You were just a kid. And now, as an adult, you're trying to make your way. You have your own life to live."

"I'm going to make sure you get out. I never believed you did it." The automated voice came on and told us the call was ending in one minute.

He sighed. "Look, there's no shortage of blame to go around, but I never once blamed you for anything. I'm just glad I finally got someone to listen to me and that you believe me. I couldn't live with myself if you believed I could hurt your momma."

The automated voice announced we had only a minute left.

"Well, looks like our time is up. Love you, baby girl."

"Love you, too, Dad."

The phone system cut us off.

I dropped my face in my hands and cried. Cam moved to my side of the bed and sat beside me. He put his arm around me. "It's okay. Hopefully, he'll be out soon, and all this will seem like a bad dream. He knows you love him, and you're trying to help him."

I nodded and blew my nose. "Yeah. I guess I'm feeling a little sorry for myself. I wish I'd grown up with my family intact like you did. I sometimes wonder how differently my life might've turned out."

"You're being too hard on yourself. You've turned out pretty good, considering the circumstances."

I toyed with my wadded tissue. "You're right. I know. I just wish I'd grown up with my mom, that she'd been able to live to a ripe old age like Prim."

He rubbed soothing circles on my back. "I know. It's tough. Maybe someday you can be the mom she didn't get to be."

My eyes met his. His eyes like expansive Kentucky blue skies. Electricity sparked between us. He took my hand and squeezed it. Footsteps sounded on the stairs. I said, "Jimmy and Derek are coming."

Chapter Twelve

Jimmy entered the bedroom, and Derek leaned against the door jamb. The air crackled around us with tension. Jimmy and I hadn't talked since last night, so we hadn't even begun to smooth things over. I wasn't sure they could be smoothed over—or if I even wanted that anymore. What was the point if all we did was bicker and fight?

"Everything okay, Rook?" Jimmy glanced at Cam.

"Yeah," I shrugged. "I'm fine."

"You been crying?"

"Oh. A little. Been talking to my dad."

"Ah." He said, "Can I speak to you for a minute?"

We stepped into the hall and walked out of earshot of Cam and Derek. Jimmy took my hands and said, "Look, I'm really sorry about last night. I don't handle my feelings very well."

I chuckled. "Clearly. But I think I have some issues with that, too."

"Really? I hadn't noticed." He smiled and rolled his eyes.

I nudged him playfully.

"So, we good?"

My skin felt too tight around my bones. I managed a faint smile. His hazel eyes locked with mine, searching them. He was too smart, too savvy. He was accustomed to questioning hardened criminals and seeing through their lies. What was he seeing in my eyes? Guilt? Shame? Confusion? Love? I suddenly thought of the Eagles song, *You can't hide your lying eyes...* A sharp, focused heat landed in my chest and spread slowly over my hair and up my neck. If he saw the pink heat reach my cheeks, I was in trouble.

I was the first to break the gaze.

My mouth said yes, but my insides still felt heavy, burdened. He kissed me and I excused myself to the bathroom. It was a pale gray room scented like lavender. A few country-chic decor pieces ornamented the walls. I pressed a cold, wet paper towel to my face, and blew my nose.

Guilt and grief wrapped around my gut like barbed wire. I wished Cassidy were here. I wished my mom were here. I wished I'd helped my dad more. I wished Prim wasn't sick. I also wished, if I was being very honest, that I'd never started dating Jimmy. I came between friends and now their relationship would never be the same. It was all my fault. What had I been thinking?

I stared at myself in the mirror at my red nose, puffy eyes. I was lonely. I hadn't been thinking. I had acted instinctively. I wanted companionship. I wanted a best friend to share my life with. Like the one I once had with Cam. I wanted that back all shiny and new, like polished silver, like it was before he and I had tarnished it with our twisted emotional baggage. When Jimmy and I started dating, I saw potential, hope for love, for a future. Tears formed in my eyes, and I couldn't look at myself. I stared down at the sink. Was I trying to get back at Cam subconsciously by going after Jimmy? Or was I trying to subconsciously get close to Cam through Jimmy? Maybe some part of me thought that because Jimmy and Cam were friends, Jimmy would be a lot like Cam, so it would be like I hadn't lost him at all. Ugh. I needed a one-way ticket to the Dr. Phil show.

Whatever my subconscious was attempting to do, my conscious self and Jimmy weren't exactly working out. It was like wearing a pair of toe-pinching shoes. The shoes were cute. They got attention and compliments. I might even really like the shoes and wished they were more comfortable. I might even try to stretch the shoes to make them fit. But at the end of the day, they pinched, they hurt, they weren't comfortable, and…I looked at myself in the mirror again. And…I was glad when I took the shoes off, and my feet could breathe again.

Oh crap. I ran cold water and splashed it on my face. What was wrong with me? This was no time for life-changing epiphanies. Besides, I was just weepy. That's all. I'd just gotten off the phone with my dad, which usually made me emotional in some kind of way. Jimmy and I had been fighting a bit, but that was normal, right? After all, we were trying to find our groove, find our footing. *Stop thinking about shoes, Rook! Dang.*

I blotted my face with a paper hand towel and slapped some color back into my cheeks—hoping to slap some nonsense out of my head at the same time—and stepped out of the bathroom.

Jimmy had waited for me. "You okay?"

"Yep." Annoyance prickled under my skin. I was getting tired of everyone asking me some variant of 'are you okay.' I was fine. Peachy-stinking-keen. Absolutely a-okay. I had to be. Maybe I was being held together by gossamer stitches, but I was still together. For now. In the spirit of fake-it-till you make it, I pasted on a too-bright-toothpaste-ad-smile. "I need to put away the picture box." I wanted to tell him about everything I'd found and noticed, but Derek was too close.

Derek and Cam stood in the hall, chatting about basketball. Seeing Derek fired my anger. "Derek, why are you already packing up Cassidy's things? I saw the boxes in your room."

He stared at me and stuttered. "I-uh-uh…"

"She died last night, isn't even buried yet, and you're already trying to erase her?"

Jimmy narrowed his eyes at Derek. "She raises a good point. It doesn't look good."

Derek, flustered, said, "I couldn't stand the reminders of her. It was breaking my heart to see her things in the closet when I was getting dressed this morning. So I put her clothes in boxes. It was a moment of craziness." He opened his arms. "There are reminders of her everywhere, and it's like a knife in the heart every time I see these things. I'm just trying to keep from drowning."

Jimmy nodded. I scowled at him while I re-entered the bedroom. I didn't believe Derek. Surely, Jimmy wasn't buying his nonsense either. I picked up the pictures scattered on the bed, stacked them neatly in the container, and snapped the lid shut. I knelt to return the box to its home and noticed a pebble jutting in the corner of the shelf holding purses and shoes Derek hadn't yet packed up. I squinted and cocked my head. Something wasn't right. A crack opened upward from the pebble. It wasn't a break in the wood, it was clean-edged as though it was built that way. I pushed on the shelf, and it swung inward, opening a mouth of darkness. Oh, wow. This was some good, old-fashioned Nancy Drew stuff here.

My eyes shot wide, and a little thrill raced through me. "Uh, guys," I said. When no one answered, I shouted, "Guys! Come here!"

All three men rushed into the room, Jimmy at the lead with Cam and Derek peeking over his broad shoulders.

"What the…" Jimmy breathed.

"Oh, yeah. That's always been there," Derek said. "But the door is usually locked." He frowned.

"I guess that puts an end to the rumors about this being a haunted house," I said.

"Why isn't it locked now?" Jimmy asked.

"I don't know. Maybe Cassidy had opened it for some reason and forgot to lock it back."

"Where does it go?" Jimmy looked over his shoulder at him.

"A couple different places. One ends up under the old barn at the bottom of the hill."

I recalled the house plans on Kenton's computer that featured a barn.

Derek continued. "There's a cellar door covering the exit. The other ends up further back, on the other side of the woods, on the neighbor's property. The exit point is a low-ceiling cave."

"Why is it there? Are you Batman?" Cam chuckled.

Derek shrugged. "Nah, this is a bourbon baron's house. In the 1800s, when J.T. Bolton first came into his money with bourbon, that was no problem. But by 1919, when Prohibition was enacted, it became a problem for a family whose lifeblood was bourbon." He had fully slipped into tour guide mode. "So, there were members of the family who wanted to continue making their spirits and did so illegally. Sometimes, they'd sell it to speakeasies in Louisville and Cincinnati. Or they'd sell it to local doctors, pharmacists, and dentists to make their *spiritus frumenti,* which was just whiskey posing as medicine. But the Boltons had had a few too many run-ins with local authorities, and they couldn't get the permits to sell their bourbon legally to medical professionals." He leaned on the door jamb and crossed his arms over his chest, and crossed his ankles. "Anyway, long story short, some of the Boltons weren't legal with their undertakings, and they often ran speakeasies on this very property. In fact, we discovered an underground space under the barn where barrels were stored and where a speakeasy would've been hosted, complete with gambling, jazz music, and dancing."

I'm not going to lie. I wanted to see that space.

Derek added, "Cassidy wanted to eventually add the speakeasy space to our events and tours, but we wanted to be certain it was structurally sound first. At any rate, the pathway"—he pointed to the secret passage—"would've been one of many escape routes from the house in the event law enforcement came to bust up the fun."

"Where else are these located?" Jimmy asked.

"So far, I've located one in the cellar and the one in the billiard room, but they are locked with gates behind the door panel. The gates had been installed sometime after Prohibition."

"Man," Cam whistled. "This place is like a maze. That's wild."

Derek shrugged. "People have always gone underground when the stuff above ground wasn't to their liking."

"Why isn't there a gate on this passage?" I asked.

"The previous owner didn't install one. We were eventually going to do it, but it was a last priority."

Jimmy said, "These tunnels could've been used to sneak in or escape detection. Why didn't you tell us about these yesterday?"

"I'm sorry. My wife had just been murdered. I wasn't thinking straight."

Jimmy eyed him with doubt. "Who else knows about the tunnel system?"

He shrugged. "Hard to say. Of course, Cass and me. The real estate agent and company. And I'd say everyone who works at the permit office, the historic records at the library…" He rubbed the back of his head. "Probably dozens of people, at least. It's not exactly a secret that these old bourbon barons did this sort of thing."

Jimmy winced with disappointment and stared into the darkness. "Can we go in there? Is it safe?" Jimmy asked.

"Safe enough for us probably, but you enter at your own risk. The last thing I need is an insurance incident."

Jimmy frowned and held up Eagle Scout fingers. "I won't file an insurance claim. Scout's honor."

Derek motioned toward the door. "All right then. Do what you want."

We all hit flashlight mode on our phones and shined them into the darkness.

"I want to go," I said, my curiosity to see the speakeasy getting the better of me.

"I'm going, too," Cam said, pushing around Derek.

Chapter Thirteen

We followed a narrow path through the house and down a flight of stairs. When we passed out of the house to the underground section, the space grew cooler and wider. The walls were covered in cement, buttressed by thick wood columns and ceiling rails. Clearly, a lot of money had gone into the construction of the underground trail, but the bourbon barons had plenty of money to throw around. After a couple hundred feet, the tunnel opened up into a large space with low ceilings. Sconces hung along the walls where torches would've been lit, and the ceiling was made of cement, now cracking, laced in webs, and scorched with the smoke from long-ago torches. A floor-to-ceiling barrel rick ran the length of one wall where barrels of bourbon would've been stored.At the front of the room was a slightly elevated space where a jazz band might perform. The wall behind the stage was made of mirrors, cracked in some places, now covered in ages of dust and spiderwebs. The floor was cement inlaid with tile, also layered in dust and rubble.

"This is so cool," I gasped. In my mind I could just hear the bouncy jazz music and see the flapper girls kicking and twisting their way across the floor with their partners, fueling the party from illegal glasses. I turned to Derek. "How long was this space in use? When was the last party?"

"At least through the thirties. Cassidy and I found journals from people of the day who reported to have met Al Capone and some of his associates here. So this place probably fell out of use when prohibition ended in 1933."

"Wow. What did it look like when you first bought this place?" I asked.

"There were tables all through this area here and a piano in the corner of the stage over there. And on this wall over here was a bar stocked with dusty, broken glasses and bottles. We cleaned all that out. Cassidy thought this space would be a really neat attraction to people, but we're waiting on the permits to ensure its safety."

Jimmy and Cam paced, shining their lights on the walls, inspecting the room.

"Plenty of shoe prints in the dust," Jimmy said. "It looks like there's been some recent activity here. When's the last time you, Cassidy, or workers were in here?"

"Maybe a couple of weeks ago."

"And what did you all do?"

"We had an inspector in here. A couple of contractors and electricians to discuss design plans and get estimates. Of course, Cassidy and I were in here."

"Hm," Jimmy said. "Too bad. If a killer came through here recently, we'd never know. I'll need you to make me a list of people who've been in this area before I leave." He shined his light overhead. "The barn is above us, right?"

"Right." Derek nodded.

"Is there an entrance from the barn to this room?"

"Yep, right over here." Derek stepped over to the wall adjacent to the bar, where there was a little alcove with a pink velvet seat blanketed in webs and dust. Tattered pea-green curtains hung over the alcove. He reached behind the curtain and pulled a lever, causing the alcove to creak open. He pulled the door open to reveal several iron stairs leading up to a door on the barn floor. "Right up there."

Jimmy shined the light up the staircase, then pulled back and nodded.

I moved behind the bar and looked at the empty shelves. A long black curtain hung to my right. I pushed it back to reveal a small, rusted sink. To my surprise, there was also a small cot that did not have dust or webs on it. In fact, it appeared rather fresh and new. Along the opposite wall were several built-in shelves, empty. Around the be,d someone had taped pictures, pictures that were clearly decades old.

I bent to get a closer look at them. "Oh. My. Lord. That's my mom! My mom!"

The men all rushed to my side. In one of the pictures, Mom was wearing a green velvet dress. She held a red solo cup in one hand and was laughing with a hand lifted near her mouth. On that arm was a silver bracelet with a turquoise stone in the center. It looked like the ring on my middle finger. A Christmas tree was behind her. Perhaps this was a Christmas party. I didn't recognize any of the other people or the room, so it didn't appear to be a family function.

Next to this picture, was a picture of *me.* It had been taken on the day Jimmy and I had visited Cassidy and Derek when she'd been sitting on the roof and gave me a tour of the house. We were standing on the front porch, talking. Though Cassidy was in the picture, I was clearly the focus. Ice cubes tripped down my spine. My brain went dark and numb as if a vacuum powered up to suck every thought out of my head. Panic and fear whirled into the emptied space, throwing me into full freak-out mode.

My voice climbed to the point of screechiness as I spit out a barrage of questions. "Why are my mom's pictures here? Who did this? How? How did that creep get these pictures? Did he know her? Did he steal these? And why is *my* picture there? What is going on?"

Derek held his head. "This is wild. I have no idea who could be doing this or who would even have access to this room."

Jimmy leaned in to study the pics. "I don't know, but I aim to find out."

Cam put his arm around me. He whispered. "It's okay. Don't worry."

I couldn't take my eyes off my mom. She was so pretty, so happy. A person I barely remembered now. "I know I can't have that picture because it's evidence, but can you take a picture of it and send it to me?"

Jimmy studied me. "Sure." He bent over, snapped a picture, and sent it to me. "Everyone out. I'm calling a forensic team to come out and examine this area." He shooed us away and opened his phone. "No bars. I'll call once we reach the top." He took more pictures of the room.

The cave seemed to be closing in and getting darker. It was getting harder to breathe. I extracted myself from Cam's hold. I wanted to get out of this old ghost of a speakeasy, but the thought of going back through the dark, narrow tunnel was insupportable. "I need to get out of here."

Jimmy said, "The upshot is I'd say our guy was probably pretty relaxed in handling these, so the techs might have a better chance of finding fingerprints here."

I paced the larger space of the speakeasy, opening up my lungs a little more. What in the world were we dealing with here? This creep must've known my mom, and now, all these years later, was he thinking about targeting me, too? I mean, he had a picture of me, so something like that must've been going through his mind. If so, why? And who? Why did he target my mom all those years ago? And what would compel him to now come after me? And was he the same guy who killed Cassidy? I hugged myself and looked around the room. Why was he set up down here? It seemed a strange location.

I turned to Derek. "Who lives down here? Do you know anything at all about this?"

His narrow brown brows cut into his tanned forehead as he shook his head. "No. I had no idea anyone was down here and can't imagine who it would be or why they're hanging out here. I mean, did this guy kill Cassidy? Or is he just some creepy squatter?"

Cam scoffed. "More like a stalker using your place as a hideout."

"But why here?"

Jimmy said, "It's the last place anyone would look or care about. It's a neutral territory that would make it harder to connect anything to him."

I hugged myself, unable to shake the chill clinging to me like a spiderweb. Jimmy finally emerged from the backroom. "Derek, I think you should consider staying somewhere else tonight."

"Nah. I'm not going to be chased away from my house by some creep. I'll make sure I lock and block the door in the closet, and I'll double check the other entrances. Besides, it seems he's more interested in stalking women than in coming after me, don't you think?"

"Possibly, but for your safety—"

"I'm not going anywhere."

Jimmy sighed. "Well, I can't make you leave, but take all precautions."

"I will."

Jimmy said, "How do we get out of here?"

"This way." Derek led us toward the rickety stairs in the alcove. "I recommend one person at a time. I'm not sure how much weight these stairs can support."

Derek went first. After a brief time of listening to him climb, we heard a door slam open.

"Rook, you go next," Cam said, guiding me toward the door with his hand on the small of my back.

Using my phone light to guide my steps, I scrambled up them as fast as I could, the stairs wobbling beneath me.

Relief washed over me as I reached the sunlight pouring in through the old wood slats of the barn. I brushed the dirt and spiderwebs off my clothes as I looked around. The loft and stalls were empty, and stray bits of hay flecked the dirt floor. Sparrows flitted in the rafters, causing flakes of straw, dust, and feathers to rain down. Dust motes danced in the golden beams, and the scent of moldy and mildewed straw and damp earth filled the air. This barn hadn't been used regularly in years. It was sad, really.

Cam and Jimmy soon emerged from the darkness. Jimmy closed the door, sending a big puff of dirt and straw into the air.

Derek pointed to the barn door. "We can exit through here." He opened a door on the side of the building and then closed it behind us.

Jimmy said, "Maybe you should consider finding a way of locking this up so the creep can't gain access to the speakeasy area any longer."

"I can lock up all the areas I know about. But there could be a tunnel I'm unaware of through which he's gaining access."

Jimmy nodded.

"I'll do what I can."

I squinted against the bright sun hanging among the grand, puffy, white clouds in the sapphire sky. The J.T. Bolton House sat on a hill among a patchwork of autumn-colored trees about the distance of at least a few football fields away. It was amazing to think we'd traveled so far. A creek trickled near the barn among a copse of trees. A crumbling stone fence surrounded the property. I made a beeline for the house, walking as fast as I could through the lumpy pasture.

Jimmy paused to place a call to the techs.

Cam jogged up behind me. "Wait. Rook. Hold up."

I looked over my shoulder and slowed a little, but didn't dare stop.

"You okay?"

"No, Cam, I'm not. I don't understand any of this, and I'm freaked out."

"I can see that, but if there's something positive to take away from this, maybe you'll finally discover who killed your mom."

I glanced at him. He was right and a part of me grasped at the wisp of hope he offered. I had never been so close to the truth. It could mean freedom for my dad, too, and possibly a chance at rebuilding our relationship. Unfortunately, catching that sort of hope was like catching bubbles. As soon as I touched it, it popped. "That's a big maybe. And at what cost? I don't like being in this guy's sights. He's clearly dangerous. And, frankly, I've had quite enough danger these last few months. I'm not a police officer or a soldier. I didn't sign up for this kind of life." Tears pressured my sinuses and my eyes. I inhaled deeply to fight them off. "I didn't ask for any of this. All I ever wanted was a simple life. I wanted to be married. Maybe have a couple kids. A decent job. A home. A couple dogs. Maybe a small farm to support my little family. Go to church. Teach Sunday school. That life. That's the life I wanted. And I don't have any of it." I cut my hands through the air. "It's all been turned upside down, and nothing is like I wanted it."

He stopped. "I'm sorry, Rook."

A sadness in his voice halted me. I turned to him. Jimmy and Derek were several yards away, but closing in.

Cam said, "I've been thinking a lot. It's my fault. When things weren't working between us, I ran away instead of staying to fight for you, for us. If I'd stuck around, tried harder, maybe you'd have the life you wanted. We both would."

I froze. I couldn't wrap my head around this right now. I sped up my pace. "Nonsense. My life is my fault. I'm the one to blame."

"Seriously, I didn't know how to communicate, to say the right words to make you stay, to keep us together. I failed us. I failed you. I thought if I ran away, losing you would hurt less because staying around to watch us drift apart was killing me."

I stopped and turned to him. Anxiety lifted inside me like a balloon. As Jimmy and Derek closed the gap, I angled my body toward them as if I was waiting. Last thing I needed was for Jimmy's jealousy to rear its ugly head right now.

I didn't know what to say. Thoughts swirled inside my brain, colliding with my fear over a crazed killer and crashing against the bits of my torn and conflicting emotions over Cam and Jimmy. Words stuck on my tongue like burrs in a hunting dog's fur. I opened my mouth to speak, to say something that might feed the expectation in his frosty blue eyes, electric blue in the sunlight. "Oh, Cam. I-I-I…" My mouth usually had a mind of its own. Where was it now? Jimmy and Derek were almost in earshot. I couldn't say anything now because I didn't want to cause more drama. I didn't want to deal with Jimmy's jealousy or cause any further issues between him and Cam. I whispered. "I forgave everything a long time ago. This is a bad time. We can't talk about it now."

Jimmy and Derek joined us, panting. Jimmy said sarcastically, "Thanks for waiting for us."

I found my voice, my throat dry as cotton. "Sorry. I had to get away from there. It's too much to handle. Seeing those pictures…" I shuddered. "It's the stuff of nightmares."

Jimmy rubbed his hand across my back. It was meant to be soothing, but it grated on me like sandpaper. I fought the urge to shrug him off. "I know you're a little freaked out right now. But I'm not going to let this guy get away. Okay?"

I nodded, looking at the grass, then glanced through my eyelashes at Cam. He scanned the horizon like a farmer, hoping to get the harvest in before the rain came. I turned away, rattled. This was the wrong time for romantic concerns. Some psycho, who might've killed my mom and Cassidy, had pictures of me in his little hideaway. I didn't have time to be thinking about matters of the heart and past wrongs. "C'mon. Let's go." I nudged Jimmy, and we all walked toward the fence stile. Cam fell in beside me, his hands in his pockets, and bumped into me. I gave him a side glance, bumped into him, and smiled.

The stile was nothing more than an old tree stump. I stepped up on it, straddled the stone fence and, swinging a leg around, jumped to the ground. The guys decided to show off for each other, vaulting over like gymnasts. After about ten minutes of walking, we made it to the back porch of the J.T. Bolton House and entered through the kitchen door.

Jimmy hooked his thumb in his uniform belt. "I'll see y'all later. I've got to get this back to the tech." He looked at me. "Are you free tonight?"

My face grew warm, and I pretended to be busy with my phone, looking at the texts that had been sent to me about Cassidy's memorial. I glanced at Cam. "We have a few more stops, and then I'll be home the rest of the afternoon to work on the memorial gathering."

"All right. I'll be over later." He pecked my lips. "Anything you need me to pick up on my way in?"

"No, but hold on. I want to walk you to your truck. I need to give you something." I ran upstairs, grabbed the folder from Derek's bed, and ran downstairs. Jimmy and I stepped outside, and I walked him to his truck.

"What is it?"

"We need to get in the truck."

"You're being weird."

"You'll see why in a minute."

We climbed in the truck. He said, "What's up?"

"I know we just made up, but you're about to be annoyed with me."

"What did you do?"

I removed the pictures of Cassidy and handed him the folder. "I found it in Kenton's room." I pulled my phone out of my pocket and sent him all the pictures I'd taken. "I also got these pictures. I can't put it all together yet, but Kenton is up to some shady business. It looks like he's trying to forge those insurance papers to make himself the beneficiary of Derek and Cassidy's insurance. He might also be trying to get his hands on their land."

"I don't know where to begin." He stared out the windshield and shook his head. "I won't thank you because this is wrong, and you know it. But…" He licked his lips and tapped the corner of the folder on his steering wheel. "This is really important information. This evidence won't be admissible because of the way it was obtained. But I also don't want to get rid of it. Maybe I can run a background check on Kenton, see if there's some reason I can search his room to justify my possession of these documents. I need to think about this, see if I can figure out a legal workaround." He thought for a moment.

"Oh, there's something else." I told him about the conversation I'd heard between Kenton and Derek earlier.

"That's interesting."

"Right? Kenton seems pretty focused on convincing Derek to sell."

"I wonder if he was working on Cassidy about selling too?"

"I bet he was."

"Sounds like a motive for killing her."

"It does."

"I never did care much for Kenton. He was always a slimy, manipulative guy."

"Do you think Derek is safe?"

"I don't know. Surely Kenton wouldn't be so bold as to try something with an investigation going on."

"I would hope not. But sometimes desperate people will do desperate things."

"I should warn Derek again. Tell him he might be in danger from Kenton."

Cam and Derek stepped out on the porch. Jimmy sighed. "Okay. Let me go talk to Derek again."

I lifted a brow. "You're not mad at me?"

"Of course I am, but right now, I just don't feel like arguing with you. I have a job to do."

I jumped out of the truck, waved to Cam, and shouted, "Let's go!"

Cam shook hands with Derek and jogged toward me, waving bye to Jimmy, who was heading back to the house to talk to Derek.

Chapter Fourteen

C am and I got in his truck. "Where to next?" He acted breezy, as if a huge melodrama hadn't just unfolded between us in the pasture. "The party store. I need stuff to make the memory board."

I hoped Cam didn't revisit our conversation in the field. I didn't want to rehash the past or my feelings right now. I felt like a paper doll torn right down the middle by an errant child—who was also me. What I really wanted, more than anything, was to get my car back, then drive straight to a secluded beach in Florida, plop my rear in the sand, and do nothing but stare at the ocean.

My phone rang.

"Hey, girl," Patrice said. "I just left the church, and they let me use their easel."

"Thank you so much. I really appreciate it."

Patrice continued, "I'm heading out to the grocery right now. What can I get? I'm going to gather stuff for the punch: some tea, water bottles, sodas, and lemonade. What else can I bring? You think we need a meat and cheese tray?"

"If you want, but I'm sure we'll have plenty of food."

"Maybe I'll get some olives, too."

"You're doing everything. Leave something for me to do."

"Oh, nonsense. I've got this covered. You've got plenty to do with Prim and all. Then, since Bonnie Cutler's greenhouse is right down the street, I'll run by there and pick up the white rose bushes. And my cousin, Clay, said he'd bring the bench out to the Bolton House tomorrow. He's working on engraving the nameplate and getting it attached now."

"You've been such a big help. I couldn't do this without you. Truly."

"That's what we do, hon. We help each other. I've got to go. If there's anything you need, you text me, okay?"

"Okay."

"What time should I be at the house tomorrow?"

"I guess if you're there right after church at noon, that'll give us plenty of time to get everything set up. I'm keeping it real informal."

"Sounds good. Bye, sweetie."

We hung up.

Cam said, "Before we go to the party store, can we grab something to eat? I'm starving."

My stomach wasn't going to argue. "Sounds good."

"Mexican?"

"Only if we can go to Hacienda Lupita. I love that place."

"Deal."

We passed the carved wooden statues of Mariachi players and the mosaic fountain in the foyer and followed the host to a booth beside a fresco painting of a desert sunset on a buff-colored stucco wall. Multi-colored string lights garlanded the wall, and upbeat Mexican music blared from the speakers. A stocky man in a black shirt and black jeans placed a basket of nacho chips on the table with a bowl of salsa and handed us menus, though I didn't need one. I got the same dish every time: chicken chimichanga, no beans or rice, and an iced tea. Cam ordered his usual steak fajitas and a Coke.

For a brief moment, I was slapped with nostalgia, where it felt as if we were living in an alternate dimension, had never separated, never divorced—a dimension where we were living our happily ever after. A flash of sadness mixed with wistfulness swept over me like a breeze then swept out of the room. I shivered.

"You cold?" Cam asked, crunching a chip.

"I guess. A little." It was difficult to be this close to him and look at him after what had transpired in the pasture.

"How's Prim? I haven't spent much time with her lately."

"She's…" I scooped up a pile of the delicious pico de gallo. "Hanging in there the best she can. She's weak. Tired."

"Have you tried to talk her into the treatments?"

"I tried for a while, but it only made her angry, so I stopped."

"Why's she so pig-headed?"

"She's afraid of leaving me with a ton of medical debt. And she hasn't said it aloud, but I think she may be afraid of the side effects from the therapy. It can be rough. Especially for older people like her."

He shook his head, poked at his ice with his straw, then took a sip of Coke. "It's sad all around. I hate it for both of you." He leveled his blue eyes at me. "So, how're things with Jimmy? Have y'all made up?"

I chuckled and shook my head. "I'm not going to talk about that with you. It's not fair to him."

He flashed a side glance and a smile. "I only want to know if you're happy."

I scooped a clump of salsa and crunched a chip, the fresh tomato and cilantro dancing against my tongue. "Whatever. If the tables were turned, and you and I were still together, you wouldn't like it if I blabbed to Jimmy the things going on between us."

He laughed. "True. You don't have to go into details, though. I only want to know if you're happy. Because if you're not, I might still have a chance."

I rolled my eyes to look at the ceiling. "Cam…" I sighed. I didn't really want to discuss this, but I also didn't want to leave him hanging. "What you said in the pasture today…I appreciate it. It was beautiful. I'm not going to lie, I've been thinking about you a lot too. I wonder, though, if we should just remain friends. I don't ever want to lose you and I guess I'm afraid if we tried again, we would destroy everything, even the friendship. Maybe being friends is safer for us."

"I think we can do better. Prim thinks—"

I coughed, choking on my food, and held up my hand. "Hold on a hot minute. Prim? You've been talking to Prim?"

He paused as if busted, stealing the last cookie from the cookie jar. "I, uh, well…yeah." He relaxed against the booth. "I wasn't supposed to say anything."

"When did you and Prim talk about this?"

"Whenever I'd watch her."

My mind rolled over all the times I'd asked Cam to watch Prim, to help her remember her pills and such while I went to work or ran an errand. There were a ton of opportunities for those two to conspire against me. I shook my head. "I can't believe this."

The server set down two large plates of sizzling food and rushed off.

I stared at my chimichanga drowning in queso blanco, then lifted my confused gaze to Cam's face. "How could y'all do that? What gave you the right to interfere?"

He sat up, unwrapped his tortillas, and filled one with the steak, onion, and pepper mix. "I wouldn't say we were interfering. How did I interfere?"

"Okay, fair enough. But I resent that you two are talking about me and Jimmy. What sorts of things were y'all talking about?"

He chewed his food. "You act like we were sitting around in dark shadows, conspiring against you. It wasn't like that."

"Then what was it like? Enlighten me."

He took a long sip of Coke. "She's worried about you. That's all. She'd tell me about her worries and how she thought you and I made a mistake to get divorced. She thought because we got married young, and you had baggage from your parents' issues, that we didn't really know how to handle marriage. And she said…" He hemmed then shook his head, seeming to think better of saying anything. "Nah. I can't."

"What?"

He finished off the last bite of one fajita and moved on to fill another. "If I tell you, you're going to get mad, and then you'll fuss at Prim, and I don't want you to do that."

I wanted to know what was said so I had only one option before me. I had to promise. "I promise I won't say anything to her. I won't even bring it up."

He stared at his plate. "She thinks you still love me, but you're too stubborn to admit it to yourself." He lifted his eyes to look at me.

I flushed. A dead giveaway. I averted my gaze and brought my glass up under the guise of taking a drink, but instead hoped to shield my face. I was certain the AC in the restaurant was broken. Why else was it getting so hot in here? I took a long drink from my tea glass. "Prim is confused, and she shouldn't be talking about something she knows nothing about. You shouldn't encourage her and give her false hopes, Cam."

"I did no such thing. She has her own ideas."

"Well, stop encouraging her." I sawed a piece from my chicken chimichanga, stabbed it, and popped it in my mouth. I chewed angrily, not sure I could keep my promise to not confront Prim.

"Look, I'm not trying to make you mad. I'm sorry. But I happen to think she's right. My mom and Prim also both think you and I made a mistake, and I'm not going to hang up my hopes just yet."

"Your mom? Geez Louise, Cam…" I grit my teeth. "Why don't y'all just call out to the TV station and have it broadcast over the greater Lexington area?"

"I didn't say anything. Prim's been talking to her about it."

I was definitely going to have a talk with Prim now.

"I don't want to talk about this anymore. I'm with Jimmy." For now.

After some tense silence, Cam brought up a conversation about the new show *Only Murders in the Building* and we finished our meal talking about the antics of Mabel, Oliver, and Charles and when the new season was going to release.

We finished up our lunch, paid, and drove to the party store. We turned left by the Walmart and crossed the access road to the small plaza that housed the party store. I was itching to get the errand done, get back home, work on the memorial board, and have a talk with Prim. So I ran in and buzzed through the store for my supplies and then we headed home.

Cam said, "I need to stop for gas." He pulled in at the convenience store.

I noticed the West Landscaping truck that had been at the bourbon event the night Cassidy died. Though Kenton and Derek were certainly at the top of my list, Trigg West couldn't be discounted yet. After all, Cassidy had been found strangled with a weed eater string.

Cam filled up the truck. I watched Trigg go inside the convenience store. I got out and said to Cam, "I'm going in for a drink. You want anything?"

"Nah, I'm good."

I ran inside, followed Trigg's white ball cap, and sidled up to him at the soda cooler. I didn't really have a plan. I just wanted to get a read on him. "Hey, Trigg, right?"

He looked at me with confusion and curiosity. He clearly didn't remember me.

"Rook Campbell. I met you at the J.T. Bolton House a few weeks ago."

"Oh, yeah. Hey. How're you doing?"

"All right. I guess you heard about Cassidy?"

"Yeah." He nodded, studying the rows of sodas and energy drinks. "I hated to hear it."

"Have the police talked to you?"

"Yep." He opened the door and reached for a Dr. Pepper.

"It seems kind of coincidental. You were there, arguing with her before she died, and she happened to be choked with a weed eater string."

"Are you with the police?"

"No. But I'm Cassidy's friend, and I want to know what happened to her."

"It wasn't me." He turned and scanned the aisle of snacks and candy. "I don't know how the string got around her throat. I say whoever did it knew about my argument with her and was trying to frame me. I hope you find who you're looking for."

"Kenton never paid you, did he?"

"No, he didn't. And now Cassidy is dead. I figure I'll never see the money now." He grabbed a bag of cashews and a jerky stick.

"Why?"

He scoffed. "Derek is notorious for not paying his bills or trying to pay less than he actually owes. All kinds of contractors and subcontractors have complaints against him."

"I'm sorry to hear it."

"Yeah, well, sorry for your loss." He walked up to the cash register to pay for his stuff.

Trigg seemed pretty sincere. I pushed him way down on my suspect list. And it would've been easy enough for Kenton or Derek, who both knew about Cassidy's fight with Trigg, to frame him.

Chapter Fifteen

Cam dropped me off at home.

I stood in the open passenger door, gathering my things. "I appreciate you chauffeuring me around today."

He pushed his mirrored sunglasses up on his head, one wrist hooked on the steering wheel. "Happy to do it. You need help carrying that stuff?"

My hands full of my purchases, purse, and Cassidy's pictures, I shook my head. "Nah. I'm good."

"Tell Prim I said 'hi.'"

"I'll tell her. But she'll be annoyed you didn't come in to see her." I widened my eyes. "She probably wants to collude with you some more."

He laughed. "Next time. I'll need to come by real soon and spend some time with her so we can develop a top-secret plan."

"Ha. Ha. Very funny."

A crooked smile teetered on his lips. "Do I need to come by tomorrow to pick y'all up?"

"I hate to inconvenience you…"

"It's no trouble. I'll bring my parents' van. There'll be plenty of room." He glanced past me at Batrene's house. "You think Batrene will need a ride?"

"Probably not. I'd say her sister, Bonnie, will probably come get her. But she's inside with Prim, so I'll ask when I go in. I'll text you and let you know."

"Sounds good." His gaze lingered on my face. "I'll see you tomorrow."

"Okay, thanks again." I stepped back to shut the door.

"Hey…"

I froze. "What?"

"I meant what I said today. I'm not going to get between you two, but I'm also not giving up."

My skin tingled and tightened around my muscles like an ill-fitting suit. I flushed and looked up at him through my eyelashes. I didn't know what to say. "I've got to go. Bye."

When I entered the house, I dumped everything on the kitchen table and found Batrene and Prim in the living room. Both had fallen asleep with crochet needles and yarn in their hands, the television blaring an episode of *Father Brown*. Prim's head had fallen to the side and Batrene's chin rested on her chest. I hated to wake them up, but Batrene had spent so much time at our house watching Prim, I wanted her to enjoy her free time.

"Hey, y'all." I leaned against the entrance.

Batrene's eyes fluttered open, and Prim nestled deeper under her afghan. "Hey, hon." Batrene cleared her throat and sat up stiffly, rubbing her eyes under her wireframes. "I guess I fell asleep."

"You and Prim both."

"I haven't been sleeping well."

"Are you okay?"

"Oh, yeah. It's just one of those things. Us older people don't sleep like you young'uns." She smiled.

I didn't want to burst her bubble, but this particular "young'un" hadn't had a solid night's sleep in years. Probably not since…No. Really? I hadn't had a good night's sleep since about a year before Cam and I divorced. Was that the last time I felt truly secure, safe, and at peace? I shoved the thought away. I didn't want to think about him now.

"Have y'all had lunch?"

"Oh, yeah. I made some grilled cheese sandwiches and tomato soup. Prim ate about half of her food."

"That's not bad. Some days, she won't eat even that. I appreciate you staying with her while I went out to get supplies and take care of some things."

"No problem. I always have a good time with Prim." She pushed herself to the edge of the couch, wound her crochet project around a yarn ball, and stuffed it in her bag. "Did you get everything you needed? Is there anything I can do?"

"I got everything. Patrice did so much already. Just bring something for the potluck tomorrow. Do you need a ride to the Bolton House tomorrow? Cam is going to come pick up Prim and me."

"Nah." She stood with stiffness and a soft grunt. "Bonnie's going to come get me."

We said our goodbyes, and I sat down at the kitchen table to work on the memorial board while Prim slept. I still had a couple hours before needing to prepare dinner, so if I worked quickly, I could get it done. I used stencils to write *Cassidy—Forever in Our Hearts* in the center of the board. Then, I used corner tabs to secure the pictures all around the words. The hardest part was trying to tie a pretty bow out of the teal ribbon. I had to watch a YouTube video tutorial about six times to finally get it right. I put a little silver and teal glitter around the edges and smiled. Cassidy loved glittery things. After a couple of hours, my back ached from bending over the table, so I stood, stretched, and searched the fridge and cabinets for items to prepare for supper. I wasn't particularly hungry since Cam and I had a large and late lunch.

Prim woke up. "Hey, hon. I didn't know you were here. When did you come in?" She sat up in her recliner, blinking. She tried to push the footrest down, but it wouldn't budge. I rushed to help her. "Thanks. Batrene was telling me about those electric lift chairs where a push of the button will raise and lower the foot thing and it'll lift up the back end of the chair to help me stand. Have you ever heard of such a thing?"

"No, I haven't." I helped her to stand. She was wearing a pink floral duster and a thick pink cardigan I bought her for her birthday.

"I sure would love to have one of those. It's getting harder and harder to get out of that thing." She looked at the chair. "But I'd hate to give it up. It was your Papaw's." She patted my arm. "Did you have a good day?"

"I did. What do you want for supper?"

She shuffled down the hall to the powder room. "It doesn't matter. Whatever you want. I'll make do."

I resumed my hunt for food. I wanted something light. I shouted, "How about breakfast for supper?"

"If you want," she said from the bathroom.

I began the preparations for eggs, bacon, toast, and coffee.

Prim emerged from the hall, looking as brittle as dried leaves. A stiff wind could have blown her right over.

She sat down in her chair at the kitchen table with the thick cushion on the seat. I handed her a ginger ale and checked the clock on the wall. "It's about time for your medicine. Let's go ahead and get your pills in you before the pain sets in." I kept an eye on the bacon while I extracted Prim's pills from the cabinet and set out her dosage on the table.

I recalled my earlier conversation with Cam. I wanted to confront Prim, but in a gentle way since she was likely to be cranky from her nap. "Cam and I had a conversation today."

"Yeah? How's he doing? Why didn't he come in to see me?"

"He's good. He said he'll see you tomorrow when he picks us up for Cassidy's memorial."

She studied the memorial board I'd put together. "It's a shame about that poor girl. She sure was pretty, wasn't she?"

"She was."

"So young. What I wouldn't do with that youth if I had it right now." She chuckled. "I remember her. She used to do those horse shows. Jumping those bars and stuff. The church put on a bake sale for her one year to help her get the money together to take her horse clear across the country to compete. She won first place that year."

I had no recollection of that. It was amazing to me how much my grandmother knew and recalled about the life going on all around me, but as a kid, I was too enveloped in my own little world to see beyond my own nose. "I never knew that. How did you know her and I didn't? I didn't even know her until I met Jimmy."

"I guess y'all ran in different circles. I didn't know her real well. She went to different schools. Private schools."

I pushed the bacon onto a plate, I drained off most of the fat then dropped in the eggs with a loud sizzle. "Wait a second. If she had horses and went to private schools, why did the church need to help send her to a competition? Wouldn't she have had the money for that?"

"They *had* money and horses, but then her daddy made some bad business decisions and lost all their money."

"Oh. That's awful." I flipped the eggs.

"But after they sold off the family farm, almost all the horses, and downsized, they were able to recoup some of their losses."

I thought about the picture of Cassidy hugging the neck of her horse, giggling as it nibbled her ear. She clearly loved her horses. "How sad for her." Tears filled my eyes. Somehow, knowing she'd endured the loss of something she loved so much made her more endearing. I dropped the bread in the toaster and returned the conversation to my initial purpose. "So I was talking to Cam earlier…"

"Yeah?"

"I discovered you two have had some interesting conversations about me and him."

She puckered her lips and pulled them back a couple times. "Hm." She looked back at the poster. "I really like this picture of Cassidy." She pointed at a corner photo. Then she swiped her hand across the table. "Lord, we're going to have glitter all over everything now."

"I'd really like to discuss this." I plated the eggs with the bacon, placed the plates on the table, and went back to butter the toast and grab my coffee. "Now, I was mad at first. I'm not going to lie." I placed the toast on the table and sat down. "But now I want to know why you and Cam were talking about me. Why would you encourage him and convince him that he and I should be together? It's not fair to give him such false hopes. He needs to move on, find someone else he can be happy with."

"Because it's true." She put blackberry jam on her toast. "And I'm going to fight to get you two back together until my last breath. So you'll have to get used to that, missy."

"But Prim, I've moved on. Jimmy and I…"

"Child, you and Jimmy won't last. You keep trying to convince yourself you're happy with that boy, but I know you're not. I see the way you look at each other. I feel the energy between you. It's not right. He's more concerned about his work than he is any relationship. I'm not saying he doesn't care about you. I think he does. In his way. He's fond of you, but you'll never be first in his life. Not any time soon."

I chewed my bacon so I wouldn't have to speak. I knew she was right. I didn't want to admit it to her or myself. Obviously, something wasn't clicking with Jimmy. In fact, we spent more time bickering and fighting than enjoying each other's company, and it had never been that way with Cam—well, until right before the divorce, when everything felt lost and hopeless.

Prim continued, "You know I'm right. How many arguments have you and Jimmy been in? Y'all've only been dating for a couple of months."

"Almost three."

"That's not a happy couple, Rook. And if you stay with that man and marry him, y'all will be miserable."

"Marry? Lord, Prim. Marriage isn't anywhere on the horizon anytime soon."

"And why not?" She leaned on the table. "You're not getting any younger. Don't you want to settle down and have a family?"

"I guess. Someday. But I'm just now launching my career."

"A career?" She snorted, chewing her bacon. "What good is a career when you're my age? Sure, maybe you get a little money and some savings. *If…*" She held up a finger. "Your company actually keeps you around or stays in business. But people are disposable to companies and corporations. There's no loyalty, no real relationship, no love, no kinship. You're just a number. When you're *my* age, you want to be surrounded by a happy family, kids, and grandkids. You want to see the generations you've created and contributed to and see how they're impacting the world around them. You want to know you've raised good people who will help you when you're too frail and old to take care of yourself. *That* is true success. To love and be loved. To be fruitful. And to know the beauty of the sacrifice a mother and father make for their children. That grows you in a way you can never achieve elsewhere, child."

My eyes stung with unshed tears. I stared at my plate, willing myself not to cry as regret grabbed hold of my throat and twisted it shut.

I felt her eyes on me. "You and Cam are still young enough that you can get back together, start a family, and be truly happy. It'll never be perfect. Nothing in this life is perfect, child. Not ever. It's an immature and silly person who runs around thinking things should be perfect. But you can be happy. I'm trying, as a final good act on this planet, to protect you and offer you the happiness I've always wanted for you. It ain't Jimmy. He's a good man. Yes. He's fond of you. Yes. But he won't make you happy. You'll always be second place to his work, and that's no way to live."

A tear slipped from my eye, and I swiped it away. My pride. My stupid pride got in the way. It always did. "Well…" I stabbed at my eggs. "I'd really appreciate it if you would stop filling Cam's head with a bunch of nonsense. We're divorced. That's it. We failed."

"Oh…" She sat back and waved away the idea. "Nonsense. I've heard lots of stories of divorced people getting back together."

"Yes, but they usually don't last."

"But those stories don't have to be your story. I think you and Cam got divorced too soon. Dr. Phil says you shouldn't divorce until all your emotional bags have been unpacked, until you know for certain all your emotional issues have been resolved."

I leveled a look of disbelief at her.

She opened her hands. "He's not wrong. You and Cam still have unresolved issues, and I think you jumped the gun and got divorced too fast before y'all had even given yourselves a fair chance to work things out. Your generation is always so quick to run from your problems. You have no grit."

A heavy, low throb began behind my eyes and spread until my whole head felt numb. I wiped my face and pushed back my plate of half-eaten food. "I don't want to talk about this anymore. All I'm asking is for you to stop encouraging Cam. It's making things hard for me. It tears me up."

Prim chewed on a mouthful of pancake. "All I'm saying is you shouldn't cast your pearls before swines, baby girl."

"You've never given him a fair chance."

"Let me ask you one question." She leaned on the table and laser-focused on me. "Why is Cam taking us to the memorial tomorrow instead of Jimmy?"

I knew the answer. Jimmy had to work and would have to meet me there. *Dang it.* Why did Prim have to be right all the time? My pride wouldn't let me speak the truth. Instead, I said, "Jimmy's not a swine." I pouted.

"Don't play dumb with me. You know what the verse means." She tapped the table to emphasize her next words. "And you know the answer to my question. Avoiding the truth won't change it."

I did know what she meant about the swine, and I knew the answer to her question, but that didn't make any of this easier. The truth was often a painful and bitter pill to swallow.

I needed to get away from this subject. "You should know something weird happened today." I explained what we found in the underground room. I showed Prim the picture of Mom at the Christmas party.

Prim looked at the image, a pained smile on her face. "My beautiful girl." She pressed her lips tight, and her eyes watered. "I've never seen this picture before. I wonder who took it?"

"I don't know."

"Do you recognize the place she's at or any of the people?"

She studied the picture and then shook her head slowly. "Nope. I've never seen that place or any of the people. She's clearly at some party. Maybe your daddy took her to a party, or she went with a friend?"

"Maybe," I sighed, disappointed. "I hope Jimmy will discover something soon." I pointed at the picture. "Do you remember this bracelet? It matches the ring I'm wearing as if it's part of a set, but I've only seen it in pictures."

"Yep. Your daddy got the bracelet and ring for her birthday one year. She loved them and wore them all the time. But, one day, the bracelet went missing. She was so upset about it. She never did find it."

"How did it go missing?"

"I don't know. When they found her dead, she wasn't wearing it, though she wore it all the time. I went through all her belongings and never found it."

Chills raced over me. Had the killer taken the bracelet as some sort of trophy from my mom after killing her?

Chapter Sixteen

After dinner, I helped Prim into bed and changed into my pink pin-striped pajama pants and a red Smoky Mountains T-shirt Cam had bought for me on our honeymoon. I hadn't selected it intentionally, and I almost put it back because of the significance that could be assigned to it. But I shrugged it off. I liked the shirt. It was soft, organic cotton, and super comfy. That's all I cared about. Since the house was a little chilly, I pulled on a gray cardigan and pink fuzzy socks.

I returned downstairs to the living room to watch something comedic. I'd had enough of murder, drama, and mayhem for one day. I put the television on *Friends* and grabbed my laptop off the coffee table to check my social media and email. A knock sounded on the kitchen door.

I ran to the door and peeked through the curtain. Jimmy.

I opened the door. "Hey, come on in."

"Hey." He kissed me. His lips felt cold and stiff. Or maybe mine were. Prim had gotten in my head.

"Are you hungry? Can I get something for you?" I shut the door.

"I'd love a sandwich if you have the fixings for one."

"I think I have some ham and cheese."

"Perfect."

I made him a ham and cheese sandwich, dropped some potato chips on his plate, and poured him a glass of iced tea.

He sat at the table. "Thanks." He took a giant bite of the sandwich. With a big wad of food in one cheek, he said, "What are you up to?"

"Nothing. TV. Emails. Facebook."

He gulped down his tea and glanced at the board. "Board looks nice. I think Derek will appreciate it." He reached over and squeezed my hand. "I certainly appreciate it." His eyes watered, and he cleared his throat. "I'll miss her for sure." He stared straight ahead, crunching his chips, his mind going to some place and time before I knew him. As I watched him eat, I rolled Prim's earlier advice through my mind.

When he finished supper, he accepted my offer of a Moon Pie, and we retired to the living room. He kicked off his shoes and sat in the corner of the couch, his feet crossed, and stared at the TV. For a moment, I got a glimpse of our future, and my skin crawled. Not that I expected to be out dancing and club-hopping all night, every night. I wasn't opposed to a quiet life at home. I probably enjoyed being home more than most people my age. But I wanted a partner who was engaged, who would talk to me about his day, talk to me about my day, and show interest in what I was doing—especially early in a relationship; someone who would talk to me about future plans—even the little ones like movies to see, places to go, or books to read. Did Jimmy even enjoy reading like I did? It was as if we'd been married for twenty years instead of dating for a few months.

I curled up beside him on the couch. When he didn't seem to notice my presence, I broke the ice. "Did the techs come up with anything from the underground room?"

"Nah. Not yet."

"You probably wouldn't tell me if they did anyway."

He smiled down at me. "Probably not."

"You seem quiet tonight. Are you okay?"

"Got a lot on my mind."

"Yeah. I can see that. Want to talk about it?"

He looked at me and hesitated. His face was full of doubt and mirth, like he was working a riddle.

"What?" I said, growing uncomfortable under his gaze. Was he going to bring up something about Cam? Did one of his friends see us at lunch, draw the wrong conclusions, and tell Jimmy?

Taking a deep breath, he turned his body to face me. One arm stretched toward me along the back of the couch. "What do you think of Florida?"

Was he drumming up the courage to ask me to go on vacation with him? I wasn't sure if I was ready for a getaway this early in our relationship, so I aimed to play it a little on the cool side. "I've only been a few times. I love the beach. I'd really like to go back. Soon."

His eyes brightened. "I really like the beach, too."

"Are you thinking about taking a trip there?"

He paused and averted his gaze, and he grew distant again. "Yeah, sort of. But I have a lot of decisions to make first."

I tipped my head and stared at him, confused. My phone chimed from my purse in the kitchen, indicating a text. "Hold on." I jumped up to retrieve it.

It was a message from Gordon Meece. **Sorry if I'm contacting too late. Let's meet next week to discuss the Christmas event. I'm free Wednesday at 8A. LMK if that works for you.**

I texted back as I returned to Jimmy. **That'll be fine. I'll confirm details later.**

K

I returned to my seat and put my phone on the table.

"Who was that?"

"A potential event for the distillery."

He thought for a moment, then nodded.

"So, about Florida. What do you mean you have some decisions to make?"

He sighed. "I'm not sure I want to get into it right now. It's been a long day."

"Get into what? I didn't realize planning a vacation would be so stressful." I laughed, nudging him, then cuddling up against him, listening to his heartbeat.

"What are you talking about, Rook?"

"Aren't you talking about going on vacation to Florida?"

"No."

I shifted my head to look up at him. "Then what about Florida?"

"I might be moving there."

I shot up and pushed away from him. "What?" Now, the question Cam had asked me earlier made more sense. Had he and Jimmy been talking about Jimmy moving away?

"I put in an application to the Sarasota PD a few weeks ago. I had a Zoom interview today. I think it went all right."

I scooted to the edge of the couch and gaped at him. I was so taken aback, shocked, I couldn't wrap my head around what was happening. I pressed my fingertips over my eyes. "Hold on. Hold on, just a hot minute. You…" I shook my head. My thoughts scrambled and collided so that I couldn't catch a single thread. "Let's start at the beginning. You put in a job application in another state around the time you and I started dating?"

"Uh, yeah." He flushed.

"And you didn't think to tell me or let me know the potential for this here…" I pointed between the two of us to indicate our relationship. "Was basically *nada*?" The more I talked, the hotter I became.

"I guess so. I didn't really think—"

By now, I was certain steam was emitting from my nostrils. "You were just leading me on this whole time? You let me think we had potential, that things might get serious, and you never once thought, 'Hey, maybe I should tell Rook she might be wasting her time because I've got plans to take off to Florida!'" I threw my hands in the air to emphasize my point.

He put up his hands. "Now, calm down, Rook."

Telling me to calm down was like striking a hornet's nest with a rock.

"Calm down? Are you kidding me right now, Jimmy?" I stood and paced in front of the TV. "And here's something else. I could understand if maybe you got busy and forgot to tell me about the job application. I could give you the benefit of the doubt there. Though it's being pretty generous, I think. But here's the kicker. You were called for an interview and never told me about it. When did you know about the interview?"

He blew out a slow breath and rubbed his face. "About a week ago."

A scoffing, laughter of disbelief burst from me. "Oh-ho-ho. Wow. Fantastic." I turned my back on him and looked up at the ceiling to gather my juice for the next round. I spun on him. "And you didn't tell *me*." I slapped my chest. "The girl you're dating." I opened my arms to the ceiling.

"Why on earth would you possibly tell me?"

He stood. His face was red now. "If you'll shut up for a minute, I'll tell you what I was thinking."

"Okay." I glared at him wide-eyed, my teeth set. I crossed my arms. "Do tell."

"At first, I was thinking I'd ask you to go with me."

I blinked at him. My stomach bottomed out. Okay. I wasn't expecting that. I hadn't thought he was that serious. And I wouldn't move anyway. First, we'd only been dating for a short time. Second, such a suggestion was moving too fast, too soon. Third, I wasn't down for living with a man I wasn't married to. It was just my way. "I, uh…"

He continued, "At first, I thought you and I were working out pretty well, so I thought we could go down there together and make a life."

What made him think we were working out well? Many of our dates were interrupted by his work. We bickered or argued much of the time, and I didn't always care for the way he spoke to me. I didn't want to get into those details now. "I can't go down there and leave Prim."

"Of course, but you know there's something else, *someone* else, between us."

I shook my head and looked down at the floor. "I don't know what you're talking about." I did know. But I didn't want him to see it in my eyes, and maybe I didn't want to admit it to myself, either.

"Rook." He put his hands to his hips. "I'm not stupid. It didn't take me too long to put things together. I'm in the business of solving puzzles. Remember? It was obvious Cam would always be between us."

I spun to sit on the coffee table and dropped my face into my hands. "Gah! Does no one think I have a mind of my own?" I looked up at him. "Cam and I are *divorced*. We are friends, yes. We always have been. That hasn't changed." I clapped my hands to emphasize each word of the next point. "But we are over. I keep telling Prim that. I keep telling Cam that. And now I'm telling you. But none of this explains or excuses why you didn't tell me you were applying for a job out of state. Why didn't you tell me?"

He shook his head, and confusion etched his features. He dithered. "I-

I-I…" He huffed. "I don't know. I don't know why I didn't tell you." He scratched his forehead and winced.

I know my face expressed my utter disappointment. "You think our relationship is strong enough for me to go trotting off to Florida with you, but you didn't think you should tell me about the application and interview? Those are really big things."

Jimmy sat on the edge of Prim's recliner. "I guess I didn't want to bring it up until I knew for sure I had the job. So you wouldn't have to worry or be concerned about anything or get your hopes up."

"Because what I didn't know wouldn't hurt, right?"

"Something like that." He dropped his head, and his hands hung between his knees. "I'm sorry. I thought I was doing a good thing. I'd make a lot more money in Florida. It would be a lieutenant position. I'd be a supervisor, putting me on a path to promotion to captain and maybe someday a chief. And the bonus is I'd be near the beach."

"When will you know if you got the job?"

He shrugged. "I don't know. A few days."

Tears swelled in my eyes, and my throat tightened. I knew what this all meant. It was inevitable. "So I guess this means we're breaking up?"

"Why?"

"Because you're going to Florida."

His voice tensed. "I don't actually have the job, Rook. And who knows, you might change your mind. Maybe a new place is just the change you need. A fresh start."

"You know I can't leave Prim."

"But I also know her time is limited. Maybe we can arrange a long-distance relationship until she doesn't need you anymore."

A heavy, dull throb began beating a drum in my head. I put my head in my hands and rubbed my forehead. I stared at my pink fuzzy socks, hoping a hole would open up in the floor and pull me under.

I must've been too quiet for too long because Jimmy said, "What's wrong? What're you thinking?"

I shook my head, which was growing increasingly heavy and numb, and the sensation was spreading through my body. I needed distance. Space to think through things and space to feel. I sighed. "I'm tired, and I want to go to bed now. Tomorrow's going to be a little tough. Let's just get through the next few days. Let me sleep on this, and then we'll talk about it after the funeral, okay? Because I really can't handle this right now. I just can't. Besides, like you say, you don't actually have the job. So, I'm not going to count my chickens before they're hatched." I sighed and pushed myself to my feet. "You should probably go." I pulled my cardigan tight around me and stood nearby, watching him put on his shoes and gather his things.

I followed him to the door. He stopped, turned, and with a sad, hound dog face, he touched my hip and leaned in to kiss me. I turned my face so he'd kiss my cheek.

"See you tomorrow," he said. "I'll meet you there."

I stood on the screened porch watching him back out of the driveway, recalling what Prim had said earlier about Cam picking us up for the memorial while Jimmy was going to meet us there. Once again, Prim was right, and I was going to be left alone.

Chapter Seventeen

Needless to say, sleep avoided me. I tossed and turned all night, ruminating on my conversations with Prim and Jimmy and the weird stalker scene with my mom's pictures in the underground speakeasy. I cried into my pillow. About a lot of things. About my stupid luck. About my losses and the losses to come. Even if Jimmy didn't go to Florida, I wasn't sure I could recover from his secrecy surrounding the job application and interview. His explanation made sense, but it still hurt to think that he had something big going on and didn't share it with me when I was supposed to be his partner, his girlfriend. Was I being irrational? I was too tired to know.

But it wasn't just Jimmy. I cried over Cassidy. And my mom. And Prim. I cried until my face hurt, and my sinuses were so swollen it felt like my whole head was stuffed with thick sheep's wool. I sat up and blew my nose. It was all too much.

Until now, I managed the issues piling on me by always getting up, always moving forward, putting one foot in front of the other and just powering through the days. Trying to not think about things too much or too deeply because instinctively I knew that focusing on my problems would only make them worse, compound them. And, as I learned from Prim early on, what good would it do to wallow in the misery, anyway? How would that help anything or make it better?

And then it seemed as though I wasn't in a position to stop. I had to keep going because I had bills to pay and work to do, and people to care for. If I stopped, then nothing would get done, and people relied on me. So I kept going. But I wasn't sure how much more I could take. Would there be a time when I couldn't get up anymore? When the desire to curl up in a fetal position would be so strong and overpowering that I'd completely lose the ability to get up and keep going? I pulled the jar of vapor rub out of the bedside table and rubbed it on my face to open my sinuses and then sprayed saline into each nostril. I flopped down on the bed in a fetal position and stared at the moonlight slicing across the wall. A good night's sleep would make things look better in the morning—if I could sleep. But over and over the thoughts slashed through my head, each thought a little razor delivering a painful cut.

I turned to the issue of Cassidy's death to distract my mind from going deeper into the self-pity pit. I'd almost marked Trigg off my list. Clearly, someone used the weed eater string to guide police toward him, but after speaking to him, I couldn't see him as the killer. And to kill her for only two thousand dollars was asinine. Of course, people have been killed for much less, but Trigg was too obvious. He wasn't stupid. Why would he use a weapon so obvious? Nope. Had to be someone else. Someone who knew about Cassidy's fight with Trigg, perhaps. Like Kenton.

Kenton knew about the fight. Heck, Kenton *caused* the fight when he didn't pay Trigg. And, if Kenton was trying to forge documents to make himself Cassidy's beneficiary, then he would have motive for getting rid of her to claim the money. Then I thought about the conversation he'd had with Derek about the land. He seemed determined to convince Derek to sell. And desperate. Would he be desperate enough to kill? To kill his own half-sister? Maybe. Maybe he believed Cassidy was his primary obstacle. And maybe he thought that by removing her, he could easily convince Derek to sell because he knew Derek wasn't as emotionally invested in the J.T. Bolton House.

The Meece's were somehow connected to this, too. Kenton worked with their property company. The Meece's were interested in the J.T. Bolton House. Maybe Gordon Meece thought he could make Kenton's negotiations with Derek easier by taking out the primary obstacle to selling—Cassidy. I thought about Gordon Meece. Handsome, charming, rich, mysterious.

But was he a killer? There was something about him that seemed too soft for such a thing. His brother, Louis, however. I shuddered. He sent my creep-radar into high alert. I couldn't explain it. His presence caused a deep revulsion to pulse through my body. Would he kill someone on his brother's orders? I don't know. Gordon Meece didn't seem like the sort of person who would order a woman's death just because he wanted her land. After all, I found him kind, generous, and easy-going. But I also didn't really know the Meece's.

There was Derek. He had at least a million reasons for killing his wife. If the policy I found on his desk was legitimate. But what if that was something planted to frame him? After all, Kenton had had documents in his room. Yet, maybe he and Kenton were working together to get the land from Cassidy to make money from it. Was he then also complicit in Cassidy's death?

Finally, my brain and body gave out to exhaustion until I was ripped from sleep by my alarm. Seven. I sat up in bed, my brain so numb and dumb that producing a thought felt like trying to start a campfire with wet wood. I rubbed my face and pushed myself to stand. Prim would be up soon and Cam would arrive in a couple hours. I needed to get dressed so I could help Prim dress.

I had just finished dressing Prim in her navy dress and pearls and settled her at the kitchen table to take her medicine when Cam knocked on the kitchen door. He held a rectangular box from Irene's. Joy hopped across my chest like the little bird on my windowsill. I let him in, thankful I didn't need to make breakfast.

"Good morning. I'm about to make coffee."

"I brought the best donuts in the world to the best girls in the world." Cam was a sight for my puffy eyes in his black slacks and form-fitting gray shirt. He didn't dress up often. He had little reason to when he split his life between the bar and the farm, but when he did dress up, it made all the difference. If only men knew how much women loved a dressed-up man. I didn't know he even owned these clothes.

"Hey." My mouth was suddenly dry. "You look...nice." He smelled good too—a clean, but musky scent. Sandalwood and fresh linen.

He smiled. "So do you." He set down the box of donuts. "And you should know. These are the only dress clothes I have, so I'm wearing them again for the wake and the funeral. I got the suit jacket and tie at home."

I laughed and shook my head. *Typical Cam.* "I don't doubt it a bit. But that's okay. Where's your parents? Aren't they coming?"

"They decided it would be best to come only to the funeral. But mom sent green bean casserole. It's in the van."

He and Prim met for a hug. She kissed his clean-shaven cheek, leaving a smudge of pink lipstick. "Oops." She rubbed at the mark. "I got lipstick on you."

"That's all right. It's a souvenir from my favorite girl."

She waved her hand at him. "Oh, you're too silly. But you look so handsome." She patted his hand. "Come, sit. sit." She pulled out a chair. "Let me get you some coffee for your donuts."

She scuffed eagerly toward the coffee pot and filled up a mug for him, complete with the amount of cream he preferred. She placed the mug in front of him and sat at the head of the table to his left.

"Prim, your pills and ginger ale are there on the table."

"I see them." She took her medicine and washed them down with a swig of ginger ale.

I handed out small plates and napkins for everyone's donuts.

Cam opened the lid. "Prim, I got your favorite right here." He lifted a Danish from the box. "A blackberry and cream-filled beauty." He placed the donut on her plate. It was topped with a dollop of cream and a single blackberry.

"Oh, thank you, hon. I can't believe you remembered."

I made a cup of coffee for Prim and myself and placed them on the table.

"Of course I did. How could I forget your favorite? That'd be like forgetting your birthday."

She chuckled and bit into the pastry delight. Her eyes twinkled with a joy I hadn't seen in a long time. She chewed and said, "Now my lipstick's going to be messed up for sure."

"Totally worth it." Cam smiled at her with a wad of apple fritter in his jaw.

"Kisses and donuts are worth all the lipstick you have."

She giggled.

I sat to Cam's right at the other table end and examined my choices. The box was filled with a bevy of delights: pumpkin spice cream, blackberry cream, cherry cream cheese Danish, raspberry-filled, apple fritter, the maple glazed, and the new flavor I'd been dying to try—the bourbon cream filled. Goodnight! Surely he didn't think I could possibly eat all those? Of course, picking my favorite donut was no difficult task. I rarely met a donut I didn't like. Anything fruit-filled or cream-filled was likely to tickle my taste buds.

I selected a bourbon cream-filled. "Thank you for the donuts."

"Anytime. I figured you'd be in a rush and wouldn't have time to do much cooking for breakfast."

"You were right." I bit into the bourbon cream-filled donut and about lost my senses. It was simply the most delicious thing I'd eaten in a long time: fried dough, covered in a chocolate glaze, topped with chopped pecans, and filled with soft, sweet cream kissed with the savory oaky flavor of bourbon. "Ohmagudnuss." I fell back against my seat to savor the flavors. I looked at Cam. "That tastes like a bourbon ball! It's amazing!"

He flashed a sly smile. "I figured you'd like it." He winked.

"Good job. Irene is a genius."

Cam laughed, sipping his coffee. "Do I know how to make you happy or what?"

That sobered me a little. He did, actually. He also knew how to make me unhappy. He knew all the buttons to push. That was both a good thing and a bad thing. That was something Jimmy hadn't figured out yet, though he probably would with time. *What time? He's going to leave me. Going to get that job. We're out of time.* But would Jimmy even have thought to get my favorite donuts? Something so simple, but endearing?

Cam was talking about his older brother, Mason, who was moving back from Louisville. "Going to be a full house now." Cam bit into his apple fritter. "But it'll be nice to see him again and to have the help on the farm. I'm hoping he'll stick around for a while."

Prim sipped her coffee. "What's he coming home for?"

"He's having problems at home. But we're trying to keep it quiet for now. We're hoping they can work it out."

"Oh, that's too bad."

"What happened?" Prim bit into her Danish.

Cam shook his head. "Not sure. He'll probably give me details when we see each other. But, sometimes, these things happen." He glanced at me, then focused on his food. "Any number of reasons why."

"Is he at least happy to be returning home?"

He scoffed. "As happy as any forty-year-old could be moving back in with his parents." He laughed. "He's not too thrilled about it. He assures us he'll move out as soon as he gets work settled, but I'm hoping he'll help me with the farm. It's starting to wear on me running the farm and the bar both. But Mom and Dad need the help. They're getting too old to manage the animals and the crops and stuff. They still do what they can, of course, but…"

"I know how it is," Prim said. "I pray they don't ever have to sell their farm or their land. It about killed me when we had to sell off some of ours back when my husband was having all those problems. We had to pay off the medical bills somehow. One of the worst days of my life was when we sold our land. Our family has worked this land for generations. Just as your family has."

He nodded.

I noticed his hands for the first time. Thick, strong, riddled with calluses and cuts.

He leaned back. "It's a good workout, though. A few hours of pitching hay, and I don't need to go to the gym all week." He chuckled.

Prim nodded. "Lord, I remember the summers. Mercy it was so hot. Sweat dripping everywhere. Felt like I was on fire. Messing with picking weeds out of the food crops, topping and cutting tobacco." Her eyes were distant, seeing days long gone. "I don't know how Henry and I survived it. I really don't."

"Thank God Mom and Dad stopped growing tobacco. The farm is much more manageable now." He and Prim laughed a silent understanding between them.

When we finished our breakfast, Prim and I reapplied our respective lipsticks. Then, I gathered and loaded the memorial supplies as Cam helped Prim into the van.

Chapter Eighteen

On the way to the J.T. Bolton House, we passed along a rural road behind the mansion with the pasture on one side and the barn on the other. In the distance, the J.T. Bolton house sat on the hill. On the other side of the road was a large pasture belonging to another farm.

My heart sank. Tacked to the barbed wire fence, a large Phoenix Properties sign announced a new housing development was coming soon.

"Hey, Cam, stop the car for a minute."

"What's the matter?"

"Please." I pointed to a gravel drive in front of the rusted metal pasture gate. "Just a minute."

He pulled the car into the drive. I got out of the van and walked a few feet down the shoulderless road lined with chicory weeds, their little purple heads bobbing in the wind. A deep ditch stretched the length of the road on the other side. I stared up at the sign. Phoenix Properties was Gordon Meece's company. A strange sensation of irritation and resentment bubbled up. I knew Gordon owned a property development company. But only when staring at the Jersey and Angus cows grazing in the pasture on borrowed time did the reality sink in. They were going to destroy this farm that had been owned for generations for the construction of a bunch of McMansions.

Of course, people needed homes to live in. I wasn't unreasonable. But Rothdale was such a small town, I knew the housing wasn't for our population. These houses were meant to satisfy the Lexington urban sprawl creeping into our tiny bedroom community. Their people were tired of living in the city with increasing crime, noise, traffic, and sky-rocketing housing prices. So, they crept into tiny bedroom communities like ours, searching for a haven of peace, quiet, and affordability.

I never liked to see farmers lose their land. Even though it wasn't my land, I took it personally. I knew firsthand the heartbreak that came with the loss of the land worked by generations of farming families. Prim and Papaw cried when they had to sell off part of their farm in order to pay for Papaw's medical bills. And he died anyway. Prim fought like the devil to keep the remainder of the farm after Papaw died. She won, but it had cost her everything and few others could afford to win.

These days, too many people weren't having children or the children they had were moving to the cities for better-paying work, so there was no one to work the land, grow crops, and tend the livestock. In many cases, the old-timers had no choice but to sell because there was no one to leave the land to. But the problem with selling was the building of unnecessary houses, warehouses, factories, the loss of peace and quiet, the loss of clean air and water. Farming was much kinder to the land than ripping it up for massive buildings of concrete and steel and enormous parking lots.

I bit the inside of my lip, staring at the large white words: COMING SOON! GREENHAVEN. I scoffed. Interesting how these developers always named their projects with titles meant to inspire peace—Greenhaven, Whispering Pines, Serenity Fields—while ripping up trees, destroying the wildlife, and pushing them into unnatural habits, crowding them out, destroying ecosystems, and tearing up viable farmland that could be used to grow food. The destruction of peace for the appearance of it. I had no problems with people building homes and businesses. But I knew there were tons of places sitting empty in Lexington. Places that could be repurposed or torn down and rebuilt *before* digging up land.

A car zipped by, blowing my hair. I gazed across the road at the old barn and pasture on the J.T. Bolton house property. Soon all this land would be gone, gobbled up by a noisy, crowded, subdivision or apartment complex. How much longer before even the beautiful historic J.T. Bolton mansion would also be destroyed by a bunch of nondescript, characterless, unbeautiful homes covered in vinyl siding? It bothered me that all around me the wild beauty of nature and beautiful architecture were disappearing into conformity, blandness, and high-priced luxury apartments few could afford.

Cam rolled down his window. "Hey. What's going on?"

"Oh, nothing. It's fine." I returned to the van and climbed inside.

"You sure? What were you looking at?"

I clicked my seat belt into place. "I was looking at that sign."

"Why?"

"Just getting a peek at the future."

We arrived at the J.T. Bolton House by eleven. Derek answered the door in his suit, his tie loose. He held a coffee cup in one hand.

"Hey." He sipped his coffee. "C'mon in."

I stepped in and caught a whiff of bourbon. "Are you drinking right now?"

A dopey grin spread over his face. "A few cups of Irish coffee for breakfast, that's all."

I shot a look of bewilderment at Cam. I didn't know what to do, but I hoped Derek wasn't going to be trouble.

"You know where everything is, right?" He swept his arm open toward the hall.

"Yes. I'm fine. If I need anything, I'll let you know."

He winked and pointed gun fingers at me. "Bingo."

The blue room was sealed with a police label and crossed with police tape. A shudder went over me as I remembered seeing Cassidy's body lying on the blue room floor.

We left Derek in the foyer and headed back to the ballroom to drop off my supplies.

Cam said, "Hold on." He swiped his thumb over my cheek. "You have glitter…"

A warm rush flooded through me. "It's okay. Cassidy loved glittery things. So it seems appropriate. And actually…" I rubbed his nose. "It's on you, too."

"Oh, man." He wiped his face as I giggled.

"We need to get busy. We'll worry about the glitter later." I pointed at the door in the corner. "Cam, get a chair out of that closet for Prim, please. We'll need chairs and tables for the guests too. I'll be right back."

I headed back to the kitchen. Dirty dishes, empty containers, and liquor bottles littered the countertop. Apparently, Derek and Kenton had a big time last night. I grabbed a bowl of soggy cereal off the table and dumped it into the garbage disposal with a huff. Already Cassidy's beautiful kitchen was falling into chaos and disorder. I snatched the empty containers from the countertops and table, stuffed them into the garbage can, and gathered up the dirty dishes. The stench of rotten food hit me in the face when I opened the dishwasher. The dishes hadn't been done in days, so I filled the reservoir with detergent and started the dishwasher.

Pushing up my sleeves, I washed the remaining dishes, looking out the window across the backyard. Kenton paced in circles in the backyard while on the phone. His face was red, and he seemed upset. I eased the window open to try to hear something.

"Let me tell you something," Kenton said. "I've done everything I could. I'm out." He paused to listen. "I've tried talking to him." He paused again. "What am I supposed to do? I can't just take it, can I? My hands are tied here." He paused. "There are cops all over the place. Maybe we should wait until things settle down. Okay. I'll do what I can. I'll talk to him again."

Kenton seemed pretty desperate.

Kenton rubbed his face. "Okay. I'll try again. Right. Right. I know. Well, I will say this. He wants more than you're offering."

My mouth dropped open. He didn't say it explicitly, but I was pretty sure he was talking about the J.T. Bolton home, Cassidy's dream she had worked so hard for.

Kenton raised his voice. "You do that to me, and I'll blow the lid off this whole thing, and you won't get squat. You'd better watch your step, buddy. No. Don't you threaten me. I was working on it and would've succeeded if you hadn't messed it up." He screamed a curse word, hung up, and shoved his phone into his jeans pocket. I pushed down the window as he rubbed his face and turned back to the house. I quickly closed the shades over the window and busied myself with the dishes, my ears primed on listening for his entrance. He entered the kitchen and slammed the door.

He paused when he saw me.

"Hey. Just doing up these dishes real quick. No telling how long Derek has left them sitting around. You might want to change clothes. People will be arriving for the memorial soon."

His nostrils flared. "Rook Campbell. The nosy girl who's stirring up a bunch of trouble."

I blinked at him. "Excuse me?"

He inched toward me, his fists clenched. "I saw you yesterday, hovering outside the door, eavesdropping on my conversation with Derek."

"I wasn't eavesdropping," I lied. "I had just arrived at the room and was about to knock when the door opened."

"Really? Then why are you telling your boyfriend to have me investigated?" He was close enough for me to smell his sour coffee breath.

"He's a police officer. He's investigating anyone connected to Cassidy. You happen to be one of the people closest to her."

He smirked, a malicious light in his eyes. "Well, somehow, he got it in his head that I was trying to convince Cassidy and Derek to sell this place. How would he come to that conclusion if you didn't hear my conversation with Derek and then run off to tattle-tell?"

He was too close. "I don't know. He's a cop. He's good at his job. Maybe Derek told him."

"Nah. I think you did. Now, I've got a mess on my hands because *you...*" He poked his finger in my face, mere centimeters from my nose. "Can't mind your business. Because *you* like to run your mouth." He backed me against the fridge. "In fact, I've got a good mind to—"

"A mind to do what?" Said a voice behind him.

Cam.

Kenton turned around. "This ain't got nothing to do with you, buddy."

Cam stormed toward us. "Wrong. It has *everything* to do with me."

I pulled a knife from the nearby knife block in case things went sideways quickly.

Kenton backed up and put his hands in the air. "Look—"

Cam stepped up and shoved his chest, causing Kenton to stagger backward. "I see how it is. You only want to threaten women, huh?" He shoved him again. "What ya want to say to me, huh? Got anything to say to *me*?"

"You don't understand—"

"Nah, I *do* understand." He shoved him again, backing Kenton out of the kitchen. "Let's go, big boy. Let's dance."

Kenton pointed at me and shouted. "She's messing up my business deals."

"I don't care. You threaten her, you deal with me."

"I wasn't threatening her. I was-was-was—"

"Save it, *buddy*. Get out of here. Now. And if I see you even looking at her, it'll be your last time. Got it?"

He gave him one last shove, causing Kenton to stumble against the hallway wall. Kenton turned and marched away, shouting, "Y'all don't know who you're dealing with."

"Yeah, right." Cam sneered. "Get out of here, punk."

When Kenton had disappeared, Cam turned to me. "You all right?"

I sighed in relief. "I'm fine."

"Did he put hands on you?"

"No." I returned the knife to its home. "He was just in my face."

"What was that about?"

"He thought I told Jimmy to investigate him, so he's mad at me."

"If he comes around you again, you tell me." He opened the refrigerator. "Okay."

He held up a water bottle. "Came to get this for Prim."

"Thanks," I smiled. "I'll be in the ballroom to help you in a minute. I wanted to clean up this mess first."

"No worries." He strode out of the kitchen.

As I finished up the dishes, a blizzard of questions flew at me. Who had Kenton been talking to? My guess was Gordon Meece. What exactly was he involved in, and why? He clearly wanted to get his hands on the B&B, but to what extent was Derek involved? How much did he know?

Even though Derek was behaving strangely for a grieving husband, I struggled to believe he was a murderer. He and Cassidy had been together for years, had recently married, and seemed to have the same hopes and dreams. They seemed so in love. However, I'd seen enough *Forensic Files* and *Datelines* to know that psychopaths could pretend to be anything for a while to fool the people around them. He could certainly fool me because I didn't know much about him, but could he fool Jimmy? I couldn't believe he could. Not for long.

Further, Cassidy wasn't the sort of person who would go around airing her dirty laundry to people—especially if she'd thought her relationship was failing or if she'd believed herself to be married to a wicked man. So, if Derek was rotten, no one was likely to hear it from Cassidy.

My insides squirmed. I didn't want to turn Cassidy's memorial into an investigation, but since her mom and sisters were going to be here, maybe I could find out a little more about Derek. Maybe he wasn't as much in love with Cassidy as he seemed to be. Maybe he was having a hard time with grief and expressing it appropriately. Crazier things have happened.

Chapter Nineteen

I finished up the dishes and returned to the ballroom. It looked ghostly compared to what it had been on Friday evening. When I hit the light switch, the dim room transformed into a bright, welcoming space.

Prim sat against the wall, watching Cam pull tables and chairs from the closet. I jumped in to help. Derek sauntered in and set chairs around the tables while holding his coffee cup. We might've been better off without his involvement.

Kenton came into the room. He had exchanged his jeans for black slacks, a lavender button-down, and a purple and gray striped tie. He put his hands on his hips. He spoke to Derek, "So this is where the thing is going to be today?"

"Yep."

He nodded. "All right. How long do you think it's going to be?" He pulled his phone out of his pants and began texting.

Weird. His half-sister was only two days dead, and he seemed like he had better things to do than to be at her memorial service.

"I don't know," Derek said. "It takes as long as it takes."

"It should only be a few hours," I interjected.

Kenton didn't acknowledge me.

"Well, I've got a meeting. So that's why I'm asking." Kenton spoke to Derek.

I glared at him. I couldn't listen to his mouth any longer. I said, my voice echoing in the room, "Your half-sister is dead, and we're honoring her memory today. Shouldn't you care more about that?"

He glanced between me and Cam. He ignored me and continued speaking to Derek. "I might not be able to stay for the whole thing."

"You gotta do what you gotta do," Derek said.

Cam and I looked at each other as we rolled a table to its position on the floor. I whispered, "I'm beginning to think he had something to do with his sister's death."

He scoffed as we unfolded the table. "You think? Who schedules a meeting on Sunday? And the same day as the memorial, too? Does Jimmy know?"

"I gave him the information I found yesterday. I'm sure he's looking into it."

Cam and I finished pulling out the long tables, covering them with paper tablecloths, and setting up the folding chairs. I dove into the stuff I'd brought with me.

Holding up the ribbon and scissors, I said, "Cam, would you care to tie ribbons around the porch rail and the tree in the front yard, please?"

"Sure." He left the room as Patrice entered, wearing a black pencil skirt and gray ruffled shirt under a black cardigan. She stopped him in the doorway and spoke with him, then approached me.

We greeted each other with a tight embrace.

"I'm so glad you're doing this. I know her family is so thankful, too." Patrice smiled wanly from behind her wireframes and a mop of tousled gray hair.

Patrice's daughter, Millie, followed behind her, carrying two potted roses. Millie and I had practically grown up together, joined at the hip from kindergarten through high school until I went off to college, and she went into yoga and massage therapy training.

She sat the roses down, and we hugged. "Hey, girl. I can't believe you put this together in such a short time." Millie wore a black sheath dress topped with a long, sheer purple paisley duster. Her thick, dark hair was pushed back from her face with a purple beaded headband she'd made herself. The faint scent of jasmine surrounded her.

"I didn't do it alone." I reached for Patrice's hand and squeezed. "Your momma did a ton. She's the superstar."

Patrice wrinkled her nose to acknowledge the compliment, but quickly ran off to hug Prim and chat with her.

When Cam entered with a box of foodstuffs, Patrice tripped along behind him. "Oh, thank you, Cam, for bringing that in for me. Just set it over on the table, and I'll take care of it." She said to me, "Also, Clay put the bench on the front porch. Where do you want it, Rook?"

"Near that magnolia tree in the backyard. We'll plant the roses by the bench."

Cam didn't even give anyone a chance to ask. He said, "I'm on it." He picked up the roses and headed toward the door.

Patrice added, "Oh, Cam, hon, on your way back, would you also get that box of drinks out of the back seat of my car?"

"Yes, ma'am."

Poor Cam. He was getting his workout today. But he was the only one we could rely on. Kenton and Derek had both made themselves scarce, and Jimmy hadn't shown up yet. I checked my phone. He also hadn't texted or called to let me know when he might arrive.

As he walked away, Patrice bragged loudly enough for him to hear. "He's such a sweetheart. I understand he's a huge help on his family's farm. And all while managing his own business. He sure is something."

I smiled. "He sure is."

Cam flexed his arm muscles like a superhero as he passed out of the door. I chuckled and shook my head.

Patrice said, "Where is Jimmy? I figured he'd be here since Cassidy was his cousin."

My cheeks grew hotter as the pride I felt about Cam swiveled and morphed into irritation toward Jimmy. I tamped down the rise in the negative feelings swelling up inside me and put on my best poker face. "He'll be here later. He has to work." The word "work" turned into a barb against my tongue.

"I see. Well….Maybe we should put this food out." Patrice pulled a meat and cheese tray, an assortment of olives, and a cookie platter out of the box. She directed Millie on how to display them while chatting about who she expected to come to the memorial and sharing any rumors or gossip she'd picked up recently.

Soon, Cam entered with another box and pulled out 2-liters of sodas and gallon jugs of tea and lemonade. Within thirty minutes, other guests began to pour into the room with consolation casseroles and desserts, and it became apparent we were going to need another table. Cam and I rushed to set up and cover another table while people stood around chatting, holding their dishes. Some people plopped down packs of plates, plastic utensils, and Solo cups. Others brought in bottles of water or coolers of ice. The room filled with a deafening cacophony of voices. It was amazing how many people were close to Cassidy and her family and could attend on such short notice.

Husbands trailed behind their wives with plants, flowers, and sympathy gifts or carrying a second food item. They stopped to shake hands with other men. Cassidy's mother and sisters filed into the room, looking worn. They hugged and greeted people who flocked around them to offer their heartfelt condolences and sympathy.

I scanned the room. Everything seemed to be in place. Except Jimmy hadn't shown up yet. And Derek. Where were Derek and Kenton? They should both be here, too. I slipped out in search of them, hoping I wouldn't be missed.

With no sign of either one on the main floor, I climbed the stairs to check their bedrooms. Derek wasn't in his room. I knocked on Kenton's room. He didn't answer, so I cracked the door and peeked in. The lights were off, and the room was empty. The desire to snoop further pulled at me, but I didn't want to be in this room longer than necessary. I slipped out of the room and eased the door closed.

I jogged down the stairs and descended into the basement den where Derek spent most of his time these days. The television was on. He'd been there recently, but wasn't there now. Throwing up my hands in frustration, I ran back upstairs, where I met Cam and Derek in the hall. They were chatting about the new college basketball season.

"Hey, there you are." I said to Derek, "Cassidy's family is here. You should probably go see them."

He nodded. "Yeah, I'll head in there in a minute."

"Have you seen Kenton?" I didn't really care where that jerk was, but since he was family, it was only right to wait for him to start the memorial service.

Derek shook his head and took a drink of beer. "Nope. Don't know where he is."

"Well, I hate to go on without him, but everyone else is already here. I'm not sure what to do."

"Go on without him." Derek took a sip of his beer.

I looked at the bottle in his hand. "Also," I hissed. "Can you have the decency to stop drinking until after the memorial?"

He snorted and walked away, swigging his beer.

Cam said, "I'll try to handle it." He rushed to Derek's side. "Hey man. Look, I know you're upset about Cassidy and everything, but we're trying to do something nice for her and her family. It'd be great if you could…" He reached for the beer bottle—"Put this aside for now."

Derek jerked his hand away. "Get away from me, man."

"C'mon, man. You don't want to do this. It's not going to be a good look for you. Seriously."

"Leave me alone." Derek grew louder and walked away.

"Cam," I said. "Let it go for now."

He lifted his hands. "I tried."

"I know. We'll manage the best we can. I wonder if Cassidy was dealing with this. If he has always been a heavy drinker?"

"I don't know." He sighed. "But if I was a betting man, I'd say he's been like this for a while."

"People sure are surprising, aren't they?"

He chuckled. "You've got that right. I'll try to hang near him and keep him cool during

the event, okay?"

"That would be amazing. Thank you."

"Happy to do it." He put his arm around me and hugged me against his side like we'd just lost a softball game.

Jimmy entered the house. Disappointment flashed over his features before his police face slid into place. "Hey, y'all." He was still in his uniform.

Aggravation prickled through me as I recalled our disagreement last night and how he'd bombed me with the revelation that he was interviewing for a job in Florida.

"Hey," I said. "Didn't you bring some clothes to change into?"

"I think this'll be okay. I have to get right back to work after this anyway."

Whatever. I wasn't going to argue. He shook hands with Cam. Jimmy didn't try to hug or kiss me. He squeezed my arm as though he wanted the affection, but couldn't bring himself to seek it out. It was for the best, anyway. After our fight last night, I was sure invisible quills jutted out from my skin like a protective forcefield.

"I see there are a bunch of cars here, so I guess the event has started?"

"Yes." I pointed down the hall. "The food is in the ballroom. We'll eat first, then dedicate the bench and roses afterward."

He nodded and started toward the ballroom. Cam and I followed.

Jimmy looked around the room. "Wow. Thanks for doing this. I talked to the morgue today, and they should be releasing the body to the funeral home today. So Derek and some of the family are going over to the funeral home after this."

"Maybe that's why Derek has been misbehaving today."

"What's he done?"

"He's drinking."

"Great." He rolled his eyes. "I imagine the visitation will be tomorrow, maybe Tuesday. Funeral on Tuesday or Wednesday. Hopefully, those details will be worked out today." Though Jimmy and I were having problems and were broken up, I still sympathized, ached, for his loss. I rubbed his back. "I'm really sorry about Cassidy."

Tears pooled in his eyes, and he nodded. "Yeah, me too."

People milled around the ballroom, talking, eating, crying, looking at the pictures of Cassidy and telling their favorite stories about her. It was just what a memorial service should be and I was happy I pulled it off—with a bunch of help from some amazing men and women. My muscles loosened into something like relief and relaxation until Derek appeared with a beer bottle in his hand.

"Hey, Deputy Jimbo. Glad you could make it." He clapped his hand into Jimmy's and shook it. Jimmy gave me a side glance of concern. "And looking all official in your uniform. That's what I'm talking about." He guffawed.

Jimmy spoke quietly. "I'm sorry about the uniform. I have to go to work after this."

"Hey…" Derek suppressed a belch. "I understand. You got all those bad guys to catch, right?" Then he broke into the COPS song, bobbing in rhythm. "Bad boys, bad boys, whatcha gonna do? Whatcha gonna do when they come for you?"

Jimmy studied him. "Yeah. Something like that. So, how many of those have you had today, Derek?" He nodded at the beer bottle.

Derek pursed his lips and shrugged. "Not enough."

Jimmy's brows shot up, and he chuckled. "Oh, I think you've had more than enough, my friend."

"Hey!" Derek held up a finger. "Listen to me. This is my home, and I can drink what I want, when I want, in *my* home."

Jimmy put his hand on his shoulder. "True. But right now, as your friend, I'm trying to help you out and let you know that you're embarrassing yourself and your in-laws. And you have to go to the funeral home after this."

Derek blew a raspberry. "Whatever. They've been embarrassed of me from the beginning. Nothing new there." He snort-laughed. "No one was good enough for their princess."

He turned to the picture of Cassidy and began singing to her picture. At first, his voice was quiet as he sang the first lines of Lynard Skynard's "Free Bird." "If I leave here tomorrow, would you still remember me?"But his voice gradually grew louder, drawing the attention of people in the room again. "For I must be traveling on now. 'Cause there's too many places I've got to see…" Silence captured the room.

Jimmy frowned and grabbed his arm. "That's enough. Let's go."

Derek broke free and continued singing at the top of his lungs. "But if I stay here with you, girl, things just couldn't be the same…"

Jimmy grabbed him again, as did Cam, and they wrestled him out the door, but Derek continued to shout the song, his voice cracking against the volume. "'Cause I'm as free as a bird now…And this bird you cannot change…"

As confused stares swung in my direction, I felt compelled to say something. "Uh. I'm really sorry, y'all. He's beside himself with grief."

Cassidy's sister, Lindy, rolled her eyes and scoffed. "Yeah, right," she muttered. She moved to the food table to refill her drink.

"It's okay," I told everyone. "Jimmy and Cam will take care of the situation. Please return to honoring Cassidy's memory. We don't want to take away from that." Thankfully, the crowd turned their attention back to talking and food.

Now was my chance to talk to her, to see if I could find out more about Derek. I beelined to Lindy's side. "Hey," I said. "Sorry about Derek. I was hoping we could get through this memorial without incident."

Lindy was Cassidy's younger sister, the middle child. She had straight, shiny, chestnut hair pulled back into a low ponytail, a round face with bright brown eyes that shone with the same firecracker spirit as Cassidy's. She wore a knee-length black dress with cowboy boots. "That's okay," she said. "If that's the only issue, we'll be doing good." She smiled crookedly, revealing a dimple in her cheek. She placed a few crackers on her paper plate and spooned some of Oda Dean Spurlock's amazing jalapeno, bacon, and cheese ball onto her plate. "Honestly, I wouldn't expect any less from Derek."

I didn't really want to eat, but I grabbed a plate to buy myself some time with Lindy. "Oh, really? Why?"

"He's always been too happy about drinking. If you catch my drift." She put a scoop of broccoli salad on her plate. "I tried to warn her about him, but she wouldn't listen. You know Cassidy. She could be stubborn. She saw a lot of good in him. Smart, good job, funny. I guess there is some of that. She loved him. God knows why. She thought the good outweighed the bad, and she could change the bad." She shook her head. "She always did love a project. I don't know why women will marry men, thinking they can change them. Happens all the time, though. And then women have the nerve to wonder how they end up in the messes they get in when the man was telling them up front, 'Hey, this is who I am and who I enjoy being.' If you watch and listen close enough, men will always tell a woman who they are. But…" She shook her head. "Women like Cassidy think they're somehow going to be the exception. They will be the one woman to fix the man and make him perfect." She dumped a spoonful of chicken and dumplings on her plate. Have you ever had Birdie Harper's chicken and dumplings? Best stuff you'll ever eat. She won a prize for them last year at the state fair."

"No, I haven't had them." The balls of dough swimming in the creamy broth among chunks of chicken made my mouth water. I scooped some onto the plate.

Lindy continued, "I guess you think I'm being awfully hard on my sister. Maybe I am. But I hate that she married him against our family's wishes, and now she's dead. And I bet he had something to do with it." Her brown eyes glimmered with fire.

"Why do you think so?"

"I don't think he really wanted to marry. I heard them arguing before the wedding. He was trying to back out, but she convinced him to go through with it. I think it was because she was pregnant."

I put my hand over my mouth and whispered. "A baby?" My heart wrenched. "Oh, no. I had no idea."

"Yeah," Her voice shook. "I was so excited to be an aunt. But he took all that away. You know how some guys will try to do the honorable thing. I guess I can't fault him for trying. But I think he couldn't make it work, so he killed her."

"That's a pretty bold claim, Lindy."

She stared at me with venom. "They had million-dollar insurance policies on each other. They have this beautiful property and business. Worth a fortune. He could have all this and no wife and kid to tie him down. You do the math."

I blinked at her. It did seem to add up. I couldn't deny that. "It does sound shady. Have you talked to the police yet about your suspicions?"

Jimmy and Cam re-entered the room. Cam checked on Prim, and Jimmy hugged and chatted with family members.

"I was interviewed yesterday, and I received a follow-up call from an officer today. I'll meet with him tomorrow."

"That's probably a good idea. If Derek is guilty, then I hope he's locked up." I squeezed her arm to reassure her.

The heat in her eyes dwindled into kind warmth, and she pressed my hand. "Thank you for putting this together for Cassidy, for us."

"I had a lot of help, but we were happy to do it."

We parted with a smile, and I headed toward Jimmy and Cam, who had re-entered the room. "Do either of you want this food?"

Jimmy grabbed it. "Thanks."

"How's Derek?"

"Good," Jimmy said, digging into the food. "He's down in his den. He promised to stay down there."

I nodded. "You should speak to Lindy. She has some pretty strong theories."

He nodded, chewing. "Okay. Is there something to drink?"

"There are drinks over on the table. Help yourself." Maybe I could go talk to Derek and get a feel for him.

"Where are you going?" Jimmy asked.

"I'll be right back." I wanted to speak with Derek before he passed out. I rushed out of the room, down the hall, and dashed down the stairs to Derek's man cave.

Chapter Twenty

The television was turned way up, playing some sort of action-packed program complete with the sounds of fighting. Then I heard the identifiable voice of Chris Tucker say, "Which one of y'all hit me?"

I rounded the corner. He sat on the sofa in the dark, still drinking, staring dully at the *Rush Hour* movie.

"Hey, Derek," I said. "How're you doing?"

"Fine. Just want to be left alone. Go have your party and leave me be."

I sat on the edge of a nearby recliner made of brown leather. "It's not a party. It's a memorial for your wife."

"Whatever."

"You don't seem to care that she's gone, Derek, and that troubles me."

"I'm not *happy* she's gone, if that's what you mean." The menace in his eyes chilled me. For the first time, I could see maybe he could be a murderer. An uneasiness filled me. Maybe I'd made a mistake coming down here to see him. I didn't know how volatile he was as a drunk, so I approached gently. I waited a few minutes, giving him some space, then tried again. "Did you love her?"

He scoffed, shook his head, and sipped his beer. "Of course…"

"Then why are you behaving like this? Why aren't you upstairs honoring her memory?"

I studied his features in the light of the television. "Y'all were together for a long time."

"Right. I loved her, but I didn't want to get married." He set the bottle on the table. He leaned his elbows on his knees and rubbed his face, propping his cheek against his hand. "I felt pressured because of the baby. Pressure from her. Pressure from our families. Her sisters hated me and didn't want us to be together, but Cassidy's dad was on my case hard to step up and do the right thing. I tried. I failed. Big surprise. Me failing. It's the story of my life. Derek the screwup."

Maybe if I boosted his ego a bit, it'd loosen his lips a little more. "I don't think you're a screwup. I mean, you bought this bed and breakfast, set up a beautiful business, and established an important historical landmark for Kentucky. And all while working a full-time job as an accountant. Those are all good things."

"I guess."

"And you married her, trying to do the right thing. That's honorable."

"That's not the way our families saw it. They were not happy about the pregnancy at first. Cassidy's family thought she could do better. They finally came around and were excited about the baby once we were engaged. If I'd just been a couple months sooner."

"What do you mean?"

He took a swig of his beer. "I was working up the nerve to break up with her. If I'd had the guts to break up with her, maybe we wouldn't be here, none of this would've happened, and she'd still be alive." He shook his head and dropped his face in his hands. He broke down in sobs. "It's all my fault. Because I didn't have the guts to let her go sooner."

"I'm really sorry, Derek. It sounds like a bunch of bad luck and bad timing."

He nodded and sucked down his sobs, sniffling, as he wiped his eyes on the back of his arm. "It was. I was trying to make the best out of a messed-up situation."

"I get that. So if Cassidy were still alive, you'd try to stay married to her?"

"Of course. For as long as we could make it."

For once since her death, he seemed genuine—which moved Kenton further up my suspect list.

"What about Kenton?"

"What about him?"

"He and Cassidy had a rocky relationship. Do you think he could've done anything to hurt her?"

He narrowed his eyes. "Are you digging for information on behalf of your cop boyfriend?"

"No. I came here on my own. I'm just trying to understand where you're coming from. I'm trying to understand why someone would want to kill a beautiful, bright spirit like Cassidy."

"I don't know. But I didn't do it. And I'm not happy she's dead, either. Maybe I didn't want to be married, but I didn't want her dead."

What a horrible situation. Of course, there was hope that Derek might've come around to love her again. I wondered how Cassidy felt about Derek. Did she still love him? Was she only trying to make things work for the sake of the child, too? Maybe it wasn't just the money or the relationship that was the issue. Maybe the pregnancy sent him over the edge. "When Cassidy told you about the baby, were you excited? Did you want it?"

He shrugged. "I don't know." He sat for a minute watching Jackie Chan with admiration. "That Jackie Chan's amazing, isn't he? Dude is like twice my age and can do stuff I can't even imagine." Then he sat up straight. "Hey. Wait a minute." He planted his hand on his thigh and glared at me. "What are you accusing me of?"

"I'm not accusing you of anything."

He looked at me with disgust. "It sure sounds like you are. Are you trying to say I killed Cassidy to get her out of my hair and collect money? Or because I didn't want the baby?"

My pulse rate increased as fear accelerated. I'd made the mistake of beginning to sympathize with him. He could be a psychopath, someone who studies people's reactions and emotions to educate himself on emotional cues. He'd turned dark quickly.

I tipped my head and looked at him. "I didn't mention anything about money, but it's interesting your mind went there."

His voice tightened. "Of course, my mind is on the money. Do you know how much money it cost us to set this place up?" He motioned around the room. "I'm in debt up to my eyeballs. It's going to take me years to dig out of this. How do you think that affects an accountant's reputation when he can't even manage his own finances?"

In spite of the fear building up, I edged closer to the fire. "The insurance money will help out with the debt, though, won't it?"

"Of course. It's a million dollars. *If* I can ever collect it. The insurance is being held up by the police investigation. Until I'm cleared as a suspect, I can't collect."

How unfortunate for you. I resisted the urge to roll my eyes. "What will you do now?"

"Wait. There's nothing else to do. But I need everything resolved as soon as possible so I can unload this property and move on with my life."

My attention perked. "What! You're going to sell this place?"

"Of course. What's the point in keeping it? It was Cassidy's dream, her idea, her work. I was along for the ride. Now that she's not here, I don't need to stay here. I didn't even want to live in Kentucky in the first place. She had a way of wearing me down. What I wanted never seemed to be a consideration. Honestly, I'd rather go back to Texas. Or Colorado." He emptied his bottle. "Besides, I can sell this and clear my debt. Most of it."

I wished I had enough money to buy the house and save it to carry on Cassidy's vision. It'd be fun to own a bed and breakfast. A ton of work, sure. But...my reverie was interrupted by another thought. "So, do you have a buyer lined up for this place already? You sound pretty sure of it being sold."

He narrowed his eyes. "Yeah, I've got someone lined up. Why do you care?"

"Who's going to buy it?"

"You sure ask a lot of questions about things that are none of your concern."

"I was just curious. I hate to see this house go. I was hoping the next buyer would keep things as they are. I mean, this is a historic landmark."

"I don't know what will happen to it, and I don't care. I just need to sell it. And I can't do anything until I'm cleared. I can't believe I'm a suspect."

"The police often look at people closest to the victim first."

"Yeah, but I would never hurt Cassidy. Maybe our relationship was falling apart, but I didn't want her hurt. Or dead."

I shrugged and said something I didn't entirely believe. "I'm sure the police will eventually discover that and clear you."

He blew out a breath and flopped back against the couch, rubbing his face. "I hope so. And soon. I've got collectors breathing down my back like crazy. Cassidy loved to spend money. She had a vision for this place and spared no expense." He sighed. "Unfortunately."

I stood. I'd extracted all the information I could from him for the moment. "It's a sad situation all around." Also, I wanted to hurt him. It was a perverse desire in my heart, but I wasn't perfect, and I couldn't stop my mouth: "More than anything, I'm really sorry Cassidy married you. You certainly didn't deserve her."

He scoffed and reached for another beer. "I told her the same thing."

I slogged up the stairs and met Pierce and his wife, Margaret, in the foyer. They were dressed in their Sunday best, he in a navy suit, she in a black dress suit. Pierce carried a large wreath of white roses, almost as white as his hair, and she carried a cake. She held it out to me. "I made this to pay our respects. It's infused with Unbridled Spirits bourbon, blackberries fresh from Engle's Orchard, and fresh cream from Grant's farm.

My stomach grumbled. "That cake sounds amazing. I might keep it myself." I smiled and chuckled, taking the cake from her. "Thank you so much."

A fragile smile wavered on her lips. "I'm awfully sorry to hear about your friend."

"Well, come on in and say something to the family. We're all back here."

She wrung her hands. "Oh, I couldn't possibly. I don't know the family, so I don't want to intrude. But it broke my heart. Such a pretty thing." She looked around the house. "And such a beautiful house."

"Thank you. She worked hard on it."

I offered again, per Southern custom, for them to join the gathering, but they refused, and left the wreath near the staircase and the cake in my hands. I carried the cake to the memorial, set it on the table, and cut off a slice for myself. The cake was amazing. A spice cake loaded with fresh blackberries, a hint of bourbon with blackberry and vanilla notes, and topped with cream cheese frosting and fresh blackberries. It was probably one of the best cakes

I'd ever eaten, moist, sweet, spicy. Monday, I was going to pester Pierce into getting the recipe from Margaret for me.

I ate my lunch in reverse: dessert first, then spooned some chicken and dumplings onto a plate and ate those, too. Then I announced we should all gather outside for the planting of the roses and the placing of the bench. It saddened me to think of Derek selling the property and the eventual destruction of the memorial. I sighed. I couldn't think about that now. Maybe it would all work out. The memorial would stand for a while, at least. Besides, nothing lasted forever.

We all moved through the front door, since it was the widest access point, down the front steps, and around the side of the house to the backyard, where Cam had placed the bench by the magnolia tree.

The day was balmy and sunny. A perfect fall day. The leaves on the trees had already changed colors. Soon, the leaves would brown and drop, leaving the trees naked, and cold winds would blow in the gray, dreary days of late fall and early winter. Recalling that made this day all the more precious.

Gordon Meece, Louis, and another man I'd never met, all dressed in suits, approached the house. I bristled. They had nerve, showing up here— especially if they were trying to take her land or if they might've had a hand in Cassidy's murder. Then I stopped myself. I had no proof that they had committed any crime. And it wasn't a crime to try to convince Cassidy to sell her home. Then I remembered they were close associates of Kenton's, so it made sense for them to pay their respects.

"Hi," I said.

Gordon winced. "I apologize. It looks like we're too late."

"Nonsense. We just finished eating. We're going to the backyard to plant the roses and have a short memorial honoring Cassidy's life." Louis hovered silently behind them, staring at me. There was something lurid in the way he looked at me as if he was a starving pit bull presented with a pork chop. I tried to ignore him and motioned toward the side of the house. "You're welcome to come with us now. When we're done, there's enough food to feed an army. So, y'all will have to stay to eat. My boss' wife made a blackberry bourbon cake that'll open up the gates of Heaven."

Gordon smiled. "Sounds good." The breeze carried his fresh and mossy cologne toward me. He turned and indicated the older man beside him. "This is my father, Stanley Meece."

Stanley Meece was tan with a thick head of gray hair. Deep lines etched around his mouth and pockets of doughy skin weighed down his green eyes. Liver spots freckled his hands. He flashed a perfectly dentured smile. He was the epitome of a distinguished man. "Good afternoon, Miss Campbell."

Though Jimmy and I had broken up or were on the verge of it, I put my hand on his shoulder. "This is my boyfriend, Deputy Jimmy Duvall." Thankfully, Jimmy played along. He shook hands with the men. I said, "I think you remember Gordon and Louis from Friday night?"

"Of course." They shook hands.

Stanley said, "My son tells me your distillery would be interested in hosting a bourbon release at my farm."

"Possibly. I'd need to see the space to ensure there will be plenty of room to set up everything."

"Of course. We have an event barn on site. I think you'll find it to your taste. I do hope you'll come out soon. We'd love to partner with Four Wild Horses. I'd say it's the premier distillery in Kentucky. Some of the finest bourbon in my collection comes from that little distillery."

"Certainly among the oldest and with the greatest heritage," Gordon said. "And the most beautiful." His demeanor was loaded with innuendo.

Oh, please. A leering, creepy guy and an awkward flirtation attempt from the younger guy was too much to stomach. I was determined to remain professional as Jimmy caught wind of Gordon's flirtation and slipped his arm around my waist. I focused on the dad. "Oh, are you a connoisseur?"

He chuckled. "I like to think so."

"My boss would be tickled to hear such high praises. Perhaps I can come out tomorrow when I'm back at work? I don't want to keep these people waiting any longer."

"Fantastic. Anytime."

Once we had gathered in the backyard, Cassidy's mother approached. She could've been Cassidy's older sister. She was tall, lean, and classy in a black dress and pearls. "Have you seen my son, Kenton? He said he was going to be here. I've been looking for him this whole time."

"I'm sorry, Miss Audrey. I saw him before the gathering, but he said he had a business meeting scheduled. I thought he would come here first."

"A business meeting? Today?" Her brows wrinkled with concern. She shook her head and tsked. "That boy. Thank you, dear." She returned to her daughters and husband.

Derek came out of the house and sat on the back porch. At least he had stopped drinking for a moment. Prim sat in one of the Adirondack chairs by the fire pit, and Cam hung by her side. People huddled around the magnolia tree and the bench.

I ran on tiptoes over to Derek and whispered, "Where's Kenton? His mom is looking for him."

"I don't know." He pulled his phone out of his pocket. "He hasn't texted or called."

"Do you think we should wait for him?"

"Maybe a few minutes." He sniffed and wiped his face.

"Don't you think you should go stand with your wife's family?"

"Nope. I want to be left alone here with my thoughts."

My hand itched with the desire to slap him clean across his face. Instead, I spun on my heel and ran back to the spot near the magnolia tree in front of the bench. The breeze gently jostled the balloons tied to the magnolia. The bench was made of maple wood, stained dark cherry, and trimmed with wrought iron. A gold plate across the back read: *In Loving Memory of Cassidy Wallace. A bright spirit who created precious memories.* On either side of the bench was a hole for the roses.

I made the first speech. "Thank y'all for coming and helping to bring this service to fruition to celebrate the life of a beautiful woman. I assure you Cassidy would've loved this as she loved each of you. In the short time I knew her, I came to adore her. She was full of life and big dreams. She was one of the kindest, most generous, and most loyal people I've ever known. I'll never forget her and I'm a better person for having known her. I only wish I could've known her longer."

Her family stood near the bench, dabbing their eyes.

I said, "Now I'm not going to take up all the time. We're going to keep this informal. Whoever wants to speak next, come on up to share your favorite stories and memories of her."

Soon, many people took turns speaking about Cassidy, sharing their fond and favorite memories of her, how she affected their lives, and informing the crowd of what they'd miss most about her. We were all in a mix of tears and laughter by the end.

After the last person spoke, the pastor we'd invited read a beautiful psalm and said, "Now we dedicate this space in loving memory of Cassidy Wallace. May her spirit rest in peace, and may whoever comes to this spot share in that peace."

Cam pulled the rose bushes out of their containers, placed them in their respective holes on each side of the bench and filled them in with dirt.

Chapter Twenty-One

The crowd began to disperse with hugs, pats on the back, and handshakes all around. Some people headed inside to carry away their dishes and fix plates of food to take home.

Cam approached with Prim on his arm. She looked tired, wilted. He said, "I'm going to take her home. She's worn slap out."

I glanced at the house. "Well, unfortunately, I need to stay and clean up. I don't want to leave the mess for Derek." Even if he probably deserved it. "Cam, why don't you take Prim home? I can probably get Jimmy…" I looked around for Jimmy, but didn't see him. "Or Batrene or Patrice to bring me home."

"Okay. I'll sit with Prim until you come home."

"Perfect. Thank you."

Cam held out his arm for Prim. "C'mon, Prim. Let's get you home and tucked in your recliner with your crochet and a ginger ale."

"Amen." Prim linked her arm in his and shuffled off. "I sure could use a nap."

"I'll be home as soon as I can," I said, watching them walk to the van. Cam measured his steps to hers, and my heart swelled. He was so kind and loving to the one person I loved most in the world. He treated her as he would his own mom. My eyes filled with tears at the tender scene.

As I watched Cam and Prim ease away, Patrice and Millie approached me. Patrice put her arm around my shoulders. "Well, lady, you sure put on a good memorial. Cassidy's family couldn't stop gushing to me about it."

"I'm glad to hear it. It was a little touch and go with Derek, though, wasn't it?" I chuckled.

"I wouldn't worry about how Derek acted," Millie said. "Everyone knew you had no control over him."

"C'mon inside," Patrice said. "We'll help you get things cleaned up." We all headed back toward the house.

As we approached the back door, Derek stumbled out. "Help! Where's Jimmy? Kenton's dead."

He was slurring his words, so it was difficult to understand him. Millie, Patrice, and I froze and looked at each other "What?"

He spoke loud and slow. "Kenton. Is. Dead."

I said to Millie and Patrice, "Y'all go to the ballroom and try to keep people out of the way. I'll call Jimmy." I dialed Jimmy's number as I ran up the steps of the back porch and followed Derek through the kitchen door.

"Hey, have you seen Kenton?" Jimmy answered. "He's got some people blocked in."

"Where are you?" I ran down the hallway.

"I'm out here on the street helping people leave in an orderly way. I've got to go to work and can't get my vehicle."

"You're not going anywhere. Derek thinks Kenton is dead." I said to Kenton, "Where is he?"

"He's upstairs in his room." Derek and I hooked the corner of the staircase, swinging around the balustrade, and ran up the stairs.

"Dead?" Jimmy said. "Are you sure?"

I shouted over my shoulder, "Are you sure he's dead? Or is he just hurt?"

"I'm pretty sure he's dead."

Jimmy's voice shook with his movement. "I'm calling back up, and I'm headed inside. Keep everyone away from the area, if you can."

After the second death in three days, the J.T. Bolton House was definitely going to have a reputation for a haunted house now. We turned the corner at the top of the stairs and ran down the hall to Kenton's room, halting in the doorway.

Kenton was splayed on his back across the bed with his tie around his neck. He had been strangled, and a handkerchief was over his face. Just like

Cassidy. "Oh, no!" I gasped and rushed forward. I took hold of his wrist to feel for a pulse.

This poor family. First Cassidy and now Kenton. Poor Miss Audrey lost both of her children in one weekend. I didn't particularly like Kenton, but I was already emotional over Cassidy, and I liked her mom and sisters. I hated how their family was going to suffer now. And Jimmy. Kenton was his cousin, too. I swiped the tears from my cheeks. There was no pulse.

What sort of Norman Bates Psycho house was this? Hidden tunnels and rooms everywhere, people dropping off like flies. After this nightmare, it wouldn't surprise me one bit if this place really was haunted.

Derek stood in the hall, his back pressed to the wall. He didn't seem overly frantic. Hectic, but not especially emotional. He slid down the wall, lay his head back, and stared at the ceiling. Had they gotten into another fight over the land, and it went terribly wrong? Interesting that Derek was the one to find him. Perhaps he was pretending he found Kenton to throw suspicion off himself. I studied his hands and face. I didn't see any defensive wounds. But that didn't necessarily mean anything. He might've ambushed Kenton, leaving him little ability to fight back.

"I'll be right back."

"Take your time."

I pulled my phone from my back pocket and snapped a couple pictures of Kenton. Just in case. His clothes were intact, and from where I stood, there didn't seem to be any other harm to his body. I scanned the room. It looked very much as it had when I'd been up there snooping earlier. I took pictures of the room.

The room was still as messy as it had been before, so if there had been a struggle, it was difficult to discern. The bed beneath Kenton was unmade and rumpled. I snapped a picture of the other angles of the room. Nothing seemed out of place at all. I lifted my phone to take a picture of the table. It too was as messy as before, except...Something was off. Something had changed. I snapped the picture, then lowered my phone. The laptop was gone.

Jimmy came up behind me, out of breath. "Hey. Watch out."

I stepped out of the way as Jimmy pushed into the room. He tried to untie the necktie, and when he couldn't, he pulled a utility knife from his belt and cut it away. He put his ear to Kenton's mouth and began CPR. He listened for breath again, took another pulse, lifted his eyelids. "C'mon, man. Not you, too. C'mon." He tried again to administer CPR. He kept working on Kenton, who was clearly gone, until the paramedics arrived. Jimmy jumped up, turned and slapped the trim around the door as he spat a curse word as the paramedics took over. He stepped into the hall and leaned on the balustrade.

I put my hand on Jimmy's back. "I'm really sorry, Jimmy."

"Yeah. Me, too." He lowered his head and cried.

I lay against him, hugging him, trying my best to comfort him. It was like trying to comfort a brick wall. His jaw knotted as he struggled against his emotions. Derek was still sitting against the wall, occasionally wiping his face with the heel of his palm.

After a few moments, the paramedics came out of the room. They sheepishly pronounced Kenton dead and recorded his time of death.

Jimmy stood, sniffling, and wiped his eyes. "Thanks, y'all. Uh, we'll have to process the scene. The techs are on their way."

They nodded and clapped Jimmy on the shoulder. One of them said, "I guess you knew him?"

"Yeah. His sister died here a couple days ago."

"Sorry, man. Rough weekend."

"You can say that again," Jimmy said.

The paramedics returned to their vehicle.

Jimmy turned to me and said, "I'll be right back." He closed himself in the bathroom.

I studied Derek. I wasn't in the mood to sugarcoat anything. "It occurs to me, Derek, you might've had cause to murder Kenton. Maybe he was the one who killed Cassidy, and you found out about it. Or maybe you discovered Cassidy had borrowed a bunch of money from him, and you didn't want to pay it back, so you got him out of your way. Or maybe you discovered he was cooking up some way of taking your land from you."

"What are you talking about?" He frowned.

"Don't pretend you didn't know about any of the ways he was attempting to steal from you."

"I didn't. When did he loan Cassidy money?"

"I don't know. But I'm sure you'll find out soon enough when the police uncover everything and arrest you." The sirens outside drew my attention to the window. Several officers and techs poured into the driveway. The attendees from the memorial service stood in the yard, gaping at the emergency vehicles and talking among themselves.

"You're crazy."

I crossed my arms over my chest. "All I know is people are dropping like flies around here, and it's *your* house."

"So—"

The bathroom door opened, and Jimmy emerged in full professional mode.

Without a word, he returned to Kenton's room. He looked it over carefully, squatted, peeked under things, took pictures, made notes, and placed his footsteps strategically through the room. More police and techs entered the house and clomped up the stairs.

Jimmy exited the room.

Derek said, "Did you find anything?"

"I didn't, but the techs might." He removed his notepad and pen from his pocket. "Let's go down to the dining room. I need to ask you a few questions."

"You don't think I did this, do you?"

"It's all part of the investigation process. I just need to talk to you." Jimmy then said to me, "Rook, if anyone is left from the memorial, ask them to stick around. We'd like to get their statements now if possible."

I ran downstairs to the people in the yard and asked them to hang around if possible. The police would like to ask them questions. If they couldn't stay, then I asked for their names and contact information so I could have the police follow up with them.

Jimmy was waiting for me in the foyer when I returned. He called me into the dining room for an initial statement. He asked if I had seen or heard anything. I told him about Kenton's conversation I'd overheard when I was doing dishes and the little run-in that Cam had broken up. "I don't know who he was talking to, but it wasn't a pleasant conversation. Based on what he was saying, someone was threatening him. Which he didn't take kindly. He said something to the effect of blowing the lid off the whole thing."

"I guess he didn't say or allude to what 'the whole thing' was?"

I shook my head. "No." I added, "A little later, when Cam and I were setting up in the ballroom, Kenton came in and asked Derek when the memorial started and how long it would last because he had a meeting. I thought it was odd to schedule the meeting on a Sunday, especially when he knew we were hosting a memorial for his half-sister. He then disappeared. I didn't see him again after that. So I don't know if he met with the person he'd been talking to on the phone or someone else."

Jimmy shrugged. "I guess some people might schedule a meeting in an emergency situation or if they didn't have time throughout the week or scheduling conflicts. If they were really dedicated to their work."

My skin tightened, and the growing irritation felt like ants crawling through my veins. "There can be too much dedication to work, perhaps. Today was meant to be a day for friends and family to honor a lost life."

"Sometimes it's necessary to do things for work when you don't expect to or want to."

I stared at him. This was quickly turning into something other than our concern for Kenton. "Anyway…" I wanted to bring the conversation back to the main topic. "That's all I know, but if I think of anything else, I'll keep you posted. I'm aware of where to find you." I smiled. "So, if it's okay, I'd like to finish cleaning up the ballroom. I need to get home to Prim."

"Sure. Go on."

I started down the hall, then turned. "Oh. There is one more thing. Whoever killed Kenton took his laptop."

"How do you know?"

"Yesterday, when I was in here and took that folder, there was a laptop on the table by the window. Now the laptop is gone."

"All right." Jimmy made a note. "What did it look like? What brand was it?"

"It was an Alienware computer with a red shell. It had a U of B Thoroughbreds basketball sticker on the palm resting near the mousepad."

Jimmy scribbled. "Okay. Thanks. Anything else? Can you think of any enemies he might've had?"

"Maybe the Meece's. But he's your cousin. You know him better than I do."

Chapter Twenty-Two

I passed the techs on my way down the stairs as I dialed Cam's cell.

When he answered, I informed him, "I'm going to be a little later than expected." I gave him the details.

"Oh, wow. Man, Jimmy, and his family can't catch a break, can they? You should probably hurry home. That's the second murder this weekend at the J.T. Bolton House. I'm not sure you should be there any more than absolutely necessary."

"I'm safe now. The place is crawling with techs and police."

"Still, be careful."

I smiled into the phone. "I will."

"Besides, you're needed here. I only barely have Prim under control," he laughed.

"Uh-oh. What's going on?"

"She thought she was going to cook supper for me. But I finally wrangled her into submission and made a deal with her. I'll do the actual cooking if she shouts out the instructions."

I laughed. "Sounds about right. What are y'all having?"

"We're keeping it simple tonight because my skills are limited. Salmon croquettes, green beans, and fried corn. Dessert is fried apples."

My mouth watered. Though there was plenty of food at the memorial, I didn't have time to eat much. And Prim's fried corn was the best I'd ever eaten, with bacon drippings, a bit of jalapeno, onions, and red pepper; it was amazing stuff. I was suddenly hit with the notion that Prim's days were numbered and most of her recipes were locked inside her. I should get her recipes written down so I'll have something of her when…I shook off those thoughts. I'd had too much sadness the past couple of days. "Well, it sounds like y'all are having a big time."

"Always." He wasn't being sarcastic.

"I'll be home as soon as I can. Do I need to pick up anything on my way in?"

"Nope. I think we're good."

We hung up, and I peeked out the front window. The yard was still full. Fuller now because of the official vehicles. People stood around, talking, watching the house, taking pictures and videos with their cell phones. Jimmy and other deputies were questioning the remaining guests, and the sheriff was talking to the coroner. Jimmy would be here for hours, and I was tired. I didn't want to wait for him to be done in order to get a ride home. I returned to the ballroom and found Patrice and Millie tossing garbage and packing up the tables and chairs. I jumped in to help.

I wadded up the paper tablecloths and shoved them into a garbage bag. "Hey, do y'all mind taking me home when we're done here? Jimmy's working on Kenton's case, and I need to get home."

"Sure, hon," Patrice said, dumping some used Solo cups in a garbage can."

Millie held up a stuffed trash bag. "Where do I put this?"

"Set it by the door. I'll take it out," I said, carrying folded chairs into the storage closet.

We scurried around to finish the cleanup, and when the room had been returned to normal, I handed the supplies I'd brought with me to Millie and Patrice and asked them to wait for me in the car. I grabbed the garbage bags. "I'll be right out."

I walked down the hall toward the kitchen, through the back door, and to the shed in the backyard. Behind the shed was a garbage can enclosure. As I opened the gate, something in the distance slammed. It sounded wooden and hollow. I peeked around the building and saw someone's leg disappear around the corner of the house. I could only tell it was a man by the shoes and pants; nothing else was apparent.

Strange. I quickly dumped the garbage in the can and ran to the far side of the house. I peeked around the corner in hopes of glimpsing the person, but they had already vanished. My skin crawled with terror. With everything going on at the J.T. Bolton House, I didn't like being out here, alone, at the back of the house. I looked around to see what might've made the noise. The best I could figure, it was the wooden cellar doors. The doors to the cellar were closed but slightly askew and unlocked. Inching toward the cellar, I noticed a black cord hanging from under the lip of the door. It looked like a power cord to a computer.

I texted Jimmy. **Get to the back of the house. Now.**

In moments, he ran around the house like running to score the winning field goal.

"What's wrong?" His hand rested on the butt of his gun. The latch undone, ready to draw.

"This." I pointed at the cord.

"Is that a computer power cord?"

"Might be. What do you want to bet it belongs to an Alienware computer?"

"I'm betting whoever took the computer used the tunnels to access the cellar and escape." He scanned the back of the house.

"I bet you're right. Seems I remember Derek saying something about the cellar being one of the tunnel access points."

"Did you see anything?" He squatted to study the ground around the cellar.

"I heard something slam. I assume it was these doors. I tried to see who came out, but they had already disappeared around the corner of the house. I could tell it was a man, though. Men's black dress shoes and pants."

"That only describes ninety-nine percent of the men here."

"Right. But why would the person come up out of the cellar instead of running back through the tunnel?"

Jimmy said, "They weren't counting on you or anyone being back here. They probably thought it would be easier to duck out this way." He thought for a moment. "Seems to me that whoever killed him was an attendee at the memorial then."

"How do you know it's not a stranger?"

"They probably needed to be here at this site, probably needed to leave soon, might've been with someone who was waiting on them or expecting them. And they needed to come out in an area where they wouldn't be noticed carrying a laptop."

I nodded. "Understandable. But who? Who would have a reason to kill Kenton?"

"I don't know, but we'll see if we can find out." He pulled a pair of gloves from his back pocket. "I'm glad you spotted this. Maybe I can pull some prints." He stood. "Dang it. I need an evidence bag. Will you get a bag out of my truck? I'll make sure nothing happens to this."

I ran to his truck, rummaged through his glove box, console, and behind his seat until I found an evidence bag, then ran back to him. He was lying on the ground, his phone in his hand, groaning.

"Jimmy!" I ran and dropped to my knees at his side. I searched him for blood, running my hands over his arms and torso. "Are you okay?" I shouted over my shoulder at the top of my voice. "Help! Help! Back here. Officer down!"

Jimmy groaned. "My head." His eyes fluttered, but they didn't open.

"What happened?"

"Someone whacked me in the head." He said, "My mic." He reached for the radio mic on his shoulder.

In my panic, I'd forgotten about his shoulder mic. I pushed the button and leaned over to speak into it. "Help! Officer down behind the J.T. Bolton House. Head injury." I ran my hand over his forehead. "Did you see who did it?"

"No." He winced.

"Hold on. Someone will be here in a minute." I pushed my fingers under his head and felt a distinct knot and something warm and wet. Blood. The soft thud of footsteps in the grass sounded behind me. A deputy and a paramedic. I stood and showed them my hand. "He's cut."

The paramedic dropped down to work on Jimmy while the officer riddled me with questions. "I couldn't get much information from him. Someone hit him from behind. He didn't see who it was."

"Why was he back here?"

I explained and said, "I was gone only a couple minutes to get this evidence bag so he could put the cord…" I pointed to the cellar door where the cord had been. "It's not there." I lifted the door. No cord on the steps. "There was a computer cord right here." My eyes widened, I bet whoever stole the computer, came back for the cord, and attacked Jimmy.

"Any ideas about who might've been involved."

"No clue." I spotted an indention in the grass. "Look there." I pointed, and we surrounded a copper pipe with a nut on it. Bits of hair clung to the nut.

The officer said, "Looks like you found the weapon."

Chapter Twenty-Three

The day had taken more of a toll on me than I'd realized. As Patrice pulled into the driveway at my house, tension sloughed off of me like layers of an onion. By the time I reached the screened in back porch, my legs felt heavy as iron as I dragged into the kitchen. I dumped my stuff by the door and kicked off my shoes.

Cam met me in the kitchen, holding a ball of Prim's yarn. "Hey! There you are. We were getting worried."

"It's been an eventful day, to say the least." I dropped my rear into the nearest chair. I looked at the frazzled ball of yarn. "What's going on there?"

He tossed it between his hands. "Prim got her yarn all in a twist, so I'm trying to get the knots out for her."

I rubbed my face and took my hair down, feeling my scalp loosen.

"I made a plate for you. It's in the microwave. You want it?"

"Sure."

He tossed the yarn ball on the table. I grabbed it up and worked on the knots while he heated up my meal. "What do you want to drink?" he asked.

"Iced tea is fine."

He pulled down a glass, filled it with ice, and poured the tea. The ice popped and cracked. "So, what's going on over at the J.T. Bolton House?"

"Kenton was killed, and Jimmy was knocked in the head. He has a concussion and had to have a few stitches."

"Is he okay?" Cam frowned.

"Yeah. He's fine. He made the paramedics put stitch glue on the wound so he could go back to work."

Prim shuffled into the kitchen, and Cam pulled out a seat for her. "He went back to work? Doesn't he need to rest?"

"He's afraid of falling asleep since that could be dangerous. So he insisted on staying on his feet and taking statements from people."

He put the plate of food in front of me with silverware. "With all the deaths, people are going to be too afraid to ever go there."

"I know. It's sad. It's a gorgeous house and would make a wonderful bed and breakfast." I dug into my supper of salmon croquettes, fried corn, green beans, and fried apples.

Cam sat with me. "I don't know how Derek will be able to run the place with the reputation for murder it's developing."

"Hm." I swallowed my food. "I don't think it's going to matter."

"Why not?"

"He told me he's thinking about selling it."

Cam's brows shot up. "Really? I wonder how much?"

"He didn't say. He did say someone has expressed an interest in it."

"Hm." Cam nodded and sipped his tea. His gaze was distant, as if he were rolling something over in his mind.

Prim said, "What's wrong, Rook?"

I scooped up some corn, staring at my plate. "It's been a long day. Lots of death and sadness recently."

"True. But I suspect something else is wrong."

"I've got a lot on my mind."

"Like what?"

I smiled faintly. "How much time do you have?"

"Does it have to do with Jimmy?"

"Somewhat."

"Are y'all fighting again?"

"He interviewed for a position in Florida without telling me."

Prim and Cam sat silent, exchanging a glance.

"I'm sure y'all are happy about that."

"No," Prim said. "I'm not happy about your heart getting broken."

I recalled an earlier conversation with Cam when he'd asked me about

Florida. I looked at him. "Did you know about him applying for a position in Florida?"

He looked down at the ball of yarn in his hand. "Kind of. I went by his house one day. We were going to the gym together, and I noticed he was looking for homes in Florida on his computer."

"Really? When?"

"About a couple of weeks ago. He told me about the application and swore me to secrecy. He didn't want to upset you unless and until he absolutely had to."

"Did he get the job?" Prim asked, perking up.

"I don't know yet. But I suspect he will," I said.

Cam worked on untangling the yarn while I worked on my salmon croquette. After a long, loaded silence, he spoke carefully. "If he goes, will you go with him?"

"I won't leave Prim. That's not even an option." I squeezed her hand.

Prim patted my hand. "Of course, I don't want you to go, but if you decide to, I'll support you in it. You need to live your life and do what's best for you."

Cam said, "Would you take Prim with you?"

Prim scoffed. "Lord, no! I have no interest in traveling all the way to Florida. My traveling days are over except to go from the bedroom to my recliner." She cackled.

I laughed. "I'd never take you away from the house you and Papaw built anyway."

Cam's thick fingers picked at the thin worsted weight yarn, delicately pulling apart the knot. He eased into his next question. "So…does that mean you and Jimmy will try to have a long-distance relationship?"

A long-distance relationship could drag on for years. That certainly wasn't feasible. I couldn't put my life in a limbo of dating, but not dating, for months or years. "No. I can't imagine that being the best solution. It would be different if he was moving to Louisville or Cincinnati, but all the way to Florida? That's too big of an ask." I popped a load of fried corn in my mouth, enjoying the flavors of peppers, bacon, sweet, farm-fresh corn, with a kiss of jalapenos. "I don't want to put myself on hold for an undetermined time, you know? I'm not getting any younger. I'll be thirty in a couple years. I'd like to settle down, get married, and have a family. My own family."

"You have a family. You have Prim."

"I know. And my biggest dream is for Prim to meet at least one of her great-grandkids. Wouldn't that be cool?" I smiled at her.

She chuckled. "You'd better hurry then."

"I know, right?"

Cam pulled apart the last knot and, focusing on the yarn ball, he said, "Yeah, I think about having kids someday, too."

"You do?" He rarely mentioned kids when we were married. Who was this new Cam? It was as if he had become a full-fledged grown-up in the last twenty months.

"Oh, yeah. A little boy who looks like me and hunts, fishes, and plays sports. You know, a real rough and tumble little guy. And a little girl who…well…" He shrugged, winding the untangled yarn around the ball. "Maybe someday. If I play my cards right and get very, very lucky."

Chapter Twenty-Four

After Prim went to bed and Cam went home, I changed into a pair of cotton pajama bottoms and an oversized sweatshirt. A cup of hot cocoa in hand and the box of my mother's case files at my feet, I curled up on the couch under one of Prim's crocheted afghans. I flipped on the TV for some background noise and let the *Seinfeld* marathon fill my too-quiet house.

I couldn't stay up too late because I had to work in the morning, but I needed to get started on reviewing the files in hopes of helping the lawyers or my dad. At the very least, I hoped I might help my own understanding of my mom's case.

I removed the lid and selected the first binder. Several pages in, I saw a line in a report she'd filed stating she'd believed she was being followed, but she couldn't be sure who it was. I highlighted that line and put a sticky note on it. Whoever stalked her was clearly still out there. He had a creepy little hiding spot in a barn on the J.T. Bolton property. I noted that and, on another paper, wrote: *the perp is somehow connected to the property, Derek, Kenton, Cassidy.* After all, how else would he have access to the hiding spot? Unless he only happened upon the place in the barn? On another sheet, I wrote the names of the people who'd made statements or had been interviewed. I flipped the page and found one of her statements written in her own hand. On the third page, a single line, stating she had come home one evening and found one of her dresses laid out on the bed with a white rose resting on top of the dress.

I sat up and gasped. That was creepy. I highlighted and starred the line. It was definitely serious stalker territory. This wasn't some pervy little peeping Tom running amok. "Ohmigosh."

I put a sticky note on the edge of the paper. Back in the day, that line probably meant nothing to the sheriff and the deputies, especially when she and Dad were separated. They probably chalked it up to an angry or jealous husband messing with his wife's head. But in recent years, enough research and forensics work about serial killers and stalkers had educated both the police and the public about stalker behavior.

I tried to continue my research, but by the fiftieth page, my eyes were growing heavy, and there were still at least a few hundred pages to get through. If I kept reading, I'd fall asleep for sure, or worse, miss something important, so I marked my spot with a sticky note. This was going to be a marathon, not a sprint.

Putting the notebook aside, I selected a manila file folder marked "Pictures." I paused. I had never seen all the pictures of my mom's murder scene. I'd never summoned the courage before. I didn't want those images in my head—especially back when her death had been new and raw.

However, it had been almost twenty years. I still hurt and missed my mom, but time and distance had created a callus over my heart. It'd been so long since I'd seen or spoken to my mom; she almost didn't seem like she'd been a real person. I couldn't remember the sound of her voice or her laughter, and many of my memories had faded or been twisted by mistaken memories. Maybe now I could look at the pictures with some emotional distance.

With a deep, cleansing breath, I eased open the cover on the folder and willed myself to try to see the body on the cold ground as someone unconnected to me. I started with the feet, bare, smeared with dirt, and worked my way up her form clad in a flannel nightgown and a blanket. My mind fizzled. My heart clenched, and the few memories I had retained of her flooded me. Her face was covered with a handkerchief.

I shot up off the couch and threw off the afghan. "You're kidding me!" I shouted. Then I paused, clapped my hand over my mouth, and shrunk, listening for signs I'd awakened Prim. All was quiet. I focused again on the picture. This was too similar to the deaths of Cassidy and Kenton to be a coincidence.

I called Jimmy, pacing in tight little circles in my living room, bouncing between the recliner, the coffee table, and the television stand like a pinball.

Jimmy answered. His exhaustion was apparent. "Hey, Rook. What's up?" There were voices in the background.

"Where are you?"

"At the station."

"What? Shouldn't you be at home resting? You were injured today."

"Nah. I'm good. A little dizzy and nauseous still, but I'm fine."

"Jimmy, please…"

"Rook," he snipped. "Why are you calling?"

Clearly, he was in no mood to be fussed over. Sympathy wrung me out. He was one of the hardest workers I'd ever met. That alone was admirable. And trying to hold on to his professionalism while injured, grieving his cousins, and having to deal with their murders must've been almost more than any one human could bear. Now, here I was, dumping more in his lap. I was really just another source of work for him, wasn't I? Was that our only connection? Our desire to solve mysteries and fight crime? I recalled once when my dad, talking about my mom, had said she was his 'soft place to fall' and how much he needed it and missed it. When had I ever been Jimmy's soft place to fall? Had that been an issue between Cam and me, too?

"Rook?" Jimmy asked. "Are you there?"

"Oh, uh, yeah." I shook off my reverie. "Sorry. Um." I closed my eyes and pushed my fingertips to my forehead to squeeze the purpose of my call into place. "Oh. The reason I called…" I'd have to worry about being a soft place to fall later, though it probably wouldn't last for long anyway if he was moving to Florida. "I've been reading through the case files you gave me, and I found some crazy stuff."

"Oh, yeah? Like what?" He perked. Like waving a pork chop in front of a tired dog. Typical Jimmy.

I told him everything I found and the connection I'd made. "I think whoever killed my mom also killed Cassidy and Kenton. I mean, they, too, had handkerchiefs over their faces. That seems to be the killer's signature."

"It sure sounds that way."

I didn't want to hurt his feelings or be antagonistic, but I had to know. "How did y'all miss this with my mom?"

The line grew silent. Then I heard the sounds of him drinking and eating. I knew he was buying time. Finally, he said, "Rook, babe, I'm sorry. We've been so short-staffed, and with so much going on…I've been working on it, but not consistently, and clearly, it's not in-depth enough. I read a few statements and looked at a few of the pictures. I just couldn't do any real work on the case. I have a full-time job. And, in case you haven't noticed, people around here have a habit of dying lately, which then throws me into overtime."

I couldn't be angry with him. I couldn't expect him to fully focus on an old case when people today were suffering and needed his help. "I understand."

"I didn't want to let you down," he said softly.

Chapter Twenty-Five

Five in the morning is a hateful time. It didn't matter to me that somewhere in the world, someone was dragging out of bed even earlier. At that hour, I only cared about my own sleep. But I had promised myself I'd make more time to exercise and take care of myself. So I put on my tennis shoes, staggered downstairs, and plugged in a cardio DVD. I slogged my way through in my pajamas and tennis shoes and then started the coffeemaker while I ran upstairs to get dressed for work. Prim had a doctor's appointment Cam had promised to drive her to, so I needed to get her ready, too.

I slathered myself in various washes and scrubs while running through my mental to-do list. Knowing I needed to meet the Meeces to view their event space, I wanted to take a little extra care in my appearance. I was nervous about the meeting because they had been trying to get their hands on Cassidy's land. But I had to remain professional and couldn't treat them differently without any proof. Besides, if I could make this event happen, it might help me get a raise or a promotion—and my career needed all the help it could get.

I selected a pair of gray wide-legged, pin-stripe trousers, nude heeled sandals, and a thin blackberry-colored sweater suitable for the crisp mornings and balmy afternoons of a Kentucky autumn. With pearls, natural makeup, and Lavanilla Lavender to accent, I was happy enough with my ensemble.

By the time I finished putting myself together, Prim was awake. Since her lymph nodes were swollen and feverish, she didn't like wearing her normal clothes. She insisted on maximum comfort and openness. After a quick shower, I put a free-flowing, mid-length, pink tank dress on her with a soft gray cardigan and pinned her hair off her face with a pair of pink rhinestone barrettes. I helped ease her down the stairs and sat her at the table. Prim worked on swallowing her pills while I prepared our respective breakfasts—oatmeal for her and plain Greek yogurt and strawberries topped with walnuts for me. We chatted about how we slept, what I'd discovered regarding my mom's case, and how it seemed to connect to more recent events.

She blinked at me from behind her rhinestone-encrusted cat-eye glasses. "My goodness, Rook. I can't believe it. You shore are something." She lifted her glasses and dabbed at her eyes, and her voice grew watery. "I never thought I'd see the day that I'd know who killed my baby girl."

"Don't get too excited. We still don't know *who* did it. But I think it was an important clue. If the police can figure out who killed Cassidy and Kenton, they might have the guy who killed my mom."

"You know, I never did think it was your daddy." She stirred the butter, brown sugar, and cinnamon in her oatmeal.

"I know."

"Now, I don't mind telling you I never cared much for your daddy. I think your momma could've done better. But she loved him." She blew on the spoonful of oatmeal, then popped it in her mouth. "He did some things he shouldn't have, but he was crazy about Annette. And she was crazy about him." She sniffled, and a faint smile bloomed on her lips. "Reminds me a lot of you and Cam. Except I like Cam. And he's trustworthy." She chuckled.

I blushed. "I don't know. Mom and Dad never divorced like Cam and I did." I ate a spoonful of berries and yogurt.

She waved her hand. "They were separated, though. I think if your daddy didn't change his ways, Annette would've left him for sure. And it might've been the thing he needed to get himself straightened out."

"Did Mom ever say anything to you about anyone following her?"

"Not to me. But Annette was the sort of person who'd keep things to herself to keep people from worrying about her." Her eyes lit up. "Kind of like you."

Playfully, I said, "I don't know what you're talking about." I smiled, finished off my breakfast, and put our empty dishes in the sink.

Cam pulled up in his parents' Oldsmobile. He climbed out of the vehicle wearing a pair of worn jeans, an untucked green flannel shirt, and cowboy boots. The sleeves were rolled up to reveal his tanned, muscular forearms. He was like a cup of cocoa on a snowy day.

I helped Prim into her recliner, turned on the television for her, and ensured she was comfortable with a ginger ale and her crochet. "I've got to go to work. Cam is here to take you to the doctor. Y'all let me know if you need anything. I should be home on time. I'll call if I'm going to be late." I kissed her head and gathered my things, wishing I didn't have to go, wishing I could be around more, wishing I could take her to her appointment.

I met Cam in the yard on my way out. "Thank you for doing this. I really appreciate it."

"No problem. I've got to take Momma to the eye doctor, too." He motioned to his truck where his mother sat in the passenger seat. We waved to each other through the window.

I chuckled. "You're like a DoorDash for doctor's visits."

"Maybe I can start a new business."

"You need breakfast?" I asked.

"Nah, I ate already."

After much begging and promises to drive under the speed limit and keep three car-distances from other vehicles, I had managed to get Prim's permission to use her car since mine was still in the shop. I moseyed toward Four Wild Horses Distillery, my lead foot struggling to keep my promises to Prim. On the drive, I called my dad's lawyer, Glenn Winston, and told him what I'd found last night and recommended he talk to the sheriff's office. The mention of the sheriff's office reminded me of Jimmy, which turned my breakfast sour in my stomach. If I was being honest, I couldn't see a way through for us to remain together, even if he stayed in Kentucky.

Chapter Twenty-Six

Late in the morning, the marketing department had a meeting with management to discuss the unfortunate events surrounding the release of our Unbridled Spirits bourbon and the continued issues at the J.T. Bolton House.

"I hate to lose the opportunity," Pierce said. "Because a historical bourbon baron house is the perfect location for such a release. Are there any other bourbon baron homes or historical places that might in some way be connected to bourbon in Kentucky? I'd prefer to have one of those over a standard event space, if possible."

Crickets. We stared at each other.

Jeff pushed up his glasses and leaned back in his chair, crossing his thin leg over his knee. "There is another baron house in Louisville and a couple in Cincinnati, but I hate to go there. I'd rather keep everything here in the Bluegrass region. And then I know there's another house in Lawrenceburg, but it's being renovated. It's not in any condition to allow the public inside, though the exterior is in pretty decent shape. If we can't find anything else, we might be able to arrange an outdoor, tented event. We could put up some tents in the yard and a portable toilet trailer."

Pierce squinted. "That's not the worst idea, though we'd need heaters too since it'll be in December. And the weather is pretty sketchy that time of year."

Marla added, "I could call the Lawrenceburg house to see how far the renovations will progress by December. Maybe we can use only the main floor area." She wrote a note on her notepad.

Pierce nodded. "Let's get all the information we can on that house, Marla, and hold it in our back pocket as a last resort. We need a price estimate for both scenarios inside and outside the house."

"Will do." Marla made more notes.

I jumped in. "I have a meeting out at Meece Farm to look at their event space today. I know the preference is to get a historical connection to bourbon, but this could be a good second choice. Apparently, they hold events there, and the space is ready for use."

Pierce nodded. "Great. May the best price win." He chuckled. "I look forward to seeing what you dig up, Rook."

The meeting was adjourned, so I headed out to the Meece Farm to look at the event space for the re-introduction of Unbridled Spirits.

I drove out into the county where the Franklin County line butted up against Scott County and Elkhorn Creek. I crossed the bridge at one point of the creek and rolled up the long, tree-lined drive that ended in a circle with perfect landscaping and a fountain in the center. The Meece home was a three-story red brick, classic Italianette structure with a facade of tall, narrow windows. The front porch was split with stairs leading up each side to end at a tall black door. I rang the doorbell, and a middle-aged woman in a beige suit answered.

Inside, the foyer ceiling extended the full height of the house, with a gallery running along the second floor. The foyer was open, white, marble, and full of light, giving off an Old World elegance vibe. Though the space was cold and museum-like to my modern eyes, it was no less striking and awe-inspiring. Green ferns and indoor trees spotted the interior. The lady guided me to a sitting room to the right. It was rose-colored with lace curtains, marble fireplace, and a wall of bookshelves, filled with books. A large painted portrait of Stanley Meece hung over the fireplace in the tradition of old European homes where the lord of the manor hung life-sized painted portraits of themselves on the walls as a show of wealth.

Soon, Gordon and Stanley Meece entered the room, dressed in jeans, cowboy boots, flannel shirts, Stetson hats, and barn vests. We all greeted each other, and the men drove me in a golf cart to the event barn at the back of the property, with the assurance that there was another private entrance to the barn for guests to access.

As we drove, the men noted points of interest: the sorts of cows and horses they raised; the number of acres of land; the hemp, corn, and soybean crops they produced. We encountered a host of farm workers, tractors, and a variety of farm equipment kicking up dust.

We rolled over the shallow hills and valleys of bluegrass and landed on the backside of a giant rusty-brown, two-story monitor barn. As I snapped pictures of the barn's exterior, I immediately envisioned a blanket of snow on the ground (if we were lucky) and green wreaths with red ribbons hanging from the windows. If the interior was as pretty as the exterior, then I was already sold. We drove around the side of the building, which must've been at least twenty or thirty yards long, to the front. The front drive was filled with loose river pebbles.

Gordon climbed out and unlocked the front door. "I think you'll find this space perfect for your needs."

My knees almost buckled when I stepped inside the barn. The interior was cozy, with walnut wood extending from floor to raftered ceiling. A modern chandelier hung from the center of the room. To the left, in one corner, leather sofas surrounded a fireplace and chairs flanked by a wet bar space. At the front of the room was a stage, leaving the rest of the floor open for tables, dancing, and catered food setups. I took a host of pictures, like a tourist seeing a barn for the first time. I couldn't wait to show these to the rest of the marketing team. I hoped the Meece's had nothing to do with the recent deaths at the J.T. Bolton House just so my distillery could use this barn.

Gordon said, "This is the space available to guests." He pointed to a set of stairs at the back of the room. "Those stairs lead to our storage area, and we can decorate for any event. We have all kinds of tables of various sizes, chairs, fairy lights, gauze fabric to hang from the ceilings and around the poles, flowers, wreaths, candles. You name it, we have it or can get it. We can make this place look like a fairyland." He smiled.

"Who manages that?"

"The woman who answered the door. Her name is Athena Blair. She's our events coordinator, and she has connections all over the region for food, drink, and entertainment. You would work with her to make your vision come to life."

"This is one of the prettiest places I've ever seen." In my imagination the space was already filled with soft Christmas-themed jazz music, guests dressed in black-tie, sampling flights of our best bourbon offerings, fairy lights around the support beams, and the fireplace lit up among poinsettias and evergreen garland.

We could do *A Christmas Carol* theme with a Victorian-Era murder mystery dinner and do a tie-in with the spirits in the story and the Unbridled Spirits bourbon. "I want it," I breathed. I paused. *Hold on, Rook.* Everything depended on the price. I walked back a little. "I mean, of course, depending on the price. I'd need to take an estimate back to the office to see if management approves."

"Of course." They smiled. "You and Athena can sit down to discuss the details before you leave today."

We loaded up in the golf cart and exited behind the main house near an enormous patio complete with a kidney-shaped pool with a waterfall pouring over stone at one end and a grand stone fire pit for barbequing at the other; this was surrounded by a posh set of furniture under a curtained canopy. Stanley received a phone call and excused himself.

Gordon said, "I'll walk you inside." He motioned for me to head toward the door. He tucked his hands in his pockets as we strolled toward the back door. "So, it seems the J.T. Bolton House has become something of A Nightmare Inn, huh?"

"Yeah. Unfortunately. I hate for the reputation of such a beautiful historical site to be so blemished. I'm not sure the business side of the house can survive it."

He held the door open for me. "What happened? How did he die?" He paused. "If you don't mind my morbid curiosity?" He winced.

We stepped into a study warmed by an electric fireplace. There was a drink and a book on the chairside table, indicating someone had been reading there recently. "Wait. Weren't you there when it happened?" I searched my memory. Though Kenton died only yesterday, it seemed like six years ago.

"Uh, no. We, uh, couldn't stay long. Dad's been having some health problems, so we needed to get him home as fast as possible. We really just wanted to pay our respects to the family. Kind of a quick in and out. It seemed more of a private affair anyway."

"Oh, I'm sorry. I guess I hadn't noticed when you left."

"No worries." He revealed bright white, perfectly straight teeth and a dimple in his cheek. "You were pretty busy with your other guests, and you needed to pay more attention to the family. We were only acquaintances. We didn't want to bother you, so we said our goodbyes to Derek and headed out."

"Oh, I see."

"So what happened?"

I shrugged. "I wish I knew. Kenton was found dead upstairs in his bedroom. Strangled." I hugged myself and rubbed my arms, recalling the dead man.

"Do you think Derek did it? I mean, they lived under the same roof, and it's my understanding they were fighting all the time about money and the property. At least, that's what Kenton told me."

Now I had a decision to make. I could say something now: accuse Gordon Meece of somehow being complicit in trying to get Cassidy's land (though I had zero proof)—and thereby ruin a professional relationship that could be great for the distillery and result in an awesome event in their gorgeous barn. Or, I could keep my mouth shut, play dumb until I had proof, and keep the professional relationship, help the distillery, and keep the beautiful barn event.

He stared at me. "Is something wrong?"

Oh, no! What was my face doing? I scrambled to cover. "Oh, I'm fine. Sorry, I was just thinking about something. Um, with the barn and the bourbon event." I chuckled. "What was your question?" So I guess I was going with keeping my mouth shut. For now.

He repeated what he'd claimed to have heard from Kenton.

I considered the statement. Then, I eased up close to my suspicions without tipping my hand. "Maybe. I don't understand what's happening, but I believe it must have something to do with the house. And the land it's on."

Gordon continued, "I mean, everything seems to be happening around Derek, right? First his wife, then his brother-in-law. Sounds like a family thing to me. Or, I guess it could be a really bad coincidence."

Or it could be Goron Meece was working too hard to push suspicion onto Derek. "Maybe," I said. "Or, it could've been—" I clamped down on my tongue. *Shut it, Rook.* I waved my hand and smiled. "Oh, never mind. It's not important." Hopefully, he'd let it go.

"What?" Interest flickered in his eyes. "What were you going to say?"

Dang it! Of course, he wasn't going to let it go. "Nothing. It's not important."

"Really, I'd like to hear what you think."

I shrugged. My mind raced to salvage the moment. I didn't want him to think I suspected him of anything. "The police are looking at a lot of different theories and different people. They aren't ruling anything or anyone out yet." There. A nice, neutral, noncommittal, and non-accusatory answer.

His eyes darted. "Have you heard who the police are looking at, if they're not focused on Derek?"

I chuckled. "How would I know?"

He smiled. "I figured since you're dating a cop, you might've heard something." He paused and added. "I-I'm really fascinated by all this stuff, you know. I really like all those crime dramas and mysteries."

I nodded. My eyes fell on the book on the nearby table. *Mindhunter* by John Douglas. "I guess that's your book, then?" I was hoping to change the subject. "Is it good?"

He looked over his shoulder. "Nah. Louis is reading that."

I lifted my brow. "Oh." My intuition sparked, flooding the space under the surface of my skin with a subtle vibration. He was trying to get information from me. He wanted to know what I knew, maybe wanted to see if the police were looking at him or his family. I was beginning to wish I'd notified Jimmy of my whereabouts. It was time to start working on an exit strategy.

I didn't really want to talk about this anymore anyway. I was tired of thinking about death and being surrounded by it. I was about to ask for Athena when he interjected.

"C'mon, you can tell me. I promise I won't say a word. Have the police confirmed foul play? They must have suspects."

I crossed my arms over my chest and lifted one shoulder. "Seriously, I really wouldn't know." I looked toward a door that opened into the hallway and the bright white foyer. "Jimmy isn't allowed to discuss things like that with me."

He tipped his head in disbelief. "Really? I don't believe that. I bet when he comes home, he shares some of the dirt with you." He nudged me playfully with his elbow.

Now, he was trying too hard to be charming and was officially on my nerves. "I'm telling you, he can't talk about cases while they're being investigated." My voice came out with a little more edge than I'd intended.

He seemed to pick up on the hint because he only responded with, "Ah." He nodded. "Okay. I see." He shrugged. "Makes sense."

Before he had a chance to say anything else, I jumped in. "I should probably meet with Athena. I need to get back to the office…" I let my voice trail off.

"Oh, yeah, sure." He motioned toward the door. We crossed the hall, passing beneath the gallery and into the white marble foyer.

Athena's office was to the left of the front door. She sat behind the desk, typing on the computer.

Gordon knocked on the door jamb. "Knock, knock," he said.

She looked up and smiled. "Hey, there. How can I help you?"

"Miss Rook here is from the Four Wild Horses Distillery. They want to do a Christmas event here to release a new bourbon. We've shown her the space and have assured her you're the expert for getting the contract together and seeing to all the arrangements."

"Oh yes," she said enthusiastically. "Come on in. We'll get you all squared away."

Gordon extended his hand. "Miss Rook." I placed my hand in his, warm and soft. Not the hands of a man accustomed to labor. Very different from

Cam's hands. "It was good to see you again. We look forward to hosting your event. You have my contact information. If you need anything at all, don't hesitate to call us. Okay?"

"Okay. Thank you."

"All right, then. I'm going to leave you in Athena's capable hands. See you later." He left the room.

I sat in a soft leather seat across from Athena. She offered me a drink.

"I'd love a bottle of water, if you have it."

"Certainly." She checked the small fridge in the corner. "Oh, mercy. I meant to fill up my fridge first thing this morning. I got distracted and didn't get around to it. I'm sorry, sweetie, I'll be right back." She left the room, her heels echoing on the marble floor.

I looked around the room at the shelves full of photos, awards, and knickknacks. I stood and crossed the room to look at the pictures. Lots of images of Stanley and Gordon standing beside horses, beaming into the camera, holding trophies and ribbons. One of the horses wore a blanket of red roses. My brows shot up, impressed that I was doing business with owners of a Kentucky Derby winner. There were other pictures of Athena with her bosses at Churchill Downs, in Derby clothes, holding mint juleps. Athena with her family. Athena and the Meeces with other employees and friends at Christmas parties, playing horseshoes at barbeques.

Then my eyes fell to another picture on the bottom shelf. It was an older picture. Judging by the graininess of the image, it had to be from around the late nineties or early two-thousands. And there, with dark-lined eyes, dark red lips, and Julia Roberts waves was my mom, in a green dress. Based on her clothes, the people, and the background, this picture was from the same party as the picture we found in the underground room at the J.T. Bolton House. Shock rattled my bones, and I jerked the frame off the shelf to look at it closer. There was a tree in the background strung with colorful lights, so it was a Christmas party.

I could now see that the picture had been taken in the foyer of the Meece home; it had the same white marble background and the same door and window placement. Mom had the same hair as my last Christmas picture with her, so this was likely the same year—only a couple of months before her murder. In the picture was a much younger Stanley Meece with his arm around my mom, several other people smiling and holding cocktails. One of them appeared to be a much younger Athena. And, off to the side, a younger man I didn't recognize, though he looked vaguely familiar. His gaze seemed to be focused to the side, at my mom. I pulled my phone out of my pocket and took a picture of the photo, and texted it to Jimmy. Why was my mom at a Meece Christmas party? And how did she know them?

And, more importantly, if this picture was taken at the same place and time as the underground room picture, then…my mind exploded. Did one of the Meece's have something to do with my mom's murder? *Wait. Hold on, Rook. Slow down.* There could be a simple explanation for this. Maybe the killer was at the Meece Christmas party. None of this was absolute proof the Meece's were in any way involved.

I'd been so laser-focused on the photo I didn't hear the click-clack of Athena's return through the house, because the next thing I heard was her voice apologizing for the wait. I jumped and yelped, clapping my hand over my heart.

"Oh, I'm sorry," she chuckled, cradling several bottles of water. "I didn't mean to scare you." She held up a small bottle of water. "Here you go."

I accepted the water as my heart slowed its pace. "Thank you."

She turned to place the other bottles in her fridge. When she sat behind her desk, I joined her and showed her the photo. "I saw this on your shelf. Where is this from?"

She held the picture and studied it. "Oh, yes. Such a long time ago. That must have been almost twenty years ago." A nostalgic smile touched her face. "It's from a company Christmas party, when the Meeces first started out."

"What do you mean?"

"Well, this company wasn't always in the business of property development. We started out as a small independent realty company. Stanley founded the company, and then, as his sons grew up and joined the business, it expanded into property development and other ventures. I had only been with the company a few months." She turned the picture around and pointed at a mousy woman in a white sweater and a permed wedge haircut. "That's me. Look at my hair." She laughed and rolled her eyes. "What was I thinking? But that was the style then."

I was going to take advantage of her willingness to talk about the picture. "Who are the other people?"

She pointed at each one. "That's Stanley. His son, Gordon. He's just a baby there. Maybe early twenties? He helped clean the homes as they sold and was working toward his real estate license and a business degree."

"Busy guy."

"Yes, indeed. He's a go-getter for sure. Just like his daddy." Then she listed off the names of other people irrelevant to me. Then she touched the lady in the green dress. I knew it was my mom, but I just wanted to hear it confirmed. I bounced my knee with nervous anticipation. "That's Annette Daniels." The shock was a punch in the gut. "I loved her. Such a sweet lady, but really a sad end."

"What do you mean?" I prodded.

"She was the secretary for the real estate firm. Had been there probably a few months before I'd arrived. She showed me the ropes. She was going to move up into real estate sales, was about to take her test to get licensed, and I was training to be her replacement." She sighed. "But, not long after this picture, she was found murdered in her home."

"Oh my gosh. That's awful. Who did it?" It was painful to pretend not to know my mom.

"Well, her husband…" She looked down at her desk and tapped her fingers. "I can't quite remember his name. He didn't come around much. And it seems, if memory serves, they were separated at the time of this picture. Gosh. I can't remember what his name was. Anyway…" She swiped the air, signaling my dad's irrelevance. "The police seemed to be convinced he did it because he went to prison for it. But…" Disappointment loaded her voice. "I wasn't sure. It didn't seem right."

"Why?"

"I don't know." She sighed and put the photo aside. "She and I weren't super close, but she would talk sometimes about strange events surrounding her, like she thought she was being followed. She told me once someone had been in her room going through her things."

My eyes widened. This seemed to be on par with what I'd found in her file. I encouraged her to keep talking. "It's so awful. You hear these stories all the time on *Dateline* or in the news where a man stalks a woman and ends up killing her."

"I know." She rubbed her upper arms. "Gives me chills just thinking about it. But she told me she came home one night, and a dress was laid out on her bed with a white rose laid on it."

I shuddered. Just like what I'd read in the file. "That's the stuff of nightmares."

"Right? I've never forgotten it. Could you imagine walking into your home, which you think is safe and secure, to find such a scene? I would feel so violated." She blew out a breath. "She said she'd gone to the police, but they didn't seem to think it was urgent." She shrugged. "Of course, those were different times. It seems those things weren't taken as seriously back then as they are now. Especially in a small town like this. I don't know what happened afterward. She didn't really talk about it anymore. But she did seem more agitated, stressed, tired."

"That's scary."

"Oh, yes. After her death, I started locking my doors and windows every night."

I had never known a time when I didn't lock my house down like Fort Knox. "You mean you hadn't been locking your doors prior to that?"

"Oh, no. When I was a kid, we never had to lock our doors. It was definitely a different time, a different culture. We had a tighter community. People looked out for each other." She sighed. "But things have changed. It's hard to feel safe anywhere these days."

Then I asked a question I couldn't help but ask. I knew the answer, but it was as if hearing a stranger talk about it, connecting me with my mother, made our connection real, made me part of my mother's a story, a story I'd never really felt a part of. "Did she have any kids?"

"Yes. A little girl. I met her briefly once. She seemed an energetic, sweet-natured sort of child. I don't know what happened to her. I hope she ended up in a good place. Poor thing. To lose her mom and then have her dad sent off to prison. She was practically an orphan." She shook her head. "So sad…" After a moment, she placed her hands on the desktop. "Well, I don't want to keep you here reminiscing about the old days. Let's talk about your event and the vision you have for it."

We talked about the bourbon-tasting event, but my eyes and attention kept wandering back to the photo of my beautiful mother in her pretty green dress and wavy locks, only a few years older than my current age, frozen forever in a happy moment. Finally, we worked out the details for the event, and Athena wrote up an estimate for me to take back to the distillery for approval.

I rushed out of the house, dialing Jimmy on my way to the car. As I neared the vehicle, I stopped dead in my tracks. A white rose with a long thorny stem pinned under the windshield wiper. I went limp and dropped my purse, my keys, and my phone. A breeze blew over me as I slowly turned to inspect my surroundings. Not a soul was around me or even in the near distance. A crow squawked above me in the beech tree, knocking some golden leaves to the ground. My skin crawled with the distinct feeling that I was being watched. At the side of the house sat a bush of white roses.

I snatched up my phone, ended the call, and pulled my sleeve over my hand to protect any potential fingerprints. I removed the rose from its place and ran over to the rose bush. The phone rang. I ended the call. I searched the bush and saw that the rose stem had been clipped at an angle from the bush. The inside of the stem was pale, indicating a fresh cut. I held the rose in place over the stem and took a picture to show the angles matched. My phone rang again.

"Rook?" Jimmy's voice was tense with concern. "Are you there?"

"I'm here." I ran on tiptoes across the yard to the car to retrieve my purse and its contents.

"What's wrong? You sound weird."

Fear stuck in my throat like barbed wire, and I strained to speak. "I'm at the Meece property. I came out here to look at an event space for the bourbon release."

"Yeah?"

"When I came outside to get in my car, I found a white rose under my windshield wiper."

He paused. "Okay," he said flatly.

I shoved my stuff back in my purse and put it inside the car. "Like the white rose on the green dress on the bed at the J.T. Bolton House. Like the white rose on the bed on the green dress in my mom's case file." Finding a plastic shopping bag on the floorboard, I put the rose inside and laid it gently in the back seat.

"Get in the car. Stay in the car. Lock the doors and get out of there!" He demanded. "Right now."

"I'm in the car now and locked up."

"Did you see who put it there?"

"Of course not. And I don't see anyone nearby. Did you get the picture I sent?"

"Yeah, but I didn't look closely at it yet. What about it?"

"It's my *mom*. That picture was at the Meece house. It's the same background and dress in the picture we found in the underground room at the J.T. Bolton House. The people in that picture are a young Stanley and Gordon Meece and my mom."

He expressed a soft curse.

"And, hold on, I have more pictures…" I sat behind the steering wheel. I texted the rose stem pictures to Jimmy and returned to our conversation. "That's from the rose stem. You'll see it's a fresh cut, same angle. And I'll get the rose to you. Maybe you can get prints from the stem?"

"Bring it out here now."

"Thanks." I fired up the engine.

A knock sounded on the window beside me. I jumped and screamed.

"Rook? What's wrong?" Jimmy shouted.

"Hold on," I squeaked as I stared into a pale, unsmiling face and large dark eyes. Louis. Where did he come from? I lowered my phone, leaving it on, and cracked my window. "Hey there, Louis, right?" I said loud enough for Jimmy to hear. "I almost didn't recognize you with the hat on." Looking into his eyes was like staring into the dark tunnels at the J.T. Bolton House.

"Hey," he said. "I'm sorry to hear about Kenton. I liked him. I've worked with him for years." He smiled, but his eyes were dead.

I hesitated. "Um. Thank you. I'll be sure to give Derek and Jimmy your condolences."

"Okay." His eyes held mine, locked in. For a second too long. "Do you know about the arrangements? I'd like to send flowers or a gift."

"Sorry, no. Derek might have that information. Or you could just send something directly to the Bolton House." This guy gave me the creeps, and I wanted to get away from him. I waited for him to say something else, according to the flow and rules of normal conversation, but he simply stood there, looking at me. Finally, I said, "Well, okay. I have to go. Bye." I rolled up my window and put the car in reverse. I picked up the phone to continue my conversation with Jimmy.

"Who were you talking to?"

"Louis Meece. Ugh, he gives me the willies. I'm leaving now, though."

"Good. I won't be here when you arrive. There's been some craziness going on over in Miltonville with a body found in a dumpster. Ladonna's the lead, but I've been helping her out. So you can leave the rose with the officer at reception. She'll make sure it gets put into evidence."

Chapter Twenty-Seven

After I dropped off the evidence at the sheriff's department, I headed back to the distillery to share the contract and pictures with my boss and the marketing team lead. Pierce and Jeff looked over the pictures and contract and approved the Meeces' event space. I slumped back to my cubicle and stared at the beige wall littered with sticky notes.

I'd had a change of heart. I sank back in my office chair, twisting from side to side. I didn't want to host the event at the barn now. I sighed. But I was locked in. It was only a few days and one night. Surely, for the sake of my career and the reputation of the Four Wild Horses Distillery, I could grit my teeth and white-knuckle my way through. But the thought of it sat like a stone in my gut. I should probably pick up some Tums on the way home.

Though I'd been trying to give them the benefit of the doubt, after today, I could definitely confirm that I didn't trust the Meece's. I didn't like the way Gordon tried to charm information out of me. I couldn't abide his brother, Louis McCreeperson. Finding the rose on my car freaked me completely out. And, worst of all, discovering the picture of my mom had been a gut punch, the shock of it depleting me. It was the last place I'd expected to find her. She had known the Meece's. Had worked with them. It was surreal.

Maybe there was a silver lining here. Though I didn't want to work with the Meece's any longer, maybe it would afford me an opportunity to question them about her. Maybe one of them knew something about her final days. Or heard something about the person she thought was following her. Maybe I should try to talk to Stanley. As the oldest, Meece, and the owner of the business, he probably would've known her best.

Armed with a ray of hope, I finished up a few tasks and headed home. Cam's mom's car was in the driveway when I arrived. The sun had dissolved into a deep golden pool along the horizon, hearkening to the earlier evenings and shorter days of autumn. A mist was settling along the grass, crickets chirped, and a coolness invaded the air. This would be a perfect night to curl up in cozy pajamas, fuzzy socks, and watch my favorite police procedurals while sipping on a cup of cocoa topped with whipped cream, chocolate shavings, and a sprinkle of cinnamon.

The scent of chili greeted me when I stepped inside. Perfect. My shoulders relaxed. Cam stood at the stove over a large pot, stirring. Prim sat at the kitchen table, buttering slices of bread and filling them with cheese.

"Hey, there," Cam said.

"Hey, what are you doing here? And you're cooking?" I said with pleasant surprise, dropping my stuff by the door.

"Well, I brought Prim home after her doctor's appointment, and I figured I'd hang around with her until you came home."

"Where's your mom?" I kicked off my shoes.

"I took her home first."

"How long have y'all been home?"

He shrugged. "A few hours."

My eyes popped wide. "You were at the doctor that long?"

"No," he chuckled, placing a cast iron griddle on the stove. "After the doctor I took the ladies to lunch, then we went to a couple stores to run their errands, then we came home."

"I got some new yarn," Prim said.

"And then we got hungry, so we decided to make chili and grilled cheese."

"It's the perfect weather for it," I said, filling a glass with ice and tea.

"Prim, you got my sandwiches ready yet?" Cam called out. "I'm ready for them."

"Here," I said, handing him the plate full of buttered bread and cheese.

He clapped his hands together. "All right." He took the plate from me and placed the sandwiches on the griddle with a sizzle.

"So, did you make the chili?" I said skeptically, peeking around his arm into the pot.

"Of course."

I smiled up at him. "What do *you* know about making chili?"

"Hey, I know more things than you realize. I've learned a lot in the past twenty months."

"I see. I'm impressed. You've moved up from heating cans of SpaghettiOs."

"Here, taste this." He offered me a taste of the chili.

"Wow. That's actually really good."

"You sound surprised." He placed his hand over his heart. "Darlin', I'm a man of many talents." He waggled his eyebrows at me. "Besides, Prim helped me."

"Now we're getting to the truth!" I nudged him, laughing. "You're full of more beans than that chili."

He flipped the sandwiches to reveal a beautiful golden-brown color. "You hurt my feelings," he said in mock offense.

I grabbed bowls, saucers, and silverware. "I'm sure you'll survive."

He plated the food while I placed the meal on the table and served everyone glasses of iced tea.

We sat down and enjoyed conversation about our respective days, good food, and each other's warm company. For a moment, I mentally stepped outside of myself to view this beautiful family scene like something from a Hallmark movie and felt the bloom of joy. Which was why I chose not to mention anything about my visit to the Meece Farm.

"Guess who's in town?" Cam said, eating his chili.

"Who?" I asked.

"My big brother."

"Mason? Really? When did he get in?"

"Earlier today."

"Why's he here?"

"Well, there's two stories. The public story is he's visiting for dad's birthday this weekend. But the actual story is he and Lisah are talking about divorce. Which reminds me, y'all are invited to Dad's party this weekend. We're going to grill out, play cornhole and horseshoes, and all. If the weather holds up."

"Why are they divorcing?"

He scoffed. "With Mason and Lisah, who can tell? It could be either or both of them. You know how they are."

I sure did. They were the sort of couple who loved to fight and thrived on drama. They were both hot-blooded and reactionary and loved getting under each other's skin. How those two were able to hold down their important careers, adulthood, and family life, and make the money they made was a mystery to me. He was a financial advisor, and she was a pharmacist. Together, they made more money in a year than I'd seen in a lifetime.

Prim tore off a corner of her sandwich. "They still live in Louisville?"

"Yeah, they moved to a big house near the river on the outskirts. You've been there, right?" Cam asked me.

"No. They moved there after we…" I didn't really want to mention our own divorce and spoil the happy family dynamic.

He picked up on my indirect message. "Oh, that's right."

"You don't really think they'll divorce, do you? They've threatened it before."

"Yeah, but this is the first time Mason has decided to start looking for an office to move his business."

"Oh," I said, lowering my sandwich. "I'm sorry to hear that."

"He's also talking a lot about living a simpler life, reducing his workload to about half."

"I can *not* imagine that. I mean, everything in his house talks to you. Smart this, smart that."

He laughed. "I know."

"What about the kids?" Prim asked, blowing on her chili.

"I guess they're okay. He says they are. But they're at home with Lisah. You know how the courts are. She'll get the kids. He'll get visitation. They'll split holidays. Honestly, I'm not sure she's the one who should have them. He hasn't told me everything, but he's hinting at some things that are a little unsettling."

"Yeah?"

"Like what?" Prim asked.

"Y'all don't say anything."

"Okay," we said in unison, though I was certain my ability to keep it quiet was a better bet than Prim's. As a leader in the Old Lady Network (OLN), it was possible half of Rothdale would know by the end of the week.

"He didn't say anything specific, but she seems to be suffering from some mental or emotional illness that might affect her ability to adequately care for the kids."

"Oh," Prim and I said, exchanging a glance.

"I'm sorry to hear it," Prim said.

"Me too."

The sound of a car door shutting echoed outside the house.

"Who's out there?" Prim said, sipping her tea.

"It's probably Jimmy," I said, getting up to look out the window. "Yep. It's him. I'll be right back." I stepped outside, hugging myself against the increasing chill, and jogged to meet him.

His face was tight and drawn, dark circles ringed his eyes. "You okay after your eventful afternoon?"

"Yeah. Did Rosie give you the evidence?"

"Yeah. I've got it logged. The lab is closed right now, so I'll send it first thing in the morning. Then I'll go out and talk to the Meece's. See if I can uncover anything."

"What's wrong?"

He scratched the back of his head, and sighed. "Well. I might as well keep this short and sweet." He crossed his arms over his chest and rocked back on his heels. "I got the job. I'm moving to Florida."

Though I'd anticipated this, it didn't make it any less of a shock. "Oh." It took a beat to recover. "Um. Okay. Uh, when're you leaving?"

"Few weeks. I want to be settled in as soon as possible."

"I see." I opened my car, removed the bagged rose, and handed it to him. "I guess you've got to do what you've got to do."

He nodded. "I was still hoping you and I could work something out. In spite of all the other stuff. Maybe a long-distance thing? Maybe you can move with me? Bring Prim."

I shook my head and looked down at the fallen leaves on the grass. "No. I can't do any of that. I'm not going to move my dying grandma from the only home she's known for decades. And I'm not leaving the only home I've known for decades. I like Florida. Love the beaches. But Kentucky is home. And for me to get involved in a long-distance relationship implies I'd consider moving at some point."

He pinched his lips tight and nodded. He looked at Cam's mom's car. "You'll probably be happier with him, anyway."

"We aren't together. But that's irrelevant. You should know my biggest issue is your job. It always comes first. And I don't blame you. I'm happy you have a job you love so much. I'm happy for the citizens who are protected by someone as dedicated as you. That's important. But I know I can't be happy in a relationship by myself, waiting for you to notice me."

"I understand. It's hard to love a cop."

"But not impossible. You're good-looking, fun, smart, caring. Some girl in Florida will snatch you up in a heartbeat. You may not be right for me and what I'm looking for, but you'll be perfect for another girl."

"I guess." He let out a heavy sigh. "So...this is it, then." He turned his face away, sniffed, and cleared his throat.

Tears pooled in my eyes, and my throat tightened with emotion. "Yeah." A dull throb pulsed in my head. "You should come in, though. I have some things of yours I need to return to you. Might as well take them now. And have a bite to eat if you're hungry. We're having chili and grilled cheese. There's no reason we need to part bitterly."

"You're right. We can still be friends."

"Of course."

"I haven't told Prim and Cam about this afternoon, though. I'd rather not. I just want a drama-free night for once. So don't bring it up."

"Got it."

The warm and bright kitchen embraced us as Cam and Prim greeted Jimmy.

"Have a seat. I'll get you set up; then I'll get that stuff for you." I placed supper in front of him. "I'll be right back." I heard them discussing Jimmy's news and his upcoming move as I jogged up the stairs.

Chapter Twenty-Eight

When I flipped on the light in my room, I froze, trying to understand what I was seeing. All the drawers of my dresser stood open. My teal dress from the night of the Unbridled Spirits release was laid neatly on the bed, topped with a picture of my mom, a silver bracelet, and a white rose. I staggered backward and ran downstairs.

"Cam. Are you messing with me?"

He frowned, confused. "What?"

I was shaking. "Please tell me you're messing with me. That the stuff in my bedroom…" I pointed at the ceiling. "Is a really bad, sick joke."

"Babe, I don't know what you're talking about."

Everyone stared at me as though I was speaking Klingon.

Prim said, "Hon, you're not making sense."

"If you're not messing with me, then he's been in this house."

"Who? You're scaring me, Rook." Prim pushed her glasses up on her nose. "You need to explain yourself right now."

"There's a dress with a rose and a picture of my mom lying on my bed. And all the drawers of my dresser are open."

"What!" Jimmy said, his mouth full of food. He launched back from the table. He drew his weapon. "Everyone get on the back porch and stay there until I clear the house. Go, now."

Cam ran to the closet, grabbed coats for me and Prim, and shepherded us out the kitchen door. About fifteen or twenty minutes later, Jimmy opened the door, his weapon holstered.

"Come on in. I'm calling techs. Y'all need to stay down here." He pulled out his phone and made a call.

We resumed our seats around the kitchen table. Jimmy was in officer mode. He removed his pad and pen from his front shirt pocket and started firing questions.

"How long has the dress been here?"

"I don't know," I said. "I got home not long before you showed up. I sat down to eat. It was my first time being upstairs tonight."

He asked Prim and Cam the same question. They hadn't been upstairs at all. They didn't know it was there.

"That whackadoo, whoever he is, has been in my house. What am I going to do? What if he comes back?" I said, hugging myself.

Jimmy didn't seem to be listening. He was too busy taking notes. "I'm going to go upstairs and take some pictures of the scene. I'll be right back." He ran upstairs.

Cam held my hand. "Rook, it's okay. Don't worry. We'll figure something out. Maybe you can go to a hotel for the night?"

"No. It'll be too hard on Prim. She needs to be home."

He thought for a moment. "Okay. In that case, I'm going to run home real quick and get my rifle and an air mattress. I'll stay here tonight in case he returns."

I said hesitantly, "I don't want you to be in danger, too."

Snippiness entered his voice. "What do you recommend then?"

I threw my hands up. " I don't know what to do. I guess I thought Jimmy might have some answers."

Jimmy returned to the kitchen. I can't get any techs out here tonight. But they can get here in the morning. I'm going to put tape over the door and over the entrance to the staircase.

"Can I at least get a change of clothing?"

"Sure, I have to go with you."

Prim said to Cam, "What in the world is going on?"

"There's some crazy stuff happening right now, Prim. How about you settle into your recliner where you can watch TV and crochet?"

"All right. Rook," she said. "Get your papaw's rifle from the closet. If that guy comes back, we'll fill him full of buckshot."

"Okay, Prim."

Cam helped her up and helped her get in the recliner. She worked on her crochet and watched *Jeopardy!*

Jimmy and I went upstairs to my room. He pointed to a laundry basket in the corner. "Are those clothes clean?"

"Yeah."

"Probably best to take them from there in case the intruder left behind any evidence."

"Okay." I dug out a pair of pajama bottoms, a T-shirt, and fuzzy socks. And extracted a black turtleneck and a pair of jeggings I could wear to work the next day. My arms full of clothes, I turned to him. "So what am I supposed to do? Just hope we make it through the night until I go to work? And what about Prim? I don't want to leave her here alone tomorrow." *Dang it!* I wanted to scream.

"I can try to come back and stay the night with y'all. And Cam said he was going to spend the night, too. The only thing is, I need to go back to the station for a while. I think y'all will be okay with Cam here until I get back."

"Okay."

"Check other areas to see if anything else has been messed with."

I checked Prim's room. Everything seemed untouched and in its place. I checked the guest bedroom, too. Also untouched. Great. So, my room was purposefully targeted. "There's no point in checking Prim's craft room. It always looks like a bomb has exploded in there." I chuckled. "We'd never know if the intruder messed with anything in that room."

We made our way downstairs, my stomach roiling. The thought of my home, my bedroom, my most intimate and safest spaces being breached, set me on edge. There was no way I'd be sleeping tonight. I'd feel more comfortable on the couch. Maybe Cam or Jimmy could stay in the in-law apartment in the basement, and Prim could take the guest room on the main floor.

"I'm going to change my clothes and get ready for bed." I slumped down the stairs and closed myself in the powder room to change my clothes and wash my face. The thought of a strange man in my house, in my room, rummaging through my underwear drawer and my closet, made my skin crawl. It felt tainted, wrecked.

By the time I'd exited the bathroom, Jimmy had put up police tape and left the house.

I pulled a pillow and blanket for myself from the closet in the guest bedroom on the main floor and dumped them on the couch.

Prim was fussing to Cam. "I can't believe some strange man has been inside my house. Invaded my Rook's room, went through her things. That's awful. Who is this guy?"

"We don't know yet, Prim," Cam said. "But we're hoping to find out real soon."

"You're probably tired," I said to Prim. "Do you want me to help you into the guest bedroom?"

She pulled her cardigan around her. "Not yet. I'm too riled up."

I couldn't blame her. The upstairs guest room was nicer. The one downstairs had been Papaw's room when he died. It was small and dark and left much as he left it. "How about I make you some hot cocoa? I know I could use some. Cam? You want any?"

"Not right now. I need to run home and grab a few things." He squeezed my hand. "Will you be alright until I get back? I'll only be gone for about twenty, thirty minutes."

"Yeah. We'll be okay." I tried to sound convincing. "We're going to drink hot cocoa, and I'm going to watch Prim work her crochet magic." I retrieved her shopping bag full of yarn from the kitchen and handed it to her. "Here. You can work with the new yarn you bought today. And, if you get tired, maybe you can sleep in your recliner for a while. You take naps there all the time, so I know you like it, and it's comfortable."

"Thank you, baby," she said. "Though if I try to crochet now, I might make my stitches too tight. Stress shows up in the yarnwork."

"That's right," I said, following Cam to the kitchen to start my cocoa milk. He turned and whispered, "Is your papaw's old .22 still around here?"

"Yep." I poured milk in the pot. "It's in the hall closet."

He opened the closet door and pulled the rifle out.

"Where's the ammo?"

"Top shelf." I slipped into my cardigan and closed it around me. I couldn't shake the chills.

He closed the door and carried the box of bullets and the gun to the kitchen table. He checked the chamber and toyed with the mechanics of the gun. "This thing needs to be cleaned, but it'll hold you until I get back. Then I'll clean it for you. I'll bring my cleaning kit." He inserted about five bullets into the rifle and loaded the first in the chamber. "It's all ready to go. I've put the safety on."

"Thanks." I emptied packets of cocoa mix into the mugs.

He laid the gun on the table. "Okay. If you need anything, let me know, but I'll be right back."

"I will." As soon as he stepped outside, I locked the doors and checked the locks on all the windows. When the milk began to boil, I filled up the cups.

I paced between the kitchen and living room, peeking out of the blinds in each room, waiting for Cam, keeping an eye on our surroundings.

Looking over the rim of her glasses, Prim said, "Child, you've got to sit down. You're making me nervous."

I sat down, bouncing my leg and sipping my cocoa. I needed a distraction. "Hey, I have an idea. I'd love to have some of your recipes, Prim. Why don't you tell me how you make some of my favorite foods?" I fired up my laptop and opened a Word document.

"Like fried apple pies?"

"Of course. And blackberry cobbler. Fried corn. Macaroni cheese. All of them."

"Lord, child, that'll take all night." She pulled out the stitches in the row she'd just crocheted.

"Right. But what else are we doing?"

"Okay. Which one you want first?"

"How about the fried apple pies?"

She glanced between the television and her crochet as she spilled her recipe for the pastry and the apple mix. "The secret is the sun-dried apples, you know. And it's best to use Granny Smiths. Of course, the older I get, the less patience I have to wait for the sun-dried apples. I just dry them out in the oven now. When I was a kid, my momma used to dry the apples up on the roof, with netting over it. We had a tin roof, you know." Each ingredient seemed to lead to a new memory and another story from her past. Many were stories I'd never heard about people long passed or people I'd never met. And finally, I felt a part of a family much bigger than I'd ever known, all these ghostly branches of a family tree surrounding me, cradling me with roots much deeper than I'd realized.

Car lights pan across the window.

I jumped up, peeked out the window. "It's Cam." Tension drained from my muscles. I ran to open the door for him.

Cam entered, loaded with a rifle, his gun-cleaning kit, a gym bag, and an air mattress. "You can have the in-law apartment downstairs."

He plugged in the air pump. "Nah. I need to be down here, at the ready. I'll be fine. You should take it."

"I'm not sleeping any time soon. I want to be down here."

"You need your rest, though. Don't you have to work tomorrow?"

That reminded me! I needed someone to sit with Prim, and given the circumstances, I didn't want to ask Batrene to do it in case the intruder came back. "Uh, well, now that I think about it, I'm not sure I should go to work tomorrow."

"You go to work. I'll get Mike to cover for me tomorrow and stay with Prim. He's been wanting more hours anyway. I'll stay here."

Relief washed over me. I clapped my hands together in a prayer position. "Thank you so, so much. What can I do for you? You've done so much for me. There must be something I can do. I don't have much money, but—"

He waved his hand and resumed plugging in the air pump. "Don't worry about it. Happy to do it." Then he said to Prim, "Sorry, Prim, I'm going to drown out your TV for a bit." He flipped the switch, and the air pump roared to life. While he pumped up his mattress in the corner of the living room, I ran upstairs to grab pillows and blankets for him.

After making his bed, he retreated to the kitchen to clean my papaw's gun and to get his gun ready. When he'd finished, he joined me on the couch.

Cam kicked off his shoes and propped his sock feet up on the coffee table. I sat close to him, careful not to touch him. But his presence took the edge off. I snuggled under the blanket I'd dumped on the couch earlier.

Around midnight, my phone rang, and I sat up on the couch. The TV was still on, playing *Bewitched*. Cam was curled up on his air mattress with the rifle on the floor beside him. Prim's chair was empty. He must've taken her to the guest room.

The screen indicated Jimmy was calling. "Yeah," I croaked, rubbing my eyes.

"Okay. I hate to tell you, but I won't be able to come by tonight. I'm working an incident, then I need to catch a few hours of shuteye before rolling in first thing tomorrow. Cam there?"

No surprise there. "Yeah. He is."

"He armed?"

"Yes."

"Good. Everything okay there?"

"We're all fine."

"Okay. If you need anything, please let me know."

"I will." We hung up.

Cam sat up. "Everything okay?"

"Yeah." I snuggled into my pillow. "It was Jimmy. He's not coming tonight."

"Oh." He checked the time on his phone. "Okay." He laid down and burrowed under his blankets.

"Cam?"

"Yeah?"

"Thank you for being here. I'm really grateful for it."

He lifted his head. "I had to. I couldn't live with myself if anything happened to you or Prim." He lay back down, closed his eyes, and smiled into his pillow.

Chapter Twenty-Nine

The next morning, I was thankful to open my eyes to a peaceful house. The sun poured in through the kitchen, marking a beautiful fall morning. Cam was lying on the air mattress in the corner. I breathed a sigh of relief that we'd made it through the night without incident. I texted Jimmy to let him know we were okay, then launched myself into the day.

After my shower, I called Batrene to let her know she didn't need to come by, dressed myself, then helped Prim dress while Cam made breakfast of bacon, eggs, toast, and coffee. I threw my bacon and egg between the bread to make a sandwich, filled a travel mug with coffee, and headed out the door.

I reached the office in time for an administrative, production, distribution, and marketing meeting where our boss Pierce effectively told the marketing team the words all marketers dream of: "The sky's the limit for the budget."

We looked around at each other. Marla's eyes grew wide, and Jeff nodded.

Pierce added, "Here's the thing. Our Halloween launch was a bust. I'm afraid of the reputation Unbridled Spirits might end up with as a result. We have to make this event big, bold, and extravagant so it erases the last launch and keeps the stigma from setting in around this bourbon. Understand? This is a definite case of spending money to make money."

Then the marketing team went into its own meeting where we discussed the re-launch at the Meece Farm.

"Dream big, y'all," Jeff said, rocking in his office chair. "We can't mess this up. There's too much riding on this."

Ultimately, we decided to do a Victorian Christmas theme and to have life-sized statues of the ghosts of Christmases Past, Present, and Future with a Victorian murder mystery dinner and Victorian-costumed servers. My teammates had lots of questions about tables, space, chairs, linens, and decor. They wanted to know the exact dimensions of the space before they hired an artist for the papier-mâché ghost statues, and how many tables could fit in a space where hoop dresses would be wandering through.

Marla had an additional idea as expressed through her loud gasp, wide eyes, and splayed fingers. "Y'all. What about horses and carriages?" she said. "We could park a small decorated carriage in the corner of the room to use as a photo booth option. Then outside, we could stage a horse-drawn carriage, decorated with jingle bells and lanterns, to take people on rides through the farm."

Jeff added, "And we can serve hot toddies made from Unbridled Spirits since it'll be cold. Do you think the Meeces will approve of these changes?"

I made notes of the ideas and questions as fast as my pen would write. "I'm not sure, but it never hurts to ask." When my list was complete, I went out for lunch at the Peonies Bistro, a cute little cafe in Rothdale square downtown. It was pink with a black and white striped awning and served a variety of delicious soups, paninis, teas, coffees, and pastries.

After filling up on a turkey and cheese panini, tomato bisque, and a blackberry cream cheese pastry, I decided to run out to Meece Farm to speak with Athena in person. It was a beautiful day and I had already learned in my few months of work that going in person was easier; sometimes a client needed to show me something or I needed another look at an event space.

Jimmy called. "Hey, just wanted to make sure everything is okay?"

"Yeah. I'm heading out to the Meece Farm to discuss an event space." And, if I was lucky, talk to Stanley Meece about my mom.

"Okay. Sounds good. I'm heading out there myself today to ask them some questions. Maybe I'll see you there."

"Maybe."

"Also, the techs should be at your house by now, along with a couple deputies."

"Okay."

"When you get a chance, it'd be a good idea to go to the station and make a statement."

"Will do."

I pulled down the long driveway and parked in front of the home. I rang the bell, but a maid answered instead of Athena.

I introduced myself and stepped inside the white marble foyer. Athena's office to the right was empty, so I switched plans. "Is Mr. Stanley Meece available? I'd like to talk to him for just a few moments if possible."

The maid said, "Follow me."

I followed her down a bright hall to the left. Stanley Meece was in his office on the phone. When he saw me, he motioned me into the room. It was a wood-paneled room with a large swordfish hanging over the mantle. His desk was a large cherry wood structure with plush red leather chairs in front of it.

He hung up the phone, beamed his dentures at me, and stood to greet me. "Hello, Miss Rook. What a pleasure to see you. Please, have a seat."

I sat in the red, half-moon chair across from him.

He sat down and folded his hands on his desk. "What brings you out this way today? Is everything going okay with the party planning?"

"Oh, yes. Athena's great."

"Oh, yes. She's the best. She's been with us for, gosh, almost twenty years."

"That's a long time. Must be a great company to earn that sort of loyalty."

"I'd like to think so. So, how can I help you?"

"Well, when I was out here the other day, I saw a picture in Athena's office." I pulled the picture up on my phone and showed it to him. "This one right here."

He looked down his nose at it. "Oh, yes. Lord, that was a long time ago. We have Christmas parties every year. It's my little way of rewarding my employees after their hard work all year."

"Yes. It looks like a lot of fun."

"Ooohhh." He whistled and chuckled. He lifted a finger. "What happens at the Christmas party stays at the Christmas party." He chortled.

I smiled. "Well, I promise to keep everything in the strictest confidence.

This woman right here…" I pointed to my mom. "Was my mom, Annette Daniels."

He froze, mouth agape, as though I'd just dumped a bucket of ice water on his head. "You don't say." His eyes drifted over me. "Yeees. I see it now. You look just like her. And, you know, when I first met you, I thought there was something familiar about you, but I couldn't place it." He sat back in his chair and shook his head. "My goodness. You know, I'm so sorry about what happened to your momma. She was a kind, gentle lady, a good soul. It wasn't right what happened to her."

"Thank you. I wouldn't normally bring this up, especially when my distillery has a business relationship we're trying to build with you, but her case has been reopened."

He paused. "Has it?"

"Yes. Some recent evidence has come to light which might exonerate my dad."

"Is that so?" He broke eye contact. "What sort of evidence?"

"I'm not at liberty to say. But I was wondering, since you were her boss, you probably knew her better than anyone. Did you happen to see or hear anything around the time of her death that may have seemed unusual or strange?"

"No, can't say as I did. But then, that was a very long time ago. I can't even remember what I eat for breakfast most days." He pressed a tight smile onto his face. "Now, if you don't mind, I have some work I need to finish." He stood and motioned toward the door. "It was mighty nice seeing you again, Miss Rook. I look forward to working together on the bourbon event this Christmas. You have a fabulous day now." He put on his glasses, picked up his pen, and resumed working as if I wasn't standing there.

I stood. "Wait. I have another question. Did you ever hear of someone following my mother or threatening her?"

He stopped and looked over the rim of his glasses. "Miss, I believe they caught the man responsible for hurting your momma. I'm sorry that happened to her, but there's nothing I can do to help."

Stanley Meece seemed to be acting, not exactly guilty, but as if he knew something, and I was getting annoyed. My words came out a little sharper than I'd intended. "My mom wasn't *hurt,* she was murdered. And I'd think you would want to help catch the murderer. Instead, you're trying to get me out of your sight as fast as possible."

"Young lady, I'm not a police officer. How on earth do you think I can help you catch a murderer?"

"By taking my questions seriously. Thinking about them sincerely, and answering them."

"I did."

"No. You didn't. You started acting strangely as soon as I brought the subject up."

"Well, I have nothing to add to the story I told the police almost twenty years ago. I'm sure they still have a copy of my statement if you want to know what I said. Now…" A warning entered his voice. "I said I'm done. I've got work to do. Don't forget to speak with Athena about the event before you leave. Have a nice day."

I fumed inwardly. There was no point in pressing the issue. He would double down on remaining tight-lipped, and I would only get angrier and end up costing the distillery an important business connection. I left his office in a huff. Every instinct in my body screamed *He knows something!* My muscles ached to throw a good old-fashioned hissy fit, but I refrained. Instead, I texted Jimmy. **Just spoke with old Meece about mom. He claims to know nothing. I think he does. Jerk.**

Ur still there?

Yes. Waiting to speak to Athena now.

K.

Chapter Thirty

I returned to the foyer to check Athena's office. She still hadn't returned, so I sat in one of the cushioned chairs for a moment, taking in the room. I bounced my knee, wishing I could get this visit over with and get back to work. Light from the French doors at the back of the house cut across the floor. An orange cat moved from its sunny corner spot into a room by the French doors.

An avid animal lover, I forgot my anger for the moment. I was obliged to seek out and pet the cat. I ran on tiptoes to the room and pushed open the cracked door. I squatted by the door to try to lure the cat to me. "Hey, kitty, kitty. Spspspspsps." The cat jumped up on the desk. He stared at me with cool, green eyes, swishing its tail.

"Hey, kitty," I cooed, reaching out my hand.

He was not going to meet me halfway. Fine. If kitty doesn't come to the human, the human goes to the kitty. I approached kitty, reaching my hand out to him and whispering in baby talk.

He stood and stretched, arching his back into my hand, turning, and bumping his head into my palm, purring contentedly. "Aw. You're such a sweet kitty." I scratched behind his ears.

I looked around the room, taking in all the pictures of golf courses and golfing buddies hanging on the walls and the trophies lining the shelves behind his desk. Gordon was in many of the pictures, so I assumed the office was his.

My eyes trailed across the top of the desk, all the papers, golf magazines, house magazines, house plans, and sticky notes with reminders scribbled on them. Then, under a set of plans, I saw the corner of a red laptop. I immediately thought of the laptop that had gone missing from Kenton's room.

Glancing around my shoulder, I shifted the magazines to get a good look at the computer. My heart stumbled. There it was. A red laptop with an alien face in the center and a Red River Gorge Railway Experience sticker. Kenton's laptop. *Oh, crap!* This was a huge piece of evidence. The only reason Gordon would have this laptop was if he removed it from Kenton's room, conceivably after he killed Kenton! Glancing around to ensure I was alone, I scrambled to remove my phone from my purse so I could take a picture.

I snapped the picture and texted it immediately to Jimmy.

He responded with **WTH!! Get out now. OMW.**

No problem there. I was about to put my phone away when I noticed a paper peeking out of a nearby folder with the letters C-A-S-S peeking out. Why would Gordon have an official document with Cassidy's name on it? I opened the folder. I took a picture of what appeared to be a deed to the J.T. Bolton House. How did Gordon Meece have a copy of this? Based on the conversations I'd overheard between Kenton and Derek and Kenton on the phone, Derek didn't seem interested in selling yet. That had only been a couple of days ago. Even if Derek did want to sell, the property couldn't have been transferred that quickly.

I recalled the sheets of practice signatures I'd located in Derek's office. Had Kenton copied this deed, then forged the signatures to effectively steal the land from under Cassidy and Derek and sell it to the Meece's? Or maybe Derek was involved in the scam, too. Maybe he killed her when she wouldn't go along with his desire to sell, so he forged Cassidy's signature in order to unload the land. Either way, this document was a big chunk of evidence. I thought about trying to steal the paper, so I could give it to Jimmy, but that would probably mess up his case. And wasn't it better to actually catch the evidence in the hands of the criminals?

I'd leave the folder and paper in their place, but I was for sure going to send the pictures to Jimmy. I opened the photos folder on my phone.

"What are you doing?" Gordon Meece spoke, causing me to almost jump clear out of my skin.

I spun around, slamming my hand to my heart. "Oh! You scared me!" I also, unfortunately, dropped my phone and it slid under the desk.

Gordon was dressed for the golf course in a pink polo shirt and black pants. The pink was a bad choice for his coppery hair. He crept closer to me as I knelt to pick up my phone. I kept my eyes on him, patting the floor in search of my phone.

"Why are you in my office, Rook?"

"Sorry," I laughed nervously, drumming my brains for some good stories and lies to tell to get me out of this situation. "I followed the cat in here. I-I-I love animals." Finally, my fingers fell on my phone. I grabbed it and stood up. "And I wanted to pet him. He's a really sweet cat."

The cat sat on the edge of the desk, licking his white paw without a care in the world. Would he even pause his bathtime to watch Gordon kill me?

I continued, holding up my phone. "I was going to take a picture of him."

The dark glimmer in Gordon's eyes told me he didn't believe me. He stepped closer. I stepped to the side to the best angle for the door and, hopefully, a clean getaway.

"See, I think you were snooping. I've been standing here for at least a couple of minutes. You seem to have a deep interest in that folder on my desk."

I played dumb to buy time. "What folder? No. Really...the cat."

He tsked. "I'm a lot of things, Rook. Stupid is not one of them. I didn't leave that folder open. It appears you've discovered my little secret. And that's not going to go well for you."

"I don't know what you're talking about." I put my purse on my shoulder and headed toward the door. "I came to see Athena about the event space and—"

He grabbed me. "Ah-ah-ah. I'll take the phone."

I tried to pull away. "You can't have my phone."

"And I'm not letting you leave here with those pictures, sweetheart."

He held my wrist, and I kicked at him as we walked around each other in some demented tango. He twisted my arm and forced the phone out of my hand.

I tried to run, and he grabbed me by the shirt and slammed the door in one move. "You're not leaving." He spun me around and slammed me against the wall. "You'll ruin everything I've worked for, and I can't allow that." He locked the door and stood with his back against it.

Crap! Now, what was I going to do? The only possible escape was to kill him or go through the window.

He scrolled through my phone and deleted the pictures. "I knew the moment we met you'd be a pain. You and Cassidy. You two shrews are cut from the same cloth."

While he was distracted, I peeked inside my purse to see if I had anything at my disposal I could use to get an advantage over him. The cat paced the floor, rubbing my ankles, completely oblivious to the terror unfolding in my life right now. There was nothing in my purse. What was wrong with me? Could I not at least carry a knife or pepper spray? Heck, with all the danger I'd been in lately, it would've been a good idea to at least secure a stun gun. *Stupid, Rook.*

Then I saw a little baggie of the teal and silver glitter I'd used on Cassidy's memorial board, and an idea hit me. I turned my back and dumped the glitter in my hand.

Gordon was still talking. "Now, what to do with you?"

I pressed against the wall and balled my fist around the glitter as he stalked toward me. I inched toward the door.

"Practically speaking, I can't allow you to live no more than I could allow Cassidy or Kenton to live."

"You killed them?"

"I don't like it when people get in my way. Especially if it's going to cost me money. Cassidy got in my way on the land deal. Kenton got in my way when he threatened to expose me. And now you're in my way because you've discovered my secrets."

"Did you have anything to do with my mom's death?"

He grimaced. "What are you talking about?"

"Annette Daniels."

"You killed her, didn't you?"

"Who?"

"She worked for your dad's realty company. You were young, but not too young to kill her. You did it, didn't you? She complained about someone stalking her and—"

"I don't know what you're talking about. And, you're crazy. I'll probably be doing the world a favor by getting rid of you."

Harsh. But the craziest part was I actually believed him. He didn't seem to have a clue as to what I was talking about. And, surely, a man who had just admitted he killed Cassidy and Kenton would have no compunction about admitting to a murder twenty years ago. He hadn't killed my mom.

The doorbell rang, and hope exploded inside me. Maybe that was Jimmy. I had to fight for my life.

He sighed. "It should be quiet. And, preferably, blood free. It's almost impossible to get rid of blood evidence. Strangling really does work the best."

Chills ran through me, and terror froze my body to hear him discuss my murder as casually as if he were trying to decide what to have for supper.

The doorbell rang again. Even if the visitor wasn't Jimmy, I needed to bring attention to my situation. Maybe they would alert the police. Gordon the psycho might kill me, but he wouldn't get away with it.

I slid along the wall toward the door.

He grabbed me. "Nope. You're not leaving, sweetheart. This will only hurt for a couple of minutes."

In a flash, I lifted my hand, opened it, and blew the glitter dust directly into his eyes. He cried out and swiped at his eyes. I hoped it hurt, jerkface. I imagined it felt a lot like sand in the eyes. I spun toward the door and unlocked it as he grabbed at me.

I screeched, "Get away from me!" In hopes of attracting the attention of the visitor. I tried to open the door, but Gordon threw his weight against it. I was getting out of this room if it killed me and him both. I jerked one of the golf trophies from a nearby shelf and clubbed him in the head with it as

I continued to shout and scream.

He couldn't fight me and the glitter, too. He rolled away from the door. I yanked it open and dashed across the foyer, screaming. "Help!"

The doorbell rang again. I made it to the front door, pulled it open, and ran smack into Jimmy.

Chapter Thirty-One

I smiled to see Cam's truck still at my house when I arrived. God, it was good to be home. Safe. Covered in glitter, but safe.

After I had run into Jimmy at the Meece's home, he ran into the house, gun drawn, and took over the scene. I ran to my car, locked the doors, and sat there, unable to move and scared to breathe, until I saw Jimmy emerge. Jimmy's backup arrived, and other deputies flooded the house. Soon, Jimmy led a cuffed and glittered Gordon Meece out of the house and stuffed him into the back of his cruiser. It gave me a great deal of satisfaction that something Cassidy loved, the glitter, took out Gordon. It gave me more satisfaction to think of how it would take a long time for him to get all the glitter out of his eyes and how every time he blinked, it would scratch and scrape his eyes like sand.

"You okay?" Jimmy returned my phone to me through the car window.

"Yeah." I hugged myself. "Glad you arrived when you did."

"Me too. Good job with the glitter." He smiled.

"A little help from Cassidy." I smiled.

Sadness filled his eyes. "Yeah." After a pause, he said, "I need to get a statement."

"I know. Can I do it later? I really want to go home."

"Sure. Sooner the better, though." He slapped the car hood and sauntered back to the house to finish his job.

I called work, explained my situation, and promised to be in the office early the next day to start looking for a new event space. Then I went home.

For a moment, I relished being home. Safe. Knowing Prim and Cam were inside. A warmth and relaxation spread over me like I'd just stepped onto a beach in the full sun. I turned off my car and stared across the backyard, enjoying the silence and the play of light on the colorful tree leaves. My muscles in my shoulders began to unknit.

My phone rang. *Dad. From prison.* My muscles wound up again. I answered the phone and closed my eyes.

"Hey, Rookie."

Dad was the only one who could call me Rookie and not make my skin crawl. "Hey, Dad."

"You okay? You sound tired."

He had enough to worry about in prison. I didn't need to add to his worries, so I lied. "I'm fine." Though I really wanted to talk to him about Mom.

"That doesn't sound convincing, but if you don't want to talk about it, I won't press the issue." He paused a beat, then said, "I spoke to the lawyer today, and he thinks he might have enough to get my case thrown out."

"Fantastic!"

"I have you to thank for it. He said you sent the information to him."

"I did. Unfortunately, I'm pretty sure Mom's killer is still out there. And…" I hemmed. "Well, maybe I shouldn't say anything yet."

"No. Go ahead. You can't say anything worse than what I hear on a daily basis in this place."

"I didn't want you to worry, though."

"Just say it. I only have fifteen minutes."

"You're right. There are a couple of things." I explained to him what I had learned from Athena about Mom working for Meece Farms and the weird dress scene the intruder placed on my bed.

"Whoa, creepy. Do you have protection?"

"Yeah. I have Papaw's old rifle. And Cam has been staying here with his gun, too."

"Good. I'm glad to hear it. You still dating the deputy?"

"No. We broke up. He's moving to Florida for a better job."

"Oh. Sorry. But…" He sighed. "These things happen. Life is full of heartbreak."

"True. So, why didn't you tell me Mom had once worked for the Meeces?"

"I don't know. Never came up. She had only been there for a few months to earn a little extra money. It's not like she'd worked there for years, and it was a major part of her life."

"True. Did she complain about any of the men there?" Even though I was pretty sure Gordon hadn't killed her, he might've known the killer. After all, Stanley Meece acted dubiously when I questioned him. The Meece's worked with a lot of contractors and subcontractors. It could have been any of those men, and Stanley might've been aware of it.

He thought for a moment. "Come to think of it, it was around that time she started complaining about things missing or feeling like someone was watching her."

"Did she say anything about someone at work making her feel uncomfortable or harassing her?"

"I can't think of anyone in particular. We were separated, so she wasn't really talking to me much. She only mentioned what I've told you, and when I offered to come home to protect her, she said no. She was still angry with me, so she wasn't ready for me to move back in yet. I did come over the night of the murder. I was trying to talk her into reconciliation, but she was being stubborn and refused. We got into a big argument. I left again. And then, well…You know."

"Yeah," I said softly. "So Mom was stubborn, huh?"

"Like a mule. I've never seen anything like it. She'd dig in her heels, and that was it."

I chuckled. "Sounds familiar."

"She gets it honest from Prim."

"And I get from both of them."

"Definitely a trait with the Vertrees women. Rook…" His voice grew serious. "Don't take this the wrong way."

"What?"

"Darling, you need to work on the stubborn thing. Now, it can be good in certain situations, but you need to learn discernment. It's not good to be stubborn just for the sake of it because you can't stand to be wrong or vulnerable."

Well that was a blast of cold water in the face.

He continued, "Your momma—I loved her dearly—but if she had been less stubborn, if she could've allowed herself to be a little more vulnerable and allowed me to stay that night, she might still be alive today."

Wow. His insight robbed me of my breath for a moment. "Uh, I don't know what to say."

The electronic voice came on and said we had one minute left.

"What I'm saying, Rook, is I want you to be happy. You'll never be happy if you're dedicated to your stubborn streak. You'll only find happiness through forgiveness, grace, mercy, vulnerability, and humility. All those things lead to love and connection."

"So, is Oprah or Dr. Phil in prison with you or something?"

He chuckled. "No, but I've had a lot of time to think. And read." He started speaking fast to beat the clock. "I haven't been able to be a proper daddy to you or a proper husband to your momma. It's my greatest regret. Though I haven't given you much, maybe I can give you the gift of wisdom and love with what time I have left. I love you, Rook."

Tears flooded my eyes, and my throat pinched my words. "I lo—" The phone system cut us off.

I sat there, staring out the window at the dwindling light, running my mind over what he'd just said. He was right. I'd been far too stubborn about a lot of things in my life. Not because it made sense. Not because it was the right thing to do, but because my pride got in the way. I dropped my forehead against the steering wheel. My stupid pride kept me from being wrong with humility and grace. It was okay to be wrong. The world wouldn't end because I was wrong about something. My pride kept me from proper discernment. My pride kept me from being vulnerable and open to people and possibilities.

A knock sounded on my car window. I jumped, but, thankfully, Cam's friendly face smiled back at me. Maybe I'd been wrong about Cam. Maybe my pride got in the way of that, too. I opened the door.

He frowned with concern. "You okay?"

"I'm fine. Just got off the phone with my dad." It was hard to talk with the knot in my throat.

Knowing filled his eyes. "Ah. I understand. Is he okay?"

"Yeah." I gathered my things. "He wanted to tell me that his lawyer thinks he can get him a new trial."

"That's great!"

"Yeah. I hope it works out for him." I forced a smile. I was still too rattled by what my dad had said.

"Why're you covered in glitter?"

"It's a long story."

"C'mon on inside." Cam put his arm around my shoulders. "You look like you could use some comfort food."

"Like what?" We strolled toward the house. The scent of hickory smoke from a distant fireplace hung in the air.

"Prim talked me through her fried chicken and macaroni recipes."

"Oh my! You've entered a special realm, young padawan. One few have entered."

"I feel The Force is strong with me, though."

I chuckled. "Seriously, you're pretty special if she's giving you those recipes."

"She fussed at me a bit, but we made it through fairly unscathed."

"Her fried chicken is my favorite."

He opened the screened porch door for me. "I do. That's why I chose it."

Chapter Thirty-Two

After a shower to deglitter, and a hearty supper, I tucked Prim in bed, happy things were returning to something like normal. Except, I still couldn't bring myself to sleep upstairs. I couldn't shake the feeling that my sanctuary had been invaded and thereby tainted. Cam decided to spend the night again.

"You don't need to do that, Cam. It could be months before this guy is caught. It could be never."

"It's okay. I don't mind." He knelt on the air mattress, and it sank. "Aw, man. My air mattress has a leak."

"Why don't you sleep upstairs in one of the guest rooms?"

"I don't feel right about sleeping in a bed while you're on the couch."

"I actually like the couch. It's really comfy. I spend half my nights down here, anyway."

"Are you sure?"

I snuggled under my blankets on the couch. "Yep."

"Okay. I'll sleep with the door open so I can hear if something happens."

"Sounds good. 'Night."

Cam chose the ground-floor guest room at the back of the house. I lay on the couch, willing myself to sleep, but every time I closed my eyes, I saw Gordon, heard his voice, felt his touch. I'd come close to being his third victim. All because he was greedy. He wanted land to build houses and make money. He was going to get that land through any and every method, and he wasn't going to let anyone get in his way.

Then my mind turned to my mom and dad and the things my dad had said to me, which then turned my mind to Jimmy and Cam and my own desires. I liked my job at the distillery, but I didn't want to be a career woman who sacrificed everything for the sake of a career. I wanted a husband and children. A job was fine, but it wasn't the be all, end all. It wasn't the stuff of love, happiness, future, growth, legacy—the stuff that really mattered. No one ever met their death wishing they'd worked more.

And Cam, he'd been surprising me all over the place lately. Yes, he'd broken my heart about twenty months ago, but I was pretty sure I'd broken his in equal measure—especially when I started dating his best friend. However, it was as though neither of us could really move on. He almost did. He'd been engaged recently, but it fell through. We'd both tried dating, but never really moved on. Maybe I was lying to myself about Cam and me being friends, so the divorce would hurt less. Maybe by holding on as a friend, we never really had to let each other go and endure the soul-crushing pain. He'd been so vital to my life recently. He'd been helping with Prim and with protecting the home. Honestly, in many ways, it was as though he and I had never split up.

I turned over on the couch to stare at the TV. I had to focus on something mind-numbing to get my brain off the hamster wheel so I could go to sleep.

A soft rustling sprang my eyes open. A man dressed all in black with a black burglar mask over his face stood over me. His frame was large and bulky. I gasped and jolted up, sitting up in the corner of the couch. He held a knife and a white rose.

"Hello, Annette. I've missed you. I got this for you." He extended the rose. When I didn't take it, he said, "Don't you like it? I thought white roses were your favorite. That's what you told me when you saw the rose bushes in front of my house."

I glanced at my phone on the coffee table. *Dang it!* If I screamed for Cam, how quickly could he stab me? I was afraid to try it. I was afraid if I opened my mouth to scream, I wouldn't be able to. Then what? If I couldn't make the scream loud enough to wake Cam the first time, then it was over for me. Maybe, for the moment, it was best to play along.

My voice shook. "I've missed you, too, but you have that mask on. I can't even tell who you are, silly." I chuckled and took the rose.

He lifted his mask. Louis. Louis-stinking-Meece. Did psycho run in their gene pool?

"I've come to take you with me. I have the perfect evening planned for us, Annette." His eyes were empty, distant. The lights were on, but no one was home.

"Oh, well, I can't really go out right now. I'm not ready. I'm still wearing my pajamas."

"That's okay. I laid your dress out on your bed. You should put it on."

"No. I mean, I can't go out right now, Louis. It's late, and I have to work tomorrow."

A faint smile crossed his lips. "Oh, I don't think you need to worry about that."

Everything I'd ever heard from police and forensics experts about these situations stated to never go to a second location. The second location is where my body would be found. So, this was going to be my moment to take a stand. If he was going to kill me or hurt me, it'd have to be here. My heart flung wildly against my chest, and my mind raced. I needed to find a way to keep my thoughts still enough to find a shred of clarity and think my way through this. First, I needed to get out of the corner of this couch. He was big, and it'd be difficult to get around him.

"Would you like some cocoa? It's getting colder outside, and a cup of cocoa really makes everything cozy and comfy." I tried to be natural and easy-going as I stood and edged around him. He studied me like a lion watching an antelope. My mind zoomed through about three different scenarios, but my window for action was closing. I needed to commit to a path. My best option seemed to be to run to Cam's room, but he stood between me and the hall as I edged toward the kitchen.

There was running out the kitchen door to Batrene's to call the police. But that was a huge risk. Just because this guy was big, didn't mean he was slow. I needed to catch him off guard somehow. I opened the fridge to take out the milk jug as if I were seriously going to make hot cocoa. Sitting by the stove was a can of spray oil and a cast iron skillet.

The cast iron skillet was heavy and would slow me down. The oil would be better, though it wasn't an ideal weapon. Pepper spray would've been better, but I knew from many facial treatments and suntan oil incidents how annoying oil in the eyes could be. It'd buy me some time—which was all I needed.

Taking hold of the spray oil, I rolled my eyes. "I can't believe Prim left this out. I've told her a thousand times…" I stepped toward him and sprayed him directly in the eyes, shouting, "Cam! Help! Call 9-1-1!"

Louis grunted and rubbed at his eyes with his hand and his sleeve, as he slashed wildly through the air, squinting and blinking his eyes. He cursed a blue streak at me. A fumble and crash sounded at the back of the house as if Cam had fallen out of bed.

I grabbed the skillet from the stove top and swung, but it was so heavy, I only managed to hit him in the shoulder. I turned to run for the door. My hand touched the doorknob and just as I reached for the deadbolt to unlock the door, Louis grabbed my hair and knocked my head against the door.

"Not so fast," he warned.

Pain shot through my forehead, but it made me angry more than anything, so I grabbed the broom leaning against the sideboard and cracked him in the face with the handle.

He cried out.

Then, my head throbbing, I continued to whack him as hard and as fast as I could while I shouted for Cam.

Louis grabbed the handle and yanked the broom from my grip. He swiped the knife at me. I dropped to the ground and rolled away toward the kitchen table, crawling to the opposite side of the table as I kicked a chair out to impede his advance. My head throbbed and ached.

Everything seemed to move in slow motion, though I knew this was unfolding in a matter of seconds.

"You can't get away from me, Annette."

"I'm not Annette. That was my mother, you freak." I stood and ran around the table as he chased after me. Around and around, we traveled as I played hard to get. If I could keep the kitchen table between us, I could buy time and protect myself. "Cam!" I shouted.

As I passed between the table and the wall, Louis rushed forward and shoved the table, catching me between the wall and the table.

Finally, Cam appeared in boxer shorts, bare chest, and bare feet, pointing the rifle at Louis. "Hold it right there, buddy. I will take you out before you blink. Hands up."

Louis lifted his hands.

"Drop the knife. Right now."

Louis snarled and dropped the knife.

I pushed the table off of me and ran to my phone in the living room. I dialed 9-1-1.

Prim shouted from the top of the stairs. "What's going on down there?"

"Don't come down here, Prim!" Cam shouted.

I joined Cam in the kitchen, talking to the emergency operator, who asked me to stay on the phone with her. Cam told Louis to get on the floor on his belly, then told me, "Rook, get something to tie him up with."

I pulled down the basket of miscellaneous items from the top of the fridge and extracted the duct tape. I set down the phone, pulled Louis's arms behind him, and taped his wrists together. Then I taped his ankles together. Louis wiggled and squirmed on the floor, red-faced, bug-eyed, and grunting.

Louis cursed me, spittle flying, "Annette, I only wanted to speak to you. We can be together, Annette. I need you. You love me, too. I know you do."

My stomach churned. "No. I don't. You freak. You're lucky I let you live after what you did to my mom." I taped his mouth shut and delivered a hard kick to the rib, though he deserved much more than that.

About ten minutes later, the police came rushing up my drive, sirens screaming and lights flashing. I let in the police, my gaze pulling to Prim, who stood in the hall in her robe, the rhinestones in her glasses sparking in the hall light.

"Are you kidding me? I can't sleep now. That fool got me riled up." She inched her way downstairs.

"They've already got him loaded in the car," Cam said.

"Is he the same man who killed my baby girl?"

"I think so," I said.

"Then you aren't going to be able to stop me. I want to see the wretch."

Fair enough. I helped her down the stairs.

The kitchen was mayhem. Officers filled up the space. One questioned Cam while others searched the scene.

"I want to go outside," Prim said.

I pulled a barn coat off the hook by the door, helped her into it, and helped balance her while she slipped into her gardening boots. We stepped outside, where police lights swept the darkness. I assisted her down the porch steps and across the dewy grass to the drive, where Louis, pale as a peeled cucumber, sat in the back of a police car. A young deputy recruit stood by the car and questioned us as we approached. He was talking with Jimmy, who had just arrived on the scene in plain clothes.

As we neared, the young recruit stepped forward and told us to go back inside.

Prim said, "Son, that man right there killed my daughter…" Then she pointed at me. "Her mother, almost two decades ago. We've waited a long time to face this vermin, and I think we deserve a word with him."

Jimmy clapped the recruit on the shoulder. "I got this."

Jimmy opened the door.

Prim glared at the man in silence for several minutes. Louis glared back, silent, grim.

"You killed my daughter. You scum-sucking coward." I could feel the shaking of her body as I helped her stand. "But her daughter caught you, and I can't think of a more beautiful justice than that. I'm a dying woman, but by the grace of God, I lived to see this day. I'm determined to live long enough to see you go to prison, where you deserve to rot for the rest of your life. I hope you have a long, painfully miserable life. Maybe someday I'll forgive you, but it won't be today." Her voice cracked with emotion. "You snuffed a bright light out of this world and left a dark hole in our hearts. You stole her momma and my daughter. You broke our family. For that, you deserve all the pain and the suffering and the wrath you receive." Then she sucked in a deep breath and spit right in his face.

Malice and hate glittered in his eyes. He wiped his face against his shoulder and said to me, "Annette..."

"That's enough." Jimmy shut the door and stood in front of the window so Louis couldn't see us.

As I led Prim away from the car, Louis continued to shout; his voice muffled through the door. "I won't forget you, Annette. You are mine. I'll come find you. Annette! Annette!"

Chapter Thirty-Three

After the police had taken my and Cam's initial statement and processed the scene, they all left. Jimmy lingered behind and sat at my kitchen table, probably for the last time. I prepared a pot of coffee while he chatted with Prim and Cam about the evening's events. Prim cried, thankful to finally know who killed her daughter. Cam wrapped his arm around her frail shoulders, comforting her.

Jimmy said, "Well, it was a wild case for sure. We retrieved Kenton's laptop earlier today and questioned Gordon Meece. Based on our initial findings, it looks as though Kenton was colluding with Meece to get his hands on the J.T. Bolton property."

"But Kenton loaned them a bunch of money to help fix the place up. Why would he do that?"

"Don't know. Could've been a ploy to hide his true motives. Could've loaned the money first *then* got involved with the Meece's. Based on Gordon's statement, he and Kenton were going to partner on the development. At first."

I pulled four mugs out of the cabinet and added the amount of cream and sugar according to everyone's preferences. "And they killed Cassidy because she was in the way. At least that's what Gordon told me."

"Right. It seems they tried to go about it legally at first. They made her offers on the land, but when she refused to sell, they became desperate. Kenton, acting as an intermediary, was trying to convince Cassidy to sell."

I inhaled the rich scent of coffee as it perked. "And with Cassidy dead, the marriage was dissolved, Derek would collect money and be free to sell the property to Kenton."

"Which would've worked until Kenton's greed got the better of him."

"Really?"

"Yeah. We recovered some documents where Kenton had filed to start up his own property development business. He double-crossed Gordon. Kenton created the phony life insurance forms, making him the beneficiary of the million-dollar policy. Derek didn't know it, but his time was limited. It just so happened that Gordon killed Kenton before Kenton could kill Derek and collect the life insurance and the land, too. Both from phony policies."

Prim said, "How did he double-cross Gordon then?"

"Because originally, he was going to forge the J.T. Bolton land deed into Gordon's name and sell the land to him. But then Kenton decided he wanted all the money and land for himself. When Gordon found out, he killed him, too."

"Oh." Prim sighed. "Lord, what a wicked world we live in."

We all nodded as the coffee sputtered its final drops. I filled four cups and carried them to the table.

"Man. This story is crazy." Cam sipped his coffee.

"So what's going to happen to the house?" Prim said, stirring her coffee.

"I'm not sure." Jimmy shrugged. "I doubt Derek will want to hang around. I imagine it'll go up for sale."

I thought of Cassidy's dream. The beautiful Victorian home with its mahogany wood, stained glass windows, turret, high ceilings, and the magnificent blue room. "It would be a disaster for that historic home to go to a bunch of land developers who will only tear it down and build a bunch of McMansions that few people around here can even afford."

"Right?" Cam said, looking at me with sadness. "I mean, it's a part of our history. Kentucky was built, in part, by the bourbon barons and their contributions. Heck, we built the bourbon industry here."

Prim said, "If *I* had the money, the youth, and the health, I'd buy it and turn it into one of the biggest attractions this area has to offer." She stared at me.

I smiled. Prim would, too. She'd be just the sort of spitfire the J.T. Bolton House needed. The same sort of spitfire Cassidy had been. Owner and proprietor of the J.T. Bolton House. Wow. What a dream that would be. Hard work, sure. But, to own that chunk of history; to live in with those historical spirits; to have holiday functions there. High teas. Lecture series. Heck, we could even distill our own small-batch bourbon there. *Wait. We? We, who, Rook? There is no WE.* I sighed and dragged myself back down to reality. There was no way on earth I could afford such a venture. "It's the stuff of dreams, for sure," I said. "I'm sure Gordon's daddy will snap it up, though. There's no way a business-savvy man like him is going to let prime real estate get away."

Jimmy shook his head. "I don't think so. Now that both Gordon and Louis have been arrested, the IRS and FBI will be looking at Stanley under a microscope. I'm willing to bet they're going to find a bunch more crimes and shady deals hiding in his portfolio. It wouldn't surprise me to hear about him being arrested for something, too. In fact, he's likely the ring leader."

We sat for a couple more hours, talking about the case and the crimes. For a moment, our little scene felt like family, then suddenly it didn't. There was a bittersweet nostalgia to it. A book closing. Jimmy would be packing up and leaving mine and Cam's life forever. This was an ending.

Jimmy rose to leave, and I stood, too. "Hey, Jimmy, I have some stuff to give you. I don't know when I'll see you again." I motioned for him to follow me to my room. I handed him a box of a few things he had loaned or gifted me: a friend's demo CD, a T-shirt and a jacket, a book about Jack the Ripper, and a little snow globe from our trip to Louisville Zoo. "Here's your stuff."

He peered down into the bag and removed the snow globe. He shook it and watched the snow float around the polar bear. Then he offered it to me. "This was a gift. I want you to have it."

I tipped my head, reluctant to accept it because somewhere, it might bind me to him by an invisible thread across the years and distance.

"Please?" he said.

I accepted the snow globe. "Okay. Thank you." I returned it to the top of my dresser.

He gazed at me. "I'll miss you, Rook Campbell."

I smiled. "I'll miss you, too, Jimmy Duvall. But I really think this is for the best. I think you'll be so much happier."

He nodded. "Yeah. I think you will be, too."

He set down the bag and opened his arms for a hug. I hugged him tight. "You and Cam are welcome to come visit anytime. I'm minutes from the beach."

"Oh, lucky you."

We separated. "I'm serious. It'll be nice to have friends visit."

"C'mon, I'll walk you to the door."

He hugged Prim goodbye and shook Cam's hand, giving him the same offer to visit in Florida. Then Jimmy turned to me again, smoothed his hand over my hair, and kissed my forehead. "You take care of yourself."

"You too."

"Try to stay out of trouble."

I gave him a crooked smile. "I try, but trouble always finds me. Besides, who else around here is going to keep Sheriff Goodman on his toes?"

He laughed and left the house. I stood at the kitchen window and watched him walk across the yard, get in his truck, and drive away. I swiped tears from my face. I wasn't in love with Jimmy, and we hadn't dated for very long, but goodbyes were always so hard.

Cam put his arm around my shoulder. "We'll see him again."

Chapter Thirty-Four

With two-thirds of the Meece family in jail, The Four Wild Horses Distillery could no longer use their event barn. Fortunately, by the end of the week, I discovered a new location for the Unbridled Spirits bourbon release party. I left work at noon on Friday to scout out the location and make sure it would work.

But first, I swung by the house in Prim's car, since mine was still in the shop, to pick up Prim and Batrene. I couldn't live with myself, or their fussing, if I dared to go to the Ethan's Orchard Apple Festival without them. According to the pictures I'd seen online, it seemed like a great place for the bourbon release. I was hoping to speak to a marketing coordinator and see the place for myself before making the final decision. But,by going today, we'd have the added bonus of enjoying the festival while I discussed business.

The orchard sat on hundreds of acres of gently rolling hills filled with blackberry vines, peach trees, apple trees, pumpkin and sunflower patches, and vineyards. A tractor pulling a canopied trailer carted people around the premises to the far reaches of the orchard to pick their own fruits. Children climbed on hay bales and flew down giant slides. Families enjoyed the petting zoo and cornstalk maze, old-timers sat around the fishing pond in their camping chairs, and more adventurous spirits flew down the zipline or tried their luck on the obstacle course.

The festival included a bluegrass band on the stage behind the barn, carnival style games, face painting, vendors, baking contest entries, a Cutest Apple Baby Contest, and a variety of fresh-baked goods made from the orchard produce.

The main building was a large red barn where one half housed the bakery full of homemade pies, tarts, donuts, hand pies, jams, jellies, ciders, honey, cakes, and other treats made from the fruits grown at the orchard. The other half was dedicated to a gift shop. I let Prim and Batrene loose on the festival and visited with the marketing agent upstairs. Between the two of us, we laid out a plan to rival the Victorian Christmas I'd planned at the Meeces'. We would still use the Christmas Carol theme, but make it more rustic. Fortunately, my initial plans wouldn't have to change much. Just a few tweaks. My boss, Pierce, would be really happy to know that, and I was thrilled we wouldn't be back to square one on the planning.

I trotted downstairs, light of feet and light of heart. Things seemed to be locking into place. The sun was shining, the weather warm, and the scent of fried apple pies and apple funnel cakes called my name. Life wasn't perfect, but it seemed to finally be heading in the right direction.

I stood in line at the funnel cake cart, humming along to a rendition of "Man of Constant Sorrow" when someone put their hands over my eyes from behind.

His spicy, sweet cologne betrayed him. "Cam?" I said, removing his hands to face him. "What are you doing here?"

"Just hanging out with the family. My brother has his kids this weekend so we brought them here to let them run around."

"I see. Don't you ever work anymore?"

He laughed. "Don't you?"

"Touche. I do work. In fact, I just finished securing this place for my distillery's bourbon re-release. Now I'm off the clock. Thought I'd get an apple funnel cake."

"Yeah, I had to take care of some business myself today, so I switched with Mike. I'll go into the bar later tonight. I saw Prim and Batrene, and they said you were here, too, so I came looking for you. Figures I'd find you at the funnel cake cart."

I stuck my tongue out at him. "Very funny. I've been mostly good on my diet."

He looked me over. "Hey, I ain't complaining."

I flushed and turned to place my order as Cam excused himself. I carried a coffee and a paper plate full of appley-fried bread and cinnamon powdered sugar to a nearby picnic table. It was a horrible lunch, but I scarfed it down as if I'd never eaten before. I threw my plate away, sanitized the sticky off my hands, then searched the crowd for Cam, Prim, Batrene—anyone I knew. I spotted Batrene and Prim sitting on hay bales, enticing the goats through the fence at the petting zoo. I started toward them when I saw Cam wading through the crowd carrying a bouquet of sunflowers. My favorite flower.

He beamed and shoved them at me. "These are for you."

"Thank you." I was glad they weren't white roses. It would be a long time before I'd be able to look at a white rose without fear. I cradled the happy yellow blooms and ran my fingers over the textured center.

"They're your favorite flower," he said.

"That's right. You remembered?"

"Of course. Come with me for a minute." He grabbed my hand and pulled me away from the noisiest part of the festival.

"Where are we going?"

"Don't worry about it. I just want a little privacy so I don't have to scream to talk to you."

We walked several hundred feet away from the festivities and stood under a large oak blazing with autumn colors.

He said, "Rook, I've been thinking a lot about you. About us. About life. I did something crazy today and I want you to be part of it."

"What did you do?"

He pulled a brochure out of his back pocket and handed it to me.

It was the J.T. Bolton House. "Why are you showing me this? Getting your hands on a brochure isn't that crazy, you know."

"Oh, I got my hands on more than a brochure, darlin'. I got my hands on the house."

I laughed and then realized he wasn't laughing. "Wait. What?"

"I bought the J.T. Bolton House. For you. For us. I heard what Prim said last night and I knew this was the way forward."

"You did what? Without even consulting me? What do you expect—"

"Can you just hush a minute and let me explain?"

I pinched my mouth shut.

"I know you love this house. I do, too. I love you. Always have, always will. I think you love me. Prim says so. I think she's right. I know things were rough with us before, but we're different people now. We've grown up. I don't want us to make the biggest mistakes of our lives by living one more day apart. I want to spend the rest of my life with you. Only you. I want us to live in this house…" He tapped the brochure. "I want us to make it the best bed and breakfast in all of Kentucky. I want us to fill it with kids and dogs and life. It won't work with anyone else but you."

"How did you even have the money to do this?"

"I've been saving, and my parents and brother helped. Plus, it turns out that it was going for a heavily discounted price because of the murders. Wait…" He paused and frowned. "Do you think you could live in a house where Cassidy and Kenton were murdered?"

I screwed up my face. "I'm not sure. I guess I could try it, and if it doesn't work out, we can sell it. But what about the bar? Do you want to drive all the way to Lexington every day?"

He shrugged. "I don't know how much longer I can run Tangled Up in Brew, anyway. I've been thinking about selling for a while. I'm getting older. Getting tired of working nights all the time and catering to a bunch of drunk college kids. I'm definitely tired of Lexington. It's not the biggest city, but it's still a city. I'll figure out what to do with the bar. Maybe I'll keep it as an income stream and hand it over to new management. Maybe I'll sell my shares. We can figure that out." He ran his hand down my arm and took my hand. "All I care about is you and me. Together."

Everything he said made sense. I'd been thinking about many of those things, too. I'd been yearning for kids, a home, stability. And if I hadn't been able to imagine the man to do those things with, it was because I couldn't imagine any other man but Cam. It had always been Cam. My best friend. My caretaker. My helper. My protector. The man who loved my family as much as I did. It was always him. What could it hurt to try one more time?

Life was about taking chances. I squeezed his hand. "If we do this, I want to take it slow."

He smiled and slid his arms around my waist. "Slow is fine. It'll be easier to hold on to you if you're moving slow."

"But not too slow because I want to have kids. And I'm not getting any younger."

His pale blue eyes gleamed. "Of course."

"And what about Prim?"

"She can move in with us if she wants. Or you can stay with Prim until she doesn't need you anymore. We'll figure out all the details. All I know is I've got you now, and I'll never let you go. Not ever again."

That was all I needed to hear.

Acknowledgements

I'm grateful for my readers. Thank you for taking this journey with me. I have no reason to keep going without YOU! And to my family and friends who are my bedrock. You know who you are and I love you all!

About the Author

Born and raised in the beautiful Bluegrass state of Kentucky, Michelle Bennington developed a passion for books early on that has since progressed into a mild hoarding situation and an ever-growing to-read pile. She delights in transporting readers into worlds of mystery, both contemporary and historical.

In rare moments of spare time, she can be found engaging in a wide array of arts and crafts, reading, traveling, and attending tours involving ghosts, historical homes, or distilleries.

SOCIAL MEDIA HANDLES:
Facebook: https://www.facebook.com/michellebenningtonauthor
Instagram: https://www.instagram.com/michelle.bennington.author/
Goodreads: https://www.goodreads.com/?ref=nav_home

AUTHOR WEBSITE:
www.michellebennington.com

Also by Michelle Bennington

The Small Batch Mystery Series, a contemporary mystery set in Kentucky's bourbon community, featuring amateur sleuth, Rook Campbell:
Devil's Kiss (2022), Level Best Books
Mermaid Cove (2023), Level Best Books
Unbridled Spirits (2024), Level Best Books

The Widows & Shadows Series, a historical mystery set in late Georgian England, featuring Lady Ravenna Birchfield
Widow's Blush (2023), Level Best Books
Widow's Fire (2024), Level Best Books
Widow's Peak (2025), Level Best Books

The Hazardous Hoarding Series, a contemporary mystery set in small-town Kentucky, featuring a hoarder, Birdie Harper, who lives with her husband's ghost.
Dumpster Dying (2023), Charade Media
Killer Cache (2024), Charade Media
Buried Treasure (2025), Charade Media

A Sampling of Sleuths: Discover A New Binge-Worthy Mystery Series Anthology (2023), Thalia Press